MEL SHERRATT

ONLY THE BRAVE

THOMAS & MERCER

Published by Thomas & Mercer, Seattle

www.apub.com

Amazon, the Amazon logo, and Thomas & Mercer are trademarks of Amazon.com, Inc., or its affiliates.

ISBN-13: 978-1477830628
ISBN-10: 1477830626

Cover design by bürosüd° München, www.buerosued.de

Library of Congress Control Number: 2014959844

Printed in the United States of America

For Talli Roland, for showing me the way.

January 31, 2015

Allie Shenton blinked away tears. Her long hair was scraped back in a ponytail, her pretty face scrubbed clean of makeup. She stared at her sister lying in the hospital bed. Karen had been there for two weeks now. It had been touch and go at first, and even though she was stable, she still wasn't breathing for herself. She was in an induced coma. Only time would tell if she was ever going to become strong enough to fend for herself again, and it was wearing Allie and her husband, Mark, down.

Allie had just solved her most recent murder case when she'd received a phone call from the doctor at Riverdale Residential Home. Her sister, Karen, had been a resident there ever since being attacked seventeen years ago. She'd been ill for a few weeks before she'd finally suffered another brain haemorrhage.

Since January 16, Allie had been on compassionate leave, as well as taking all the annual holiday entitlement she could have, but she was running out of days. More than that, she was wracked with guilt because she was desperate to get back to routine, cooking meals, paying the bills, day-to-day normality. Living. She hated herself for even thinking like that, but no matter how much she tried to block it out, a small part of her mind betrayed her. Everything had been taken from Karen; there was so much that they had both missed out on. It just didn't seem fair.

With a breaking heart, she looked at her sister, knowing that Karen might not survive for another month, another week, another day even. Allie couldn't begin to think what life would be like without her.

The door opened. The nurse who entered was almost as familiar to her as every line on her sister's face. Marissa – a young woman in her twenties, small but heavily built, a mop of blonde curly hair kept out of the way with the help of a large blue clip. Allie had never seen her without a smile, never heard less than a kind word. It occurred to her, as she looked at Marissa, that just as her own job in the police force was suited only to some, the same could be said about health professionals. A certain type of demeanour was required to walk the thin line between the grittiness of life and the harshness of death.

'Hello, Allie. How are you today?' Marissa asked.

'I'm good, thanks.' Allie let out a huge sigh. 'How about you? Shaken off that cold yet?'

'For now. That's the trouble with working in an environment like this. There's always something to catch. Better than the Norovirus, though.' Marissa smiled. 'I have something for you. It must have been left on the nurses' station.'

Allie frowned. 'Do you know who by?'

'Sorry, no. I've only just spotted it. Strange it's addressed to you, though.'

Marissa handed her a long white box. Tied around it was a red ribbon, a large bow in the centre of the lid. Allie froze as a feeling of déjà vu engulfed her, a sense of fear rippling through her veins. She remembered the moment three years ago when a similar packet had been laid in her hands. She pushed the thought to one side as she opened the small white envelope attached to it, trembling fingers pulling out the card from inside.

You're next, my surviving angel.

A sharp intake of breath had Marissa turning and eyeing Allie with a frown. But if the young nurse thought it was anxiety that was making Allie panic, she was wrong. It wasn't grief that she was feeling: it was sheer terror.

You're next.

Y.N.

The capital letters that had been written on a note, taped underneath a waste bin in the park during her last investigation. The envelope had been addressed to DS Shenton. Chloe Winters' battered and broken face appeared in her mind. Although DNA tests had shown that the woman had been raped by the same person who had attacked Karen, it was a shock to realise that the note itself had been some sort of warped warning to Allie.

She slid the red ribbon from the box and lifted up the lid. Just like the last time, inside it was a dying, solitary red rose, its petals dropping to the floor as she picked it up.

Just like the last time, Allie let the box drop to the ground. She ran out of the room, out of the ward and into the main building.

Outside, Mark was walking towards her down the long corridor that ran the length of the hospital wing, a newspaper under his arm and two chocolate bars in his hand. He reached for her as she moved past him.

'Allie, what's wrong?'

But Allie didn't stop. Tears poured down her face as she ran, ignoring the startled looks from hospital staff and patients alike.

She headed towards the exit, eyes darting left and right, desperately looking for a face she might recognise, checking out the people coming and going.

Was he there, waiting for her?

Could he see her?

Was he watching from somewhere?

At the main doors she slowed down and realised it was useless. He wouldn't be here now. He could be anywhere.

Mark caught up with her a few seconds later. 'Allie, what's wrong?'

'He's here,' she said between breaths.

'Who's here?'

'Him! He's watching me again.'

'Who? What do you mean *again*?' Mark pulled her to a spare seat in a row of eight fastened to the wall and sat her down. 'Tell me what you mean.'

Allie closed her eyes. She couldn't look at him, knew she would see the incredulity, the hurt and anger etched on his face when he realised what she had kept from him.

'What . . .' Mark stopped, realisation dawning on his features. 'This isn't the first time, is it?'

She shook her head, fresh tears forming. She had to come clean, no matter how deceitful she would seem.

'On New Year's Eve 2011, just after Steph Ryder was buried, I was visiting Karen and there was a delivery for her. It was a long, white box, and it had a single rose inside.'

'What? But who sent it?'

'I don't know. There were some words on a card.' Allie faltered. 'Words that meant he was still watching. Still waiting.'

'What words? What do you mean – who's watching you?'

'The man who attacked Karen! He's watching *me*.'

Mark's eyes widened. 'And you think he's coming after you now?'

Allie nodded, tears rolling down her face. She flicked them away with the back of her hand.

'I've just received another rose in a box.'

Mark recoiled. 'Does it have a note with it?'

Allie handed it to him. Watched his brow furrow as he flicked the card over to see if anything could explain what he had read.

'*You're next, my surviving angel.* What the hell does that mean?'

'I –' Tears welled in her eyes. 'I – I don't know.'

'Well, what did it say on the first note?'

Allie could recall the words by heart; she would never forget them.

Karen, until we meet again, my fallen angel.

One day you will all be mine.

And you, little sister, Allie.

Don't you ever stop looking for me.

But even though she hadn't told Mark three years ago, she wasn't about to tell him now. She shook her head.

'Really?' Mark's face dropped. 'And you told *no one* about it?'

'Except for who I needed to tell.'

'You mean Nick.'

Allie nodded.

'Three years ago!' Mark lowered his voice to a whisper. 'Three fucking years ago. And you said nothing?'

'I didn't want to worry you, okay! But now . . .' Allie began to cry again. 'It was my fault that girl was raped, can't you see? He attacked her to get back at me.'

'Of course that's not your fault.' He paused. 'Unless there's something else you're not telling me?'

Allie said nothing. Oh, God, she couldn't tell him about the note taped to the bottom of the waste bin.

Mark dropped his eyes to the floor. Allie put out a hand to him but withdrew it. She wanted *him* to put an arm around her shoulders, tell her he could understand why she had kept it to herself.

Eventually he looked up. 'You have to stop this,' he told her.

'Oh, I intend to stop him, and when I do, I –'

'No,' Mark cried, 'I mean, when Karen – you have to stop *this*. If someone is out to get you too, then he needs to be found before he hurts you. You have to leave it to Nick, not put yourself in danger by looking for him.'

'I can't.' Allie shook her head.

'Your sister is dying!'

People were looking their way. They both sat in silence for a moment.

Every emotion possible fought to get out of Allie. Anxiety for her safety, anger that he was still out there, dread at the thought of her sister's imminent death. But most of all, the fear of not catching him. Of not ever knowing who had left Karen for dead all those years ago.

She wiped at her eyes and spoke calmly to the man who had stuck with her through thick and thin. The man whom she loved with all her heart but didn't truly deserve. The man she hoped would be there for her when all this was over.

'I won't stop until he's arrested,' she told him. 'And more to the point, it doesn't seem like he wants me to forget about him, either.'

'But can't you see,' Mark took her hand and enfolded it in both of his, 'I'm not going to lose you because of some psycho who's trying to ruin your life for something that happened with your sister.'

'You won't lose me!' She said this more in hope than certainty.

'If you continue with this, Allie, it's going to ruin everything we have.'

'But –'

'I'm scared for you – can't you see that?' Mark's eyes glistened with tears. 'Don't let him ruin *us*.'

He'd been standing outside the entrance to the Royal Stoke University Hospital for over an hour when he saw them coming out of the building. Allie's eyes were red and raw. He watched her press a tissue to her cheek. Her husband, Mark, had his arm around her shoulder, pulling her to him.

He didn't really need to stand back in the shadows. He wore a woollen hat and scarf that covered most of his face and hair; he was sure she wouldn't have noticed him anyway, even though she saw him most weeks. She and Mark seemed wrapped up in each other, their pain shared as one. He supposed they were going home now. Home to their bed. How could they be so insensitive after they had just left the hospital?

He followed behind them as they crossed over the road to the car park, two figures huddled together illuminated every now and then as passing car lights caught them in the beam. Seeing them together made his blood boil. He should be comforting her. He should be the one with his arm around her, then holding her as Mark was now.

He trod silently as they went up to floor two of the multi-storey car park. Here it was lit so he kept his head down. They got into a car and he stopped nearby, hands in pockets looking like he was searching for keys, never taking his eyes from them for a minute.

Allie was crumpled in Mark's arms; Mark comforted her again.

He should be doing that. He wanted to run his hand over her hair, smell its freshly washed scent. He wanted to wipe away her tears, feel her skin underneath his fingertips. Kiss away the salt.

Had she known he'd been watching her since the night he'd attacked Karen? All those memories locked away until a few weeks ago when that stupid bastard he'd heard them dub the Alphabet Killer went on a killing spree. It was his fault; he'd dredged up the past, made him think about things again. It had been harder to put the memories away this time. And now that Karen was dying, it seemed like it was meant to be.

The engine of the car roared into life and he stooped down out of sight until they had driven past him.

Once they were gone, he headed back towards the hospital. If he hurried, he'd just make it in time for the last few minutes of visiting hours. He would have to go inside and see why Allie was crying so much. If he timed it right, there would be so many visitors coming and going that the staff might not notice him. It was the reason he'd chosen not to visit Karen too many times. He didn't want to draw attention to himself.

After the first few days, when Allie had come out in tears with every visit, she'd seemed to harden to the routine.

But now, he needed to find out what information he could.

More to the point, he wanted to see if she had received his gift.

February 5, 2015
3.00 A.M.

Jordan Johnson walked quickly along the path by the side of Harrison House. When he saw a patch of bushes on his left, he jogged over the grass to them. He shrugged off the holdall he was carrying, unzipped it and slipped his hand inside. Pulling out a smaller bag, he took a quick look around, and then up at the flats in front of him, to see if anyone was watching. When he felt satisfied they weren't, he shoved the bag underneath the hedge and made his way back to the path – he'd pick up the bag again in a while, once the drop had been made.

Still hidden in the shadows, away from the blazing street lamp that lit up the area a few yards away, he peered at his watch, trying to make out the time in the dark. It was just past three a.m. He wished whoever was coming to collect the money would hurry up. His imagination was running wild as he thought about what was waiting for him on the first floor. But after a while, his thoughts returned to the awful night he'd had.

When Kirstie had come looking for him at Flynn's nightclub, he knew she was after trouble. The stupid bitch was always accusing him of having an affair. You'd think she'd be thankful for what they'd got. They still had fun occasionally, even though he enjoyed it less and less.

They were the golden couple – Kirstie with long, smooth jet-black hair, slim-gym figure and sapphire-blue eyes that demanded authority and attention, just like her father. At thirty-one and ten years her senior, Jordan was six foot one with dark skin and hair, a six-pack he was proud of that he kept under wraps and bulging biceps always on display. He wore tailored clothes, fashionable and expensive, just because he could.

So it was one thing to put on a show to everyone that they were a united couple, but really, did Kirstie have to keep throwing it in his face, making him look like a heartless bastard all the time? He was sure she was sleeping with someone else – not that he cared but it made her antics all the more annoying. She treated him like a prick. After leaving Flynn's, he was disinclined to go home so he'd gone to The Genting Club on nearby Etruria Road and played a few tables, drunk some coffee with nice people until it was time to leave for his meeting.

He couldn't believe he still had to babysit Kirstie. It had been three years since her old man had been locked up and he'd been sent to keep an eye on things. Granted, the luxury of living in Terry Ryder's house and looking after his daughter was a major scoop but it meant he'd had to put up with so much arrogance and selfishness. Luckily, the money he was delivering should set him up for a better life. A twenty-five grand down payment to take Kirstie out of the equation, plus a ten grand fee for himself for setting it up when the time was right. Not that his brother, Ryan, knew about the ten grand. Jordan wasn't the only one who was double-crossing him.

The setup with Kirstie had been good while it lasted but he'd be glad to be out of it. He was sick of being a dogsbody – that's all he had become. Of course, he had Flynn's, something he was good at managing, but Kirstie owned it at the moment. She also swanned round, taking the glory. Everyone knew he did a good job of keeping out the riff-raff and the dealers that he didn't want in there. He had his own suppliers when necessary but he'd kept on the good side of the law purposely. Still, he wouldn't have to put up with Kirstie for much longer, once Flynn's belonged to him and Ryan.

Besides, he had fallen in love with someone else.

Jordan glanced up at the flats again, feeling a warmth rush through him at the thought of what was to come. He hadn't planned it, but now that it had happened, he felt ecstatic. Once Kirstie was out of the way, and the heat was off him and Ryan, he was getting out of Ryder's house and buying his own place. He'd just put a deposit down on a flat being built in the city centre. It was a new block; he wanted to be one of the first to live in them, plus be near to his club.

He glanced up again, smiling when he saw her window was the only one lit up on her floor. Flat 210. Sophie Nicklin was waiting – waiting for him. Sex with a beautiful woman who was a pleasure to be around. He couldn't believe his luck. He'd only met her by chance as he'd walked through the main area downstairs and seen two blokes bothering her at the bar. After getting the bouncers to move them on, he'd offered to buy her a drink to make up for the lack of quality clientele that night and had been drawn in by her charm. When she got up to leave, Jordan had asked for her number and it had started from there. Six months later, he was wondering how long he could keep up with the pretence that it was all about sex. He wanted her all to himself, whenever he wanted – without Kirstie fucking Ryder breathing down his neck as if she owned him. Luckily, he didn't have long to wait now. His plan was to make it happen soon.

Jordan heard someone approaching. He shook his head when he saw who it was. Really – Steve Burgess had been told to choose someone and he'd involved this cretin?

'What the fuck do you want?' he snapped.

Had he realised that removing the strap of the bag from his shoulder and over his head would hinder his reflexes, he would have left it where it was. He felt a hard object crash into the side of his head, let the bag drop to the floor so that he could retaliate, but it was too late. He stumbled to his knees as the second blow caught him straight across the nose. The stars in the sky mingled with the ones he could see flashing before his eyes. The toe of a boot cracked up into his chin and the blows continued to rain down.

As he took the beating of his life, all he could think of was Sophie, who would be waiting for him.

3.20 A.M.

Leah Matthews staggered, trying to negotiate the path alongside Harrison House. It was a two-mile walk from the city centre to her home at the dip of Ford Green Road. She'd been around Hanley for most of the evening and had left just after two a.m. It had taken an age but she couldn't afford a taxi after drinking away most of her money.

It had become a regular occurrence lately – after a night out, if she hadn't picked up a fella, she would grab something to eat on the walk back home and either start a fight in the kebab house on Town Road or mouth off at someone as she walked home afterwards. She never took a taxi unless she was really far out of town. She wasn't one of those women who were scared of their own shadows, terrified that someone was going to run out of an entry they were walking past, grab them around the neck, drag them into the dark and attack them. Growing up with two older brothers on one of the meanest streets in Stoke-on-Trent had given her the courage of a bear when it came to defending herself, something she had needed on many an occasion over the years with the type of men she fell for. Bad boys – she couldn't help but love them.

Almost dancing on her heels, so desperate to use the toilet after her marathon walk home, she folded her arms across her chest and shivered in the cold night air. The blouse she had on was no more than a thin piece of material covering her modesty, her fake leather leggings clinging to her uncomfortably after she'd ripped up the dance floor in Chicago Rock for an hour or more.

In the distance, she spotted her neighbour, Rita Pritchard, with her dog. It wasn't anything out of the ordinary; she often caught them out walking as she was coming in from a night out. Despite Leah's attempts to instil a sense of danger into the older woman, Rita had a mind of her own. She also liked a good natter, something Leah wasn't in the mood for. She stepped off the path and onto the grass so that the noise of her shoes wouldn't alert Rita, running past quickly, hoping to go unnoticed into Harrison House.

Two seconds later, she was flat out on the grass.

'Ow,' she cried out, turning back. Flicking strands of hair away from her face, she peered into the dark to see what she had tripped over. She stood up, brushed her clothes down and stepped a little closer. As her eyes adjusted to the night shadows, the shape came into focus.

It looked like a man lying there.

'Wake up, you drunken bastard.' She took another step forward. 'You can't stay out here. You'll bloody well freeze to death.'

He didn't make a murmur so she kicked him a bit harder.

'Oy, wake up!'

Still no sign of life. She half wondered whether to walk away, leave him there, but it might be someone from the flats, and she knew she'd take great pleasure in banging on someone's door to let them know who she had found. She nudged his shoulder with her shoe, pushing him over onto his back so that she could see his face.

'Shit.' Her hand covered her mouth.

Careful not to tread in the blood at the side of his ribcage, already pooling on top of the soil, she took another step nearer. He hadn't made a sound, not even a groan: was he dead? She grimaced at the sight of his face, an unrecognisable mishmash of bruising and swelling, his eyes like two slits in a pie. Leah was surprised to see his watch still on his wrist, gleaming in the moonlight. Maybe she should . . .

She pulled her hand away sharpish. It would leave prints. There was no way she was taking the blame for something that she hadn't done.

A white flash reflected in the bushes, catching her eye as she stooped beside the man. Peering into the darkness, she realised it wasn't her eyes playing tricks on her. She moved closer, put a hand out and reached for it. It was a black bag with a draw-through string handle. She picked it up, undid the string and peeked inside. Her eyes widened as she surveyed the contents.

Gasping, she looked around. The lamppost on the path illuminated most of the green beside it and she couldn't see a soul, not even Rita. Quickly, she pulled the string handle tight again and hooked it over her shoulder. Finders, keepers. Finders, keepers.

She stepped away again, this time turning to leave. Let someone else find him. She didn't need to get involved. She didn't want any more hassle at her door.

She did need money, though.

The bag wasn't near the man; it might not have anything to do with him. And anyway, she was right – finders, keepers.

With one more glance up and down the pathway, then up at the flats to check that the coast was still clear, she tucked the bag into her side to keep it hidden and legged it into Harrison House.

3.30 A.M.

Sophie Nicklin woke with a start when she heard a bang. It sounded like a door being shut along the walkway outside. She checked her watch: no wonder she'd been dozing on the settee. Pushing herself up, she stretched and reached for her phone, saw nothing new and sighed. There had been no messages from Jordan since he'd texted her at one a.m. Usually if he was delayed at Flynn's, or sometimes if he couldn't come at all, he'd ring her to let her know. The very least he'd do was send her a quick text message, so that she wouldn't worry.

She frowned, then moved to look out of the window. Harrison House was laid out in an L-shape, the flats having a shared-access walkway to all doors at the front of the building. She was the last flat at the end of the block so had the advantage of being able to see the side and the front of the large grassed area, as well as the path that was a cut-through from the main road to the entrance below. The times she'd stood in this particular window and waited to see Jordan appear and walk across to see her . . .

From somewhere up above, she could hear the thud of a bass beat. Since she was on the first floor, it wasn't loud enough to bother her, despite the hour. It was more part of the problem living in a block of flats as large as Harrison House. So many people housed in close proximity was a recipe for disaster – no matter how clichéd that sounded. A door banging, someone shouting, loud music, a fight breaking out. Only the other night some brave sod had called the police because the Granger brothers had been scrapping again. Boy, those twins knew how to fight, going at it like animals, as if they wanted to kill each other. Still, floor one didn't have too many rowdy residents. And it was home for now, much safer than where she'd been living this time last year in Birmingham.

She stared at her phone, willing it to ring. Sophie missed Jordan terribly when he didn't turn up, ached for him even. Longed to feel his arms wrapped around her keeping her safe, making her feel wanted, cherished. Granted, he could only stay an hour or so but that time was enough to make her feel so loved and warm that it would always get her through until the next visit.

Falling in love with him hadn't been on the agenda – then again, when is falling in love ever a plan? These things just happen. And despite him being upfront with her that he lived with someone, she believed him when he said the relationship was nothing more than a business arrangement. At first she hadn't liked it, but as she'd seen more and more of him, she couldn't help but care less and less. He consumed her every thought when he wasn't with her. He made her lonely existence bearable.

She wouldn't call him to see where he was. She knew by now that he would visit if he could. Often things would change right at the last minute and anticipation would turn to disappointment for them both in an instant. She was no fool, though – Jordan would never be her man. The woman he lived with was Kirstie Ryder and everyone knew that she was cold and callous and didn't seem to have love enough for anyone but herself. According to Jordan and her friend Stella, Kirstie swanned around Stoke-on-Trent living off her dad's reputation and money as if she were Lady of the Manor. Yet, even though Sophie knew she would be in for it if Kirstie ever did find out that she was sleeping with Jordan, she couldn't stop. Maybe she was more addicted to him than she cared to admit.

Shivering now as she stood in her pyjamas, she looked down for one last time. The path, lit by a lone lamppost at its middle, was isolated except for a woman with a small black dog. They shuffled along together, the woman using a stick to keep her balance, the dog running ahead every now and then on an extendable lead. Sophie recognised her as Rita from the ground floor. She saw her often walking the path in the early hours with – what was the dog's name? Maisie, that was it.

With a sigh, she closed the curtains. If Jordan did come now, he had a key and could let himself in. Oh, how she wanted him to climb in beside her, cuddle up to her, run his hands over her body and turn her to face him.

She turned out the light, sad to be going to bed alone.

6.00 A.M.

Allie Shenton hadn't been out of bed more than ten minutes when the familiar ringtone on her mobile phone made her groan as she ran back through to the bedroom to answer it. She sighed as she listened to the caller tell her a body had been found under suspicious circumstances. Such bloody bad timing, but incidents didn't stop happening just because she had things in her life to attend to.

As she felt the familiar thrill of excitement that washed over her whenever she got a new case, she tried to push away the guilt. Something to sink her teeth into right now would hardly be a bad thing. She wouldn't be able to spend as much time with Karen, but she might bring peace to another family who had lost a loved one.

'Why were we awake at stupid o'clock this morning? It's only just past six now,' said Mark as she joined him in the kitchen once she'd showered. He turned to hand her a mug of coffee. 'Oh, you're already dressed for work. What's happened?'

'A man's been beaten and killed.' Allie rested her back on the worktop as she took a sip of her drink. 'You won't think I'm heartless if I take the case, will you?'

Mark stared at her long enough to make her feel even guiltier. She hated to see that look of annoyance that he'd perfected over the years.

'No,' he spoke finally, 'but I can't stay at the hospital all evening on my own. It'll drive me insane.'

'I wouldn't expect you to!' Allie almost shouted her words but knew he hadn't meant it to sound like it was such a chore. 'I'll see if I can get off for a couple of hours at the same time you're there.'

'Okay.'

She touched his arm. 'It's not like it's going to be this way forever.'

'I know.'

'We – we'll most likely be planning a funeral this time next week.'

Mark drew Allie into his arms and held her for a moment. She felt the warmth of his chest, the beating of his heart. It was what she needed to keep her focused, grounded even. The past three weeks since Karen had been taken ill had been hard for both of them and she was grateful to him for keeping her spirits up, making her smile through the tears. Even more so after she'd received the rose last week and confessed that it wasn't the first one.

'Please be careful,' said Mark. 'Stay near to Perry?'

'Ugh. If I have to.' She smiled.

'And don't forget to keep a look out. I want you home in one piece.'

'I'll be here.'

6.15 A.M.

Allie pulled on a woollen hat and located her car keys. Luckily there was no ice to scrape from her car, even though the morning was still cold and dark.

Over in the north of the city, Smallthorne was less than three miles from her base in Bethesda Street and just over five miles from Allie's home in Werrington. To get to the scene of the crime, she drove along a main road that cut through a long line of modest new-build properties, the odd light illuminating a downstairs window here and there. Past a large open space with a low wall around it and next up were the flats.

Harrison House had been built in the eighties and was mostly full of renting tenants. Like anywhere, certain people were prone to causing havoc but most of the time the shouts the police received were for either low-level domestics or anti-social behaviour. Allie cast her mind back, trying to think of more serious incidents in the vicinity, but apart from a knife attack on a man in his late fifties several years back, she came up with nothing. Still, she wasn't relishing spending time there.

It was so early in the morning it took her just minutes to get through the streets. She left the main road and turned right into a cul-de-sac, the only way to drive in to Harrison House. There wasn't room there to park her car, so she squeezed it into a ridiculously small space in the car park, partly blocking in a marked police car. As she got out, she spotted DI Nick Carter's BMW. Yet again, she wondered if she would ever be ready to be in charge of her own murder investigation, or if she still wanted to stay hands-on as a detective sergeant, with her ear to the ground so to speak.

In front, she could see the path had been cordoned off with crime scene tape. In the distance, she saw the familiar sight of a white tent erected to contain and conceal evidence as well as the body. Even in the awakening first light, there were a few bystanders keen to rubberneck. Allie glanced up towards the flats as she locked the car door. There were several lights on at windows here too, people hanging over the walkway to look down upon them. She wondered as always if the killer was amongst those watching or if they had simply been woken by the noise as officers responded to the incident.

Harrison House was the type of place where everything could be going down, or nothing at all, and no one would be any the wiser. Not least the police. Everyone kept themselves to themselves, but an eye on each other too. It was going to be a hard task getting information from the people in those eighty flats. She sighed.

PC Angela Butler stood at the beginning of the path.

'He was found by a woman out walking in the early hours, Sarge,' she told Allie as she drew level with her. 'She's an old dear – couldn't sleep so was taking her dog out for a pee. Victim's face has taken a right old battering, plus he has a stab wound to the chest.'

'Thanks, Angela.' Allie signed the clipboard and put on protective clothing before stepping inside. Forensic officer Dave Barnett was closest to her as he stood up to take a look around the body.

'Morning, Dave. We meet again.' Allie smiled, despite the sombre moment.

'Hey.' Dave glanced in her direction. 'Yes, I reckon it's been, what – three, may be four weeks?'

'About that. How are you?'

'All the better for seeing your lovely face.' Dave dipped his eyes again.

'Morning, sir.' Allie greeted Nick next. She moved nearer to him and stooped down beside the body, her face screwing up when she saw the wounds that had been inflicted. The man was lying on his side, his features distorted by the beating they had taken. Swollen eyes, nose and lips. Blood had run down his cheeks from a large gash on the head; bruises were still forming even though to her mind he'd most probably died during the altercation. She noticed blood on his shirt and pointed to it.

'Cause of death is stabbing, right?' she asked.

'Can't say for certain.' Nick glanced her way. 'It's more than likely but he did take a good beating about the head as well.'

'Any weapons nearby?'

'Nothing yet. We need to get the area searched ASAP – and the bins.' Nick handed an evidence bag to her. Inside was a wallet, a wad of twenty-pound notes and a driving licence pulled out from it on the top. 'Take a closer look who it is.'

Allie glanced at it and cursed quietly. 'Jordan Johnson. That's all we need. Does his brother know yet?' Allie hadn't had too many dealings with Ryan Johnson on a professional basis lately, although she had seen him last month when he'd been with one of the victims of their last case at Car Wash City in Longton. He had tried to wind her up then, but she hadn't reacted. She assumed he'd be a little more civil when she saw him today.

'Jordan Johnson?' Dave looked at her for a moment. 'The fella who runs Flynn's nightclub over in Marsh Street?'

'The very same, and no – haven't told the family yet.' Nick nodded and stood up, his knees creaking as he straightened out.

'The brothers have some very dodgy friends as well as enemies. Allegedly they're involved with Terry Ryder and Steve Burgess, to name two that we know well.'

Allie shuddered as she checked out the state of the body. 'Do you think it was a planned attack? Payback for something? Or a mugging gone wrong?'

'I'll tell you more as soon as I know for sure. He's been moved, though.' Dave pointed to the ground. 'The blood has pooled there, indicating he was originally lying on his side. I wonder if someone was checking that he was dead before they left. And that's an expensive watch to leave behind if someone wasn't after him.'

'Someone who was bothered about leaving prints behind, then,' Nick commented.

A few minutes later, Allie left the tent. She took a deep breath as she watched people buzzing around her. It was funny to feel a sense of cautious excitement about their next case. It was a good distraction too – Karen would want her to carry on.

Nick joined her outside. 'Jordan Johnson.' He shook his head. 'His brother isn't going to be too pleased.'

'I know.' Allie wasn't at all relishing the thought of seeing him again so soon.

'You know he's still living with Kirstie Ryder, don't you?'

Memories of the last time she was at the Ryder house rushed to the forefront of her mind. 'Ah, I had hoped he'd moved on by now,' she replied, trying not to blush.

'I'll send someone to deliver the bad news to his next-of-kin but I think you and I can pay a visit to Kirstie,' Nick added. 'Can you set up things around here until then? Start with interviewing the woman who found the body. And, well, you know the drill.'

'Yes sir.'

'It's going to become a media circus, this one.'

Nick paused for a moment and Allie dreaded what was coming next. Nick had known her for too long not to say anything, no matter how awkward the situation felt.

'How's Karen?' he asked.

Allie sighed. 'No better, no worse.'

'Any time you want to come off the case, I don't expect –'

'I'm fine, Nick, thanks. I'd rather keep busy.'

'Yes, I thought as much. But, you know you can go just as soon as, well . . .' Nick's skin flushed a little too. 'You can go at any time.'

Allie nodded, holding in tears. She couldn't look at him now.

'And unless you're going to meet someone in particular off site, take an officer with you at all times – even if it's a uniformed one. Keep your eyes peeled and report to me anything that you don't like the look of.' He paused to clear his throat. 'Especially after what happened to Chloe Winters last month.'

Sifting through paperwork and searching computer files had been something to take Allie's mind off the reality of waiting to say goodbye to Karen – statistics on rapes, sexual assaults and attacks on women in Stoke-on-Trent over the past seventeen years. It hadn't been a nice task, but it was one she was working on alongside her other jobs. So far she could see no emerging pattern but during that last case, the attacker had definitely given her fair warning that it had been happening since – and that it could happen again.

She'd spent a lot of hours comparing and compiling notes, all in her own time. Except for Sam, her work colleague, no one else was aware of what she was doing. She'd interviewed seven women so far, gone back over the evidence that they'd had at the time. She'd dug deep, trying to think who would be unlikely to report a sexual or physical assault; maybe the victim knew her attacker and was frightened about what he would say, which could mean he was a powerful man or one with a violent reputation. For some reason she couldn't quite pinpoint, though, Allie didn't think any of these things. She was more inclined to think of him as a loner, someone who thought he should be more than he was, someone who used force to control women because he had no say in his day-to-day life.

Allie wanted to complain, protest that she didn't need babysitting. A risk assessment had been put into place for her at work, in case he came after her next. But as far as Nick was concerned, she'd only received that one note. Despite the possible danger, she wanted to be able to do her job without restrictions. Although she felt guilty for being dishonest, she'd decided not to tell him about the second rose she'd also received. So far she'd avoided telling Mark that Nick didn't know about it either.

'Also, stay in sight of someone all the time as per the brief,' Nick added. 'Be looked after for a change. And speak to me if anything else happens, yes?'

'Yes, sir,' she nodded.

'He might be around here today.' Nick looked in the direction of the small crowd that had gathered by the end of the path. 'This is a perfect time for someone to target you because you're busy. Just try not to drop your guard.'

As Nick walked off, she hated herself for it but she gave herself a mental shake and pushed all thoughts of her sister, and her attacker, to the back of her mind. The investigation was all she wanted to think about for now.

7.00 A.M.

Ryan Johnson woke up with a foul taste in his mouth and a fuzzy head. He lifted his arm to check the time on his watch. Groaning at the early hour, he turned over and tried to go back to sleep. But the events of the previous night came hurtling at him.

He'd only drunk so much to keep his nerves at bay. After coming home once Kirstie had left Flynn's last night, they'd stayed up for an hour getting their story straight before calling it a night and going to bed. Kirstie had played a blinder at the party. A couple of times would have been enough but in typical Ryder style, Kirstie had laid into his brother. Credit to Jordan, neither of them could stand the bitch but Jordan hadn't lashed out at her once over the three years he'd been keeping an eye on her. Even so, after only a few months living at The Gables, Ryan would be glad to be rid of the bickering that went on between them.

He stretched and yawned, running a hand over his trim torso. Although Kirstie was a looker, she had more money than sense, having loaned him and Jordan enough to buy Flynn's nightclub. She said she'd trusted them, silly cow. If Kirstie thought Daddy would be proud to see how his little girl had turned out, she'd be very much mistaken. In three weeks time Flynn's would belong to him and Jordan and, by that time, he hoped that his brother would still be in hospital, preferably unable to walk unaided thanks to the beating he'd received on Ryan's orders.

It was nothing personal with Jordan, but Ryan had to look out for himself. He was happy for his brother to continue working with him, but he was going to be the one in charge. He didn't report to anyone. When they were younger, he and Jordan had been quite close. But now he wasn't into all that blood-is-thicker-than-water shit. Ryan had been the one whom Jordan looked up to, but once Jordan had stepped in to look after Kirstie, everything had changed. He had lorded it up as if he were part of the Ryder clan. Ryan had put up with it for over two years but eventually he couldn't stand it any longer. Things with his wife had been over for a while, so moving in was perfect. From the Ryder home he could make sure he knew exactly what was going on, and he could keep an eye on his increasingly arrogant brother. Once living with them, though, he'd soon found it was all a big act between little bro and Kirstie and that they hated each other with a passion. So for him, the hit couldn't come quick enough. He couldn't stand this pussy-footing around much longer. And now that Jordan was in no fit state to look after anything, things could move on as planned. It was a big risk but hey, only the brave would dare mess with the Ryders.

His phone vibrated across the bedside table. As he reached for it, he noticed he had six missed calls. The name of the caller now wasn't a welcome one.

'What do you want?'

'I've – I've been calling you for ages. Ryan, I –'

'This had better be good, Nicole,' Ryan butted in, 'or else I'm going to string you up by that false hair of yours. What do you want?'

'It's Jordan.'

Ryan rubbed at his eye with a knuckle. Then his heart began to sink at her pregnant pause.

'He's dead, Ryan. He's been stabbed.'

⌣ ⎯⎯

'What do you mean, he's dead?' Kirstie Ryder said once Ryan had come into her room to tell her the news. She pulled back the duvet and jumped out of bed, following him as he raced into the family bathroom. 'What's happened?'

Ryan rested his forehead on the tiled wall before banging his fist on it. 'I don't know everything yet.' He turned his face to look at her, tears glistening in his eyes. 'The police told Mum that he's – he's been stabbed.'

'No.' Kirstie shook her head. 'But he can't be! That wasn't part of the plan, was it?'

'You know it wasn't.'

Kirstie began to cry. 'Did it happen at Harrison House?'

'Yes.'

'So it must have been one of Steve Burgess's men.'

'We don't have any proof.'

'Then we'll find some.' Kirstie laid a hand on his arm. 'Someone must have seen something.'

'At three o'clock in the morning?' He threw her a look. 'Yeah, everyone would be walking around then. It's the reason we chose that time. And those flats – there's no cameras. We might never find out who it was.' Ryan turned round and with his back to the wall sank to the floor. 'When I get my hands on them . . .'

Kirstie wiped at her eyes before sitting on the floor by his side. 'I'm so sorry, Ryan.' She put her arms around him, tried to bring him into her embrace but he pushed her away.

Just as quickly he was up to his feet. At the sink, he splashed cold water on his face.

'I need to go and see Steve,' he said, 'find out what went wrong.'

'Jesus Christ, Ryan,' Kirstie sobbed. 'We have to go and see your mum first.'

'I'll go afterwards.' He flicked his eyes her way. 'Are you sure you have your story straight?'

'I left Flynn's at eleven, you left at midnight and we were both here. Neither of us saw Jordan as he didn't come home.'

Ryan nodded.

'And you're sure I don't need an alibi for that hour as he was with you until midnight?'

'I'm sure.'

'Steve has that on CCTV?'

'Yeah.' Ryan ran a hand through his hair. 'Shit, I was probably one of the last people to see him alive now. This is some fucking cock-up.'

'There were lots of people who saw him last night,' Kirstie reassured. 'It was why the party was set up. Don't worry about that side of things. Although if this comes back at me, my dad'll have my arse out on the street. He said if I get into any more trouble, I'll be out and he –'

'It's always the same with you, isn't it?' Ryan turned towards her, his face creased with rage. 'Let's all think about Kirstie Ryder first. My fucking brother is DEAD.'

'Ryan, I'm –'

He pushed her out of the room abruptly. 'Leave me alone for a minute.'

'But we need to make sure we get our stories watertight. This wasn't supposed to happen!'

The door slammed in her face. Kirstie turned on her heels, padded downstairs and into the living room and located the TV remote control. She flicked through the news channels to see if anything flashed up about Jordan, but there was nothing. Maybe it was too early, or maybe it wouldn't be covered by national channels, would be kept more local. She went through into the kitchen, picked up her iPad and located Signal Radio. Perhaps something would be on the next news bulletin.

With shaking hands, she made a mug of coffee and sat down on the settee. It was at times like these that she very much wished her father was here.

Once Kirstie had gone, Ryan's knees buckled and he sat back down on the floor, head in hands. His little brother was dead and it was all his fault. Yet he hadn't told Steve to arrange for Jordan to be killed. He'd wanted him to maim him, rough him up, at the most put him in hospital for a few weeks so he'd have time to get used to the idea that Flynn's was out of his control and in the hands of his big brother now. He only wanted him out of the loop for a while, not killed!

What the hell had happened? He knew Steve had been at Flynn's last night, the party set up for his wife's birthday a ruse to ensure that they were all in one place and could give each other alibis if necessary. He knew Steve had given the job to someone else but he hadn't been keen on telling him who – said he'd be better off not knowing.

Ryan banged on the walled tiles with the flat of his hand. If it was that gormless idiot Craig Elliott, then there'd be more blood-shed before the day was over. How had a simple fight got so much out of control? Jordan could handle himself but he'd wanted him taken down by surprise, before he could retaliate. How had he ended up being stabbed? A beating, that's what he'd been told was being set up. He'd told Steve not to use any weapons.

After a few minutes, he pulled himself together. The fear of it being found out that he'd set Jordan up for something that had obviously got out of control would keep him going for now. He wasn't sure how he would face his mum if the truth ever came out. She'd be cut to the core to lose one son but to know that the other was somehow involved might send her over the edge. Her heart had been weak for some years now. Why the hell hadn't he thought of that?

It was because he'd been so cocksure that nothing would go wrong. Now, he'd have to make sure that Steve kept his mouth shut too. And if he wouldn't, then he would do some serious damage.

Once he'd showered and shaved, he felt more in control. In his room, he dressed quickly and appropriately in black jeans, a smart but casual dark tweed jacket and a white shirt. First he needed to see if the delivery had been made. He'd start with Steve Burgess, find out exactly what had gone wrong. Next, the inevitable question that would be on everyone's lips was why would Jordan be over at Harrison House in the early hours of the morning. He needed to see . . . what was her name? Sophie – Sophie Nicklin.

Then he would spend some time with his mum, go through what the police needed from the family and hopefully keep poker-faced long enough for them to believe that he didn't have anything to do with his brother's death.

More importantly, he needed to check if the money had been delivered. Because if it hadn't, he would be in much more trouble by the end of the day.

7.30 A.M.

'Allie!'

She turned at the sound of her name and saw Simon Cole, crime reporter for the city's local newspaper, *The Sentinel*, jogging towards her. Dressed in running gear, he paused when he got to her. At least with his hands on his knees while he caught his breath, he was at her eye level for once. He was six foot two to her five foot six, with kind eyes and was one of those people who never seemed to see the negative in anything, despite what he covered in his profession. His brown hair was a tad longer than he usually wore it, at a length where Allie wondered if he was trying to take on the look of a young George Best, sideburns to match. But he was too long and gangly for it to be effective. Instead it made him look awkward but cute – like a little boy on his first day at school making too much of an effort to fit in.

All around them people were gearing up for a long day ahead. In the car park, groups of uniformed officers were arriving. Except for emergency service vehicles, no one else was being allowed in to the cul-de-sac. The top of Rose Avenue, and the only way vehicles could access the car park of the flats from the main road, had been cordoned off for now.

'Never had you down as a jogger,' Allie smiled as Simon looked up at last.

'Done it for years. Even ran the Mow Cop Mile once.' The Mow Cop Mile was an annual local race, known as a fell-runner's revenge. It was run over a mile, a total climb of 550 feet without a single level step.

'Ah, the killer mile.' She screwed up her face in sympathy.

'It did nearly kill me, too!' Simon stood up to his full height. 'You got anything that I can release?'

'Male, early thirties, took a beating. Stabbed once, too. It's possible the stab wound is the cause of death. Found in the early hours of this morning, etcetera etcetera etcetera.'

'Statement coming . . .'

'Probably late afternoon, or evening. We'll be starting house-to-house – or rather door-to-door in this instance – soon. Speaking of which,' she checked her watch, 'it's early. What brings you here?'

'I was just passing,' he grinned.

She threw him a knowing look. 'If you were just passing, why didn't you bring some oatcakes for breakfast? I'm starving.'

'Want me to fetch something for you?' Simon jerked a thumb over his shoulder. 'There's a shop a few minutes away.'

'I was joking.' She shook her head. 'I don't think I could stomach any after what I've just seen.'

Simon grimaced.

'Well, I'll let you know when I have anything to share.' Allie nodded as she saw one of her detective constables, Perry Wright, striding towards them. She was pleased he was here already – he was a good police officer and a good friend too.

'Morning, boss. Simon. Christ, this is an early one.'

'An early one!' Allie tutted. 'I've been here for ages. What's up? Did you need time to do your hair?'

As Simon sniggered, Perry pressed a hand to his gel-held spiked blond cut. 'It takes time to look this good.'

'Yes, but do you have to style yourself on a sixteen-year-old gangsta rapper?'

'Matches the snazzy suit, don't you think?'

Simon laughed. 'You might want to pull your pants over the top of your trousers, though, for full effect.'

Perry rolled his eyes. 'You on the sniff already?' he mocked.

'I was just asking if Allie wanted any breakfast.' Simon's smile was one of innocence.

'You make that sound like you woke up with me this morning!' Allie swiped at Simon's arm playfully. 'And you a married man!'

'Each to their own.'

Perry smirked this time.

'Bugger off and leave us to it now.' Allie shooed him away.

'I'm going.' Simon raised his hand and made the sign for a phone call. 'Get in touch as soon as you have anything for me.'

'Will do.'

Both officers stayed quiet until he was out of hearing distance.

'How's –'

'How's Lisa doing now?' Allie interrupted. Even though she knew Perry wouldn't think anything of it, she didn't want to talk about Karen and then feel guilty that she had put her job first again.

'Great.' Perry grinned. 'Although morning sickness has taken on a whole new meaning again. Morning, noon and night at the moment.'

'Ouch. Well, at least it gives you both time to think about how much sick you'll be cleaning up once little Wrighty comes along.'

It was something Allie had thought about often, her unwillingness to have a child. She'd never had that maternal feeling, not even when holding friends' newborn babies. Not even when she and Mark had become godparents to Sam's little girl, Emily, five years ago. At first she'd thought she was strange, unwired somehow, but gradually she had come to accept it. Mark had, too, although he hadn't been too pleased at first. But it still took some explaining. People wanted them to conform, weren't happy if they didn't somehow.

'It's going to take a lot of door-to-door.' Perry glanced back at the flats. 'But someone must have seen or heard something last night. Want me to get on with that?'

'Yeah, thanks,' Allie nodded, 'and can you deal with the council officer when she gets here? Someone from the emergency call-out team is on their way to help with the co-ordination of removing the rubbish in the bins. Dave's indicated that the weapon was most likely a bat of some sort – a rounders or baseball type, round, not flat like a cricket bat. The area is cordoned off but we need to get the bins sealed off too – ask for an empty bin lorry to collect the rubbish. We might need a secure area to offload it, get it checked to see if anything has been dumped. The entrance and Rose Street at the side are closed too, as you know.'

'Yeah, I've had to park two streets away.'

'We'll need to get that open as soon as we can, the amount of people it houses. I'm going to talk to the old dear who found our victim first and then I'll head off to meet up with Nick.'

'He's been and gone?'

'Yes.' She looked at him pointedly. 'He said you need to look after me.'

Perry smirked. 'I'm down for babysitting duties today, I see.'

'Well, only until he calls me. He wants me to go with him to The Gables.'

'Oh, you're going to the Ryder's gaff?' It was Perry's turn to pull a face.

'Yes.' Allie sighed. 'I drew the short straw.'

'That'll be fun.'

'It'll be déjà vu.'

'If anything, you might lay some ghosts to rest.'

Allie said nothing. It wasn't a ghost that she was worried about. It was more of a demon. Terry Ryder had got under her skin three years ago. She'd been told to use her womanly charms to get to the truth about how involved he'd been in the murder of his wife, however politically incorrect that was. But the man had a certain charm about him, an allure that she hadn't been able to resist, and she too had fallen under his spell.

She shook her head to rid it of past memories. She hated being reminded of the night she'd almost lost everything.

7.50 A.M.

As Perry instructed the uniformed officers who had congregated near to the entrance, Allie made her way into Harrison House. She knocked on the door of flat 107 on the ground floor. With so many flats to cover over four floors, it was a lot of calls to make and log but it probably wouldn't take long, as everyone was in close proximity. This kind of door-to-door inquiry could yield nothing or could prove vital, as it had often done in cases gone by. A member of the public mentioning the tiniest of things had often led them to a conviction.

She glanced around while she waited for the door to be opened. The walkway to this floor was spotless: even the tarmac surface seemed as though it had been mopped. Not a crisp packet or a leaf in sight. A morning newspaper was sticking out of the letterbox of number 105 that she had just walked past. And even though the low-level wall in front was enough for a step-over-and-grab, there were tubs of soil ready for flowers outside the doors of two, although they were chained to the walls. It seemed strange to see such order in a block of flats renowned more for its scruffy exterior. Allie sensed a welcoming pride, found she liked it.

She wondered if the residents of Harrison House would close ranks and look after their own. Often she'd come across streets and blocks of flats where, no matter what had happened, the residents stood by their neighbours, gave them alibis, as if they were untouchable. Most of the time, the police would let them stumble, push themselves into a corner until they admitted the truth. Allie could never understand why people would want to cover up for others who had done wrong.

She turned as the door was opened. An elderly woman stood there, holding a small Yorkshire terrier in the crook of her arm. She had curls in her grey hair, rouge on her cheeks and garish pink lipstick to match her twin-set cardigan and jumper.

'Mrs Pritchard? I'm Detective Sergeant Allie Shenton.' She flashed her warrant card.

'Yes, I'm Rita. I've been expecting you. Come in.'

The door was opened enough for Allie to squeeze through.

'Have you lived here long?' she asked, following Rita slowly as she limped down a narrow hall.

'Twenty-seven years, duck, ever since the block was built. I was one of the first tenants.' Rita puffed out her chest with pride. 'I've seen some changes, mind. It gets worse as the years go by, and now this! Right outside my front door. I don't know what the world is coming to. Would you like a cup of tea?'

'No, I'm fine, thanks.'

Rita put the dog on the settee and flopped down beside her as her knees took the strain. She beckoned Allie to sit down too.

'Nice place you have here,' Allie humoured her, noting the flowered chintz curtains and matching cushion covers, the dusky pink of the fabric three-seater that was barely able to fit in the room and the pile of dolls that stood staring at her from the armchair. She hated those things, knew she would see them in her dreams that night. She always imagined one was going to get off the chair, walk towards her and kick her in the shins.

She took out her notebook after discreetly checking her phone for messages. 'Would you mind going through what happened last night for me please, Rita?'

'I couldn't sleep as usual.' Rita rolled her eyes. 'Arthritis in my knees was stopping me from getting comfortable. I got up to make a cup of tea and well, as soon as Maisie saw me, she went to the door to go out. She's twelve now, bless.' Rita laughed. 'Two old ladies with aches and pains together.'

Allie smiled. 'And what time would this be?'

'It was quarter past three.'

'Do you often wander around during the night? I'm not sure that's a wise thing to do.'

'Oh, Maisie and I only go to the end of the path and back. I walk one way, sit on the wall to catch my breath and then walk back again.' She pointed to the corner of the room where her walking stick was propped up. 'I take my trusted friend with me, but often I don't see anyone.'

'Can you remember anything different at all? Anyone hanging around, any car, anybody? Any noises, that kind of thing?'

Rita laughed. 'There are eighty flats – there's always someone making a noise. But, no, nothing out of the ordinary.'

'What happened then?'

'Well, Maisie disappeared into the bushes.' Rita looked at Allie. 'She's on an extendable lead, you see. Not that it matters much as she can only walk as fast as me. But she began to bark. And that was when I saw him, the poor thing, and rang for you and an ambulance. My granddaughter gave me a mobile phone for emergencies. I was glad I had it with me. We waited until the police arrived, stayed for a few minutes, and then came back inside again, didn't we, Maisie?' She stroked the dog's head as she lay curled up by her side.

'Did you notice anything else?' Allie tried to hurry her along as politely as she could.

'As a matter of fact, I did.' Rita caught her breath for a moment. 'Someone went into the flats while we were on the path.'

Allie looked up from taking notes. 'Go on.'

'I could see someone walking in the distance towards the entrance. I heard the entry door buzzer going off and then it was quiet again.'

'Do you have any idea who it might have been?'

'I couldn't be one hundred per cent certain – my eyesight isn't what it used to be – but it was a woman. She had dark hair, I think. Definitely long.' Rita shook her head. 'No, I can't be sure of anything else.'

'Do you know of anyone in the flats who may be out at that time of night? I reckon you must know most of your neighbours after living here for so long.'

'Well, you must be able to tell by the tidy walkway that we're all of a certain age on the ground floor,' she smiled. 'We like to take care of what we have, as well as each other. The same can't be said about the other floors though.'

'Oh?' Allie cocked her head to the side, in a manner similar to Maisie, she suspected.

'You'd be surprised about some of the things that go on around here,' Rita continued. 'I can't get out much so I do tend to nosy through the window.'

Allie smiled. 'Just what we like, Rita,' she encouraged.

'Now, let me see. There's Leah Matthews on floor one. She often goes out on her own. It could have been her. And there's a new woman on floor one too. Don't know her name though.' Rita paused to think. 'Oh, and there's Stella Elliott. Her hair is dark, not that she bothers to wash it enough, mind. She's a nosy one.

I bet she'll be outside here all day today trying to see what's going on.'

Allie knew of Stella Elliott and her delightful husband, Craig. She'd also had a few run-ins with Leah Matthews, though not so many lately. She'd have to find out what the other woman was called. She made a note of the details. When she'd finished, Rita didn't seem to have any more names for her.

'I don't suppose anyone in the flats was looking down, not at that time of morning?' Allie asked finally. 'Did you notice?'

'I'm sorry, duck, but I couldn't tell you.' Rita paused for a nanosecond. 'Do you know who he is, yet?'

'There's been no formal identification.'

Rita made a big show of sighing. 'I'm sorry I couldn't be of more help.'

'No, you've been really good, thanks.' She stood up, took a card from her pocket and handed it to her. 'If you remember anything, give me a call, please. In the meantime, I'll send an officer to take a statement from you too. I'll see myself out.'

'Do you think he'll kill anyone else?' Rita asked just as she was at the living room door.

Allie turned back to her. 'There's nothing to worry about, Rita. I'm sure we'll catch whoever did this soon.'

She saw the older woman shiver.

'Scares the life out of you, doesn't it?' Rita folded her arms across her chest. 'This sort of thing just doesn't happen around here. My poor Maisie nearly had a heart attack.'

Allie nodded in reply.

'I mean, this is Stoke-on-Trent,' Rita went on. 'I suppose you'd expect this sort of thing if we lived in a big city. It's too close for comfort, if you ask me. Do you have any, what do they call them on the telly programs?' She paused with a finger to her cheek. 'Leads! That's it – do you have any leads yet?'

'We're still making enquiries.'

'You will come back to let me know how things are going on?'

'Yes, of course. You're an important witness.'

'Will I have to go to court?'

Rita put a hand on her chest as if it would all be too much but Allie could see she seemed delighted at the prospect.

'It's early days,' she told her. 'But I will keep you informed.'

Rita smiled and nodded.

'I'd prefer you not to go out so late, though . . .' Allie urged. 'If you do think of anything else, please let me know. Anything could be vital at this stage of the investigation. No matter how small or insignificant you think it might turn out to be. Okay?'

As she made her way back outside, Allie kept her eyes peeled for anyone watching her. She felt desperate for someone to flag her down, keep her talking, show her something, tell her anything. Because she couldn't put off the inevitable for much longer.

She'd be heading for Royal Avenue before she knew it.

———

Sophie had taken a shower and made a cup of tea, and was sitting in the living room. It wasn't long before she became aware of noises outside. A car door slamming shut, and another. Then a voice, the beeps of a van reversing. She got up quickly and moved to the window, gasped when she saw several police cars, crime scene tape across the pathway near to the green holding back some of the neighbours. She craned her neck to look to her left. There was a white tent in the background, and police officers in uniform everywhere.

She checked her phone, trying to push away the rising panic that was threatening to engulf her. There was still nothing from Jordan. It was unlike him not to send her a message, unlike him not to ring. She cast her mind back to when she had last seen him. It had been Monday night, three nights ago now. She hadn't sensed an atmosphere, she didn't think. Oh, yes, she remembered opening the door to him, his hands all over her as soon as she'd closed it behind them. He'd pushed her up against the wall there and then. She pressed her fingers to her lips, still remembering the smell of him as he kissed her and then led her to the bedroom. Words weren't often spoken between them for some time. One thing she would give him credit for was that no matter how late it was in the night, two a.m., three a.m. sometimes, he was always ready to make her smile. Always ready to make her shout in some instances. No wonder she was addicted to him – her dirty little secret.

He wouldn't forget her.

She glanced out of the window again, just in time to see one of her neighbours walking past below. She ran to the front door, scrambled to undo the lock and stepped out onto the walkway.

'Stella, what's going on?' she shouted down to her over the wall.

A woman with brown hair severely tied back in a ponytail looked up. The fact that she was squinting and wore no makeup did nothing for her round face.

'Some poor bastard copped it last night,' Stella shouted back. 'Rita Pritchard found him when she took that mutt of hers for a walk. She said there was blood everywhere. Gave her a right fright.'

Sophie clasped onto the wall as the sense of dread she had felt earlier deepened. She shuddered, feeling goosebumps erupting all over her skin. She had seen Rita last night – she'd been fine then, hadn't seemed in a panic over anything. What time had that been? Half past three?

'Can't believe it, can you?'

Sophie's next-door neighbour, Jude, was leaning on the wall. She was still in her pyjamas, fluffy pink slippers in the shape of rabbits keeping her feet warm.

'You don't expect this kind of thing on your own doorstep. Awful, isn't it?'

Sophie could only nod. As well as Jude, several neighbours had come out to see what was going on. Up above, she could see people on the two floors higher than hers looking down onto the ground.

'You don't mean he's . . . ?' she shouted back to Stella, unsure she wanted to know but feeling compelled to find out.

'Yep, he's a goner.' Stella ran a finger across her throat.

'Is it anyone from the flats?'

'Not sure yet. I suppose we'll have to wait until the police tell us later.' Stella pointed to the tent in the distance. 'He was found on the grass by the path. There's not too many places around here to visit except here. I reckon someone in these flats knows something. Wonder if they'll let on.' She waggled the purse in her hand. 'I'm off to the shops for some cigs. Obviously I'm going to walk past that nice young policeman over by the front entrance and see if I can find out any gossip. I'll let you know if he tells me any. Do you want anything while I'm there?'

'No, thanks.'

Sophie went back into her flat. She glanced at the phone and then at the tent outside the window. The blood drained from her face. Surely it wasn't Jordan? She was being irrational: it couldn't be him.

Trying to stop from freaking out entirely, she tapped out a message.

'Are you okay, babe? Just busy last night? Call me, I'm worried.'

Her fingers hovered over the send button for a second. If this wasn't what she was thinking, he was going to be pissed off with her. But if it wasn't what she was thinking, she wouldn't care. She would tell him off too, for worrying her and not getting in touch. And then she would hug him and not let him go for a very long time.

It was less than a minute later when the phone began to ring. Sophie still had it in her hand. The caller display showed Jordan's name.

'Jordan!' she almost cried with relief as it was answered. 'Are you okay? Where were you last night? I've been worried sick. There's been a –'

'This is Staffordshire Police – who am I speaking to please?'

Sophie pulled the phone away from her ear and stared at it.

'Hello, is anyone there? This is the –'

She disconnected the call and switched it off, her hand covering her mouth. She walked slowly to the window, oblivious to the tears filling her eyes. Peering around the curtains, she could see a man downstairs by the side of the tent. He wore a white suit and was putting something into a plastic bag.

Sophie looked closer – was it a mobile phone?

'No,' she sobbed, dropping to the floor. 'Please don't let it be Jordan.'

⌣

Steve Burgess switched the radio on and turned down the volume to almost nothing. He made a mug of coffee, hoping not to wake anyone with the noise. The last thing he wanted was to wake his wife. Most of the family had been at Flynn's for her birthday party until way after one a.m., despite the glitch around eleven when Kirstie had turned up.

He pulled out a chair at the dining table and sat down. It had been easy to fool people into thinking he was drinking his usual tipple last night but he'd made sure to switch to Coke early in the evening. Even still, his head was pounding, caused by tension he assumed. He'd be the next one to reach a big birthday – it was only three years until he'd turn fifty. He wondered if he was getting too old for this kind of thing as he thought about the day to come. He closed his eyes for a moment. Once the money had been delivered, things would get interesting.

Steve had lived in Stoke-on-Trent all his life. He'd met his wife, Lorraine, when they were both in their early twenties. They'd stayed in the city and brought up three children. Life was good. They lived in a big house in a decent enough area. They had no money worries, something he was proud of despite some of it having been gained illegally. His background was one of poverty, getting by with handouts and hand-me-downs, another thing he'd vowed never to put his own family through. His parents had worked in the pottery industry and had both died early through breathing in all its dust and debris. He'd worked in the industry for a while, too, when he'd left school but he soon realised it wasn't for him. So began a life of flitting from one job to another, mixing with criminals to get the best for his family. So far he had avoided jail – he wasn't quite sure how.

Like a lot of people, he was proud of where he came from, ashamed of its people at times but for the most parts happy with his lot. Stoke-on-Trent was a city with a heart and a wealth of history to be proud of. The six towns were more than just areas: they were like individual neighbourhoods. Yet, with a population of just under a quarter of a million, people could slip under the radar fairly easily.

Steve had known Terry Ryder for years before he'd been sent to prison and had been delighted when he was put in charge of the Longton branch of Car Wash City after Joe Tranter had been murdered last month, something he knew Ryan was pissed off about.

The Johnson brothers had lorded it in Terry's absence for far too long, and Steve had had enough. Once he'd heard how much Terry was offering to set them up, he'd jumped at the chance.

He was halfway through his coffee when the news bulletin came on.

'Police are looking into a suspicious death in Smallthorne. A man, believed to be in his early thirties, was found brutally attacked at the side of Harrison House, off Ford Green Road, in the early hours of this morning.'

The vein in Steve's temple began to pulse as he stared out of the window onto the manicured garden he lovingly tended. He saw nothing of its beauty – not the dew glistening on the hedge like the jewels on the bracelet he'd given to Lorraine yesterday, nor the birds squabbling over the feed on the table. Instead, he listened to the rest of the bulletin with his blood rushing.

He picked up his phone and dialled a number. When there was no reply, he waited to be connected to voicemail.

'You'd better pick up this message soon and get over to the office right now. You have some fucking explaining to do.'

8.15 A.M.

Two mugs of tea in one hand and her iPad in the other, Stella Elliott nudged the bedroom door open with her bottom. She put the drinks on the bedside cabinet and sat down on the bed.

'Cup of tea,' she said.

A grunt but no movement.

She swung her legs up and rested her back on the headboard. She was due some new clothes, she reckoned, especially if the stench coming from her husband who lay snoring beside her had anything to do with it. She could always nag him in to parting with a bit of money when he had a hangover. She checked her watch: she'd give him a few more minutes and then she would wake him up.

Ten minutes later, he turned towards her and stretched an arm in the air. 'What time is it?'

'It's nearly eight thirty. I made you a cuppa.'

Craig sat up and ran a hand over his bald head, scratching at it with his palm. He was a small, squat man with a paunch that had been growing steadily over the years. With his smoke-stained teeth and a drinker's nose, he looked like a washed-up boxer who had lost too many fights. His squashed features often reminded Stella of a bulldog when he was in a temper. He'd been so much better-looking when she had married him fifteen years ago, although he must still have had something about him. If the rumours were true, he'd managed to pull a fair few women in the time they'd been together. She'd caught him out a couple of times; always taken him back afterwards, soft sod her.

But then again, she'd let herself go too. Even at thirty-five, Stella could clearly see her mother looking back at her in the mirror and it wasn't a pretty sight. Too many frown lines, the same large nose, thin lips and high forehead.

She passed him his tea.

'What're you looking at on there again?' His tone was derogatory.

'The news.' Stella gritted her teeth as she heard him slurp his tea. 'Something happened outside last night. There are police everywhere downstairs. Rita Pritchard found someone dead in the bushes and –'

Craig reached for his phone.

Stella ran a hand up his bare back. 'Fancy a quickie?'

'Give it a rest.' He slapped it away. 'I'm not in the mood.'

'Charming.' Stella pouted. 'I don't know why I bother.'

'Look, shut up will you?' He held the phone closer to his ear. 'I'm trying to listen to a voicemail.'

Stella sighed, knowing she was beat.

Craig threw back the duvet and leapt out of bed, knocking her off balance. Drips of tea slopped onto her leggings.

'Ow, be careful! What's the big hurry?' she asked, watching him pull on clothes quickly.

'Something's come up at work.' Craig pushed his feet into his boots but left the laces undone. He pulled a jumper over his T-shirt before heading out of the room. 'I have to go in.'

Stella shuffled to the end of the bed and followed him into the living room. 'Aren't you going to have breakfast first? I've bought some oatcakes.'

'No time.' He spotted his keys on the floor by a pile of change and pocketed them both.

'Well, when will you be back?' Stella folded her arms as he reached for his coat.

'I don't know!' He pushed past her and opened the front door. 'Shit.'

'What is it?'

'Police everywhere.'

'I told you so!'

They both stepped out onto the walkway and looked over the wall onto the ground below. They stood in silence watching for a few seconds. Stella could hardly hold in her glee. There was far more going on than when she'd been down there earlier.

'I have to go, but before I do,' Craig grabbed her arm and began to squeeze, 'I didn't hear a thing, did you?'

'No, I couldn't believe it when I opened the blind this morning. I –'

'What time did I get in last night?'

'I can't remember.' Stella tried to wriggle from his grip but he squeezed harder.

'I said what time did I come in last night?'

'Ow! About half past three.'

'Wrong. I was in about midnight, wasn't I?'

She stared at him. He was asking her to lie for him again and she wasn't sure she should. It was one thing to fib to his friends and family on the odd occasion but not to the police.

He squeezed a little harder. 'What time did I get in?'

'Okay, okay, I got it,' she cried. 'Just after midnight.'

'Good.' Craig glared at her, menace clear in his expression. 'And keep your big mouth shut today. I don't want you gossiping, do you hear?'

She nodded in response.

As he hurried away, Stella rubbed at her arm. She was sure she'd already have red marks on her skin where his fingers had dug in. What the hell was all that about? Had something dodgy happened at work?

Stella loved nothing more than a good gossip but when it came to keeping secrets, she was always the first to spill. The 'don't tell anyone I told you but' line was one of her favourites. She loved catching up with the girls at the fat club, or down at the pub after their weigh-in, or even at work at the chippie. She prided herself in wheedling out information. But she knew when to keep quiet as far as Craig was concerned. Maybe if he'd stopped to think for a minute, he'd perhaps realise how useful to him she might be. She could find out what was really going on inside these flats.

She went back inside and into the bathroom. Once she'd had a shower, she'd ring her friend Leah and they could go downstairs together. Whatever was going on was serious, and she was going to be the first one to find out about it.

9.00 A.M.

While she'd co-ordinated what she could, Allie had knocked on a few doors on ground level as she waited for Nick to get back to her. Rita had been right: most of them on that floor were over the age of seventy. Allie loved chatting to the elderly. Despite their moans and groans about the good old days and the community spirit that had gone missing, they were often so much more accommodating.

But none of the tenants she spoke to had heard anything. Two of them were hard of hearing and the other, although up for most of the night with sciatica, had had a radio on for company so she doubted he would have heard anything anyway. Three of them were sitting outside on the walkway now on plastic garden chairs, a pot of tea stewing and a packet of ginger nut biscuits to share.

She saw Perry speaking to two uniformed officers and walked across to him, checking her phone as she did. There were a few texts relating to work plus two from her friends Kate and Ruth, asking how Karen was. Allie didn't have time to reply to them now but she did want to give Mark a quick call.

'Hey,' he answered.

'Hey.' She smiled, glad to hear his voice, although it wasn't three hours since she'd spoken to him in person.

'I'm just going to ring to see how Karen is. Is there anything you need me to ask?'

She felt her shoulders drop. 'No, thanks, but you're a star.'

'I know – I can't help myself. How're things going for you?'

'Deadly.'

'Oh, very funny.'

'If I didn't joke about it, I'd cry. Will you ring me when you've spoken to the ward sister?' She stopped. 'If I'm busy, I'll have to deny the call but I'll ring straight back when I get the chance. Or I can call you in an hour?'

'Okay.'

She paused. 'Mark, are you sure you're all right with me not – ?'

'You don't have to convince anyone that you want to be with her. You stayed with her for two solid weeks after she was taken ill.'

'I know but I feel so –'

'But you have to be at work. Besides, it's a waiting game, isn't it?'

She nodded even though he couldn't see her.

'And you're keeping a watch out?'

Allie felt unexpected tears well in her eyes. 'I don't deserve you,' she whispered.

A silence followed and she wondered if he had been cut off. She pulled the phone away from her ear to see it was still connected. 'Mark?'

'I'm here. I was just wondering what I could get you to think about to take your mind off Karen.'

'Oh, I'm sure you'll think of something.'

'I'm sure I will.' His laugh was dirty. 'Hmm-mmm.'

'Are you listening to me?'

'I'm – fantasising.'

'Bugger off.'

She disconnected the phone with a smirk. He was trying to keep her spirits up, make her stop thinking of the inevitable, and she loved him so much for it. But the next instant, she let out a sigh. She sniffed and flicked away the lone tear that had escaped. A roller coaster of emotions flooded through her – grief, angst, anxiety.

But right now, she needed to compartmentalise her own feelings for a little longer because there was something else she had to deal with – guilt. It hadn't felt right yet, either, to let Mark know that she would be involved with another member of the Ryder family.

'Perry,' she drew level with him, 'can you do a PNC check, please – see if any of the cars here are registered to Jordan Johnson? And if it's not here, get someone to walk some of the surrounding streets, see if it's parked nearby.'

'Will do, boss.'

She pointed upwards. 'Rita Pritchard mentioned that Stella Elliott lives on floor one.'

'Yeah, I've already seen her hovering around.'

'Me too. I'm going up to speak with her and that layabout husband of hers. Although he hasn't been in trouble recently for fighting, it's a bit too close to his front door for my liking.'

'I was hoping to collar him too,' said Perry, 'but I've just spotted him going out. He was too far away to shout back.'

'Ok, let's leave that until later then. I'd like to chat to them together. I'm sure they'll cooperate the way we want them to much better that way.'

When Craig arrived at Car Wash City in Longton, there were already several vehicles lined up waiting to be scrubbed down, spruced up and polished, despite the bitter cold morning. He couldn't see the big attraction himself, hardly ever keeping his car clean. He preferred to use it as a bin until he had to empty it because there was no room for his feet.

To steady his nerves, he had a bit of banter with the lads before heading for the office at the back of the building. He counted nine of them today, all under the age of twenty, keen despite the weather, dressed in many varied layers and hats. He couldn't remember ever being that keen to do a job himself.

In front of him, the office door loomed. He didn't know what he was more scared of: going in to face the music or not going in and being on the run. There could be any number of people waiting for him in there or it could be just him and Steve. Either way, he was going to get it in the neck. No one was going to believe he hadn't been involved in Jordan's death. It had been tempting but he knew the job could lead to more of the same. He'd done several jobs like this for Steve over the past year. Craig got on with him, mostly because he scared the shit out of him.

He blew out his breath, tapped a knuckle on the office door and went in. Steel-dark eyes bore into him as Steve looked up from behind a desk. Craig swallowed.

'I've been ringing you,' Steve said. 'Where the fuck have you been?'

'I overslept.' Craig shrugged, deciding to play it cocky. He plonked a bag down on the desk.

'Close the door.'

'Prefer it open, if you don't mind.'

'I do fucking mind. Close it.'

Craig did as he was told. As he turned back, those eyes were on him again, this time flitting from him to the bag.

Steve opened the zip, his shoulders drooping when he saw that there was money inside. 'Do you want to tell me how the hell he ended up dead?' he said finally.

'I don't know.' Craig held up both hands. 'He was battered when I left him but that's all.'

In an instance all semblance of calm was gone, and Steve flew across the office, pushing Craig up against the wall. He punched him in the stomach.

Craig coughed as the wind went from him. 'I wasn't carrying a knife! I used a bat.' He pointed. 'It's in the bag.'

'You brought it here?' Steve looked like he would combust.

'I'm about to get rid of it. Could have done without waking up to coppers crawling around everywhere this morning. Luckily, I didn't take the bag home.'

When Steve remained silent, he continued.

'I'd moved my car before I went out last night – I've been seeing a bit of stuff over in Regina Street so I left it at her place, got a taxi there and back from Flynn's. That's where I was until it was time to do the job. After that, I took the money and the bat back to my car and hid them in the boot. Then I legged it in the back way.'

'I thought there was only one entrance to Harrison House, at the front.'

'There is. I'm still nimble enough to climb up a floor from the outside, though.' Craig felt the grip on him release.

'But Jordan shouldn't have died!'

'I heard on the news that he'd been stabbed. Someone must have got to him after me.'

Steve snorted. 'Like everyone is hanging around the flats at that time of the morning.'

'I'm telling you it wasn't me. You need to start thinking who it could have been.'

Steve let him go, moved around to the other side of the desk.

'Have you any ideas?' said Craig.

Steve stacked up the bundles of money. 'No, but they'll wish they'd never got involved when I get my hands on them. Wait a minute.' He counted the bundles again, frowned after a moment. 'Ryder said thirty-five grand.'

'Yeah.'

'There's only twenty-five grand in here.'

Craig shuffled forward, looked inside the bag as if more would miraculously appear, and then at the bundles of notes. A film of sweat began to develop on his forehead. 'That's all I collected, I swear!'

'Don't take me for a fucking mug.' Steve made fists of his hands and leaned on the desk. 'Where's the rest of it?'

'That's all there was!'

'You expect me to believe that?'

'I haven't been in the bag! I wouldn't do that. I know the risks – plus you paid me good money to collect it.'

'Money I want back. You fucked up on the job. You don't deserve payment. I want my five grand, too.'

'No, I –'

'You must be on a death wish stealing from Ryder.'

'Do you think I'd be stupid enough to do anything like that right outside my own front door?' Craig tried to pacify him. 'I'd be prime fucking suspect with my record.'

'It seems more than a little convenient that you live close by and some of the money goes missing.'

Steve still didn't drop his eyes. Craig felt his life depended on a little grovelling.

'When I left, he was breathing, I swear. A beating, you told me: face, body and legs. I know when to stop.'

'What about the flats? You think anyone from there is stupid enough to take it?'

'I don't know.' Craig felt the sweat begin to pool at the middle of his back. His right eye twitched, the pressure to stop it increasing every second. He wanted to be any place but here in this office, stifled by the threat of violence.

'You know why he was there? Why we chose that meeting place?'

'No.'

'He's knocking off a bird in Harrison House. Maybe you could start by finding out who she is. She might know something.'

Craig nodded.

'I want it back by this evening, Elliott.' Steve glared at him. 'Nine p.m. – no later.'

'But there are police everywhere around the flats!' Craig stepped forward, a pained expression on his face, 'I can't just –'

'Just fucking find it!' Steve came round the desk and grabbed the collar of Craig's jacket. He slung him in the direction of the door so hard that he fell to the floor. He kicked him in the stomach. 'If you don't have it by this evening, it's not my feet that I'll be using on you the next time I see you. You got that?'

9.20 A.M.

Craig clutched an arm to his stomach as he sat waiting for the traffic lights to change at Limekiln Bank. All he'd had to do was give Jordan a good beating, Steve had said. Make it enough to put him in hospital for a week or so, off his feet for a few more. He'd wanted to make a quick buck. And fighting for him was easy money. Everyone knew he was a thug. But he wasn't a killer.

His car had been given a quick once-over while he'd been at Car Wash City and the bat disposed of so it was safe to take it home now. He parked on Ford Green Road, noticing a few more neighbours' vehicles nearby. For a moment he sat looking across at Harrison House, wondering whether anyone there knew anything.

Had someone come across Jordan, seen the money nearby and run off with the stash? And if so, why only ten grand of it? Or had someone killed Jordan because they knew he would have a bag full of money, and then taken some of it from him?

Another thought crossed his mind. Could Jordan have taken some of the money himself? Maybe he had conned them all.

And what of the mystery woman that Jordan was knocking off from here? He went through a list of possibilities as to who it might be. She'd probably be quite young, definitely good-looking and maybe a little bit classy – which ruled out half the women in the flats. The other half would be too old, were single with kids or had partners, although that hadn't stopped some of them from straying.

One thing he knew for certain was that it wouldn't be anything to do with Stella. There was no way someone like Jordan would look at his wife – even he found her repulsive at times. She hardly wore any makeup – most days she would slob around the house pretending not to stuff her face on titbits as she was on this latest diet fad, rather than get off her arse and do some exercise to keep everything working. And her job in the local chippie didn't do her any favours at all. But she was always good for an alibi. And she had a nose for gossip.

He and Stella had lived at Harrison House for the past eight years. Between them they knew most of the tenants. Staring at the windows now, he crossed off the ones that didn't fit the bill. He ignored a lot of the families and couples. Discounting Stella, that left two women he could think of. Leah, the dozy bitch who was Stella's best friend, and that posh bird who had moved in next door a few months ago. He knew where he was hedging his money. And he knew just the person to ask to find out.

9.30 A.M.

Craig kept his head down as he made his way back to the flat. Near to the path they had cordoned off with crime scene tape, he saw Stella. If he threw her a line, she would go fishing for him.

He strode over to her. 'I want a word with you.' He grabbed her arm and marched her away from the crowd. Out of ear range, he turned to face her. 'What have you heard?'

'Not a lot.' Stella shook her head, pulling her arm free. 'The police won't say who it is.'

'Who found him?'

'Rita Pritchard. She was taking that mutt of hers out for –'

'Has anyone questioned you yet?'

'Only while I was here. They said they'd be coming to see us both together though.'

He nodded. 'Let me know if anything else happens.'

But Stella wouldn't let it rest. 'Why all the interest?' she asked.

Craig glanced around furtively to make sure that no one was near enough to hear him. 'It's Jordan Johnson.'

Stella's hand shot to her mouth and her eyes widened. 'Shit.'

'Keep it shut for now.' He pointed at her, inches away from her face. 'I'll know if you've said anything.'

'You can trust me.'

Craig glared at her for a moment, feeling her crumbling under his gaze.

'Rumour has it that he was knocking off someone in the flats.'

'No way!' Stella's eyes widened again.

'Find out what you can and tell me as soon as you hear something.'

'Okay.'

He let her go and jogged up the stairs, past several neighbours and a few uniformed officers knocking on the ground floor properties. Once inside the flat, he flopped into the armchair and held his head in his hands. All at once the enormity of how much trouble he was in came crashing down around him.

If he didn't get the missing money back, it was a question of who would come after him first – Steve Burgess, Ryan Johnson or someone sent by Terry Ryder.

He'd have to play safe, use his contacts, wait for the police to do their stuff and then go out once it was dark. He could use his charm, try out his persuasive tactics. Better still, he could use his fists.

At least he was good at something.

Steve knew his next visitor wasn't going to be so easy to pacify. Craig had been gone less than twenty minutes when Ryan arrived. The door reverberated off the wall as he pushed it open with force.

Steve came round the desk towards him. 'Ryan, I'm sorry. I'm –'

'I've just been consoling my mother – organising a fucking funeral!' Ryan tore across the room. 'I told you to warn him off, not fucking kill him!'

'Keep your voice down!' Steve held up his hands, noticing some of the lads looking round at the sound of raised voices again. He closed the door behind Ryan. 'I didn't have him killed. You know it wasn't part of the deal.'

'Someone stuck a knife in him, and when I'm finished with whoever it was, they're going to get the favour returned.'

'Believe me, I'll find out who did it.' Steve rested a hand on Ryan's shoulder. 'But we have another problem. There was only twenty-five grand in the bag.'

'I packed that bag myself.' Ryan eyed him suspiciously. 'There was thirty-five grand in it.'

Steve picked up the holdall and unzipped it. 'Does it look like it's all in there?'

Ryan stretched the opening with his hands and looked inside. 'There was thirty-five.' He frowned. 'Who did the job?'

'Elliott.'

'Oh, for fuck's sake.' Ryan kicked out at the leg of the desk.

'He says he didn't stab Jordan. He beat him up, just like we planned – just like he was paid to do – and then he legged it with the bag.'

'And he didn't count the money after he'd picked it up?' Ryan stared at him incredulously.

Steve raised his eyebrows. 'Would you have stood in the middle of that path and counted it out?'

'I would have counted it when it was safe!'

Steve shook his head. 'If he does have it, his days are numbered. If he's given it to someone else to keep safe until this has blown over, I want it back first and then I'll deal with Elliott. Or maybe someone did take it. Either way, he's in a lot of fucking trouble.'

'What's he doing now?'

'I've told him to put out feelers.'

Ryan's hands clenched into fists and he stepped closer to him. His eyes were dark, a vein popping in his temple. 'I trusted you to do a job.'

'I did the job!'

'You didn't do it very well!'

Steve folded his arms, wondered if what he was about to say was a good idea or not. But he had to know.

'How are you so certain that your little brother didn't siphon some of it for himself?'

'You bastard!' Ryan threw a punch, catching Steve on the chin. 'You killed my brother and now you're trying to fool me into thinking he stole the money, too?'

Steve stepped back and raised his hands in the air. 'Calm down and think rationally, will you?'

'My brother's dead!'

'How long have we worked together? Do you really think I'd be double-crossing you after all this time? We're friends, Ryan. I have your back.'

'Jordan had my back.'

'Really?' Steve raised his eyebrows. 'You're so certain of that?'

Ryan paused for a fraction. 'He had my back.'

Sensing the younger man was calming down a little, Steve continued. 'The woman he was knocking off . . . It wouldn't be anything to do with her?'

'I don't think so.'

'Do you know her?'

Ryan shook his head.

Steve thought for a moment. 'Well if you don't have the money and I don't have the money, then who the hell does?'

9.45 A.M.

Ryan screeched off the forecourt of Car Wash City. There was no way he was giving Burgess the name of the woman whom Jordan had been seeing. If she had no involvement in his murder, he didn't want to hurt his mother if anything untoward came out. Betty wouldn't want to know that he'd been disloyal, even if she didn't know the true nature of Jordan and Kirstie's relationship. She was still getting over the break-up of Jordan's marriage. Besides, he needed to check with her – this Sophie Nicklin – to see if she knew anything.

He drove down King Street, thankful of the traffic that would keep his speed down. What had Burgess been thinking? He would never have trusted Elliott to do the job. Or was this part of the plan for something to go wrong?

He didn't trust Steve – had never liked the man, just tolerated him because of who he was. The money had been arranged to do a bigger job, one that he was certain would hold him in good stead if it happened. Would it be pulled off now or would the heat of the police around Jordan's death mean that it would be put on hold? He hoped to God it wouldn't. He wanted rid of Kirstie as much as he had known his brother had.

Yet, despite his brother's death, it left Flynn's nightclub solely in his hands now come the end of March. He'd take great pleasure in sacking Burgess. He'd even enjoy throwing him off the premises. Burgess had always seemed like an undercurrent threat to him, as if he had been sent to keep an eye on him and Jordan as well as be a father figure to Kirstie. He'd often wondered why Terry hadn't sent him in to do the job that Jordan had done. Maybe it was an age thing to keep Kirstie happy. But then again, Kirstie knew when to toe the line. Ryder always put people in their places, family or not.

10.00 A.M.

When Leah woke up, she knew by the pain in her head when she moved that she wouldn't be able to recall what time she'd got in the night before – couldn't even remember getting home. Still it had been good to let off steam after the crap week she'd had. Her supervisor had hauled her into the office last night and put her on written warning after being late again. One more mark-down and she'd be out of a job. Well, that had certainly put her in a good mood for the rest of the week. It wasn't even as if she had a great job. She worked in a restaurant – it was a ten-a-penny role. But it was a position that she needed. She was up to her eyes in debt, plus she owed Kenny Webb so much money that she had to look over her shoulder every time she went out the door.

By her side, her phone beeped an incoming message. It was from her friend, Stella.

Wake up sleepyhead. I'll be along in ten minutes. Something BIG is going down! Sx.

Leah sighed. The only thing she was interested in getting down was something that would stop the nausea rolling over her every time she moved. She pulled the covers back and sat on the edge of the bed, head in hands. Her forehead was clammy. Christ, she must have been wasted last night. She tried to think who she had seen; sometimes that would trigger a memory. She hated it when she blacked out. She could have done anything, and with anyone. Still, at least she was in her own bed. That was definitely an added bonus after some of the places she'd woken up in lately.

Yet again, she wished she were in a stable relationship. The longest she'd been with a fella so far was two years and that had finished because she'd been giving more violence out than she'd been getting back. It had scared her, the loss of control on her part, so she'd got out. It had also left her lonely and, at twenty-seven, all she wanted to do now was find someone to love, maybe start a family, erase the memory of so many one-night stands. But what man in his right mind would want a woman like her?

She glanced around the chaos in the room, the floor strewn with size ten clothes and size six shoes, discarded from the night before. Her makeup bag, hair straighteners and paraphernalia dropped where she'd last used them on the floor by the window. Her knickers curled up where she had stepped out of them. *Yeah, Leah Matthews*, she chastised, *you really are quite some catch.*

As she stood up, she noticed a bag on the floor. It was black with a white trim, a drawstring for a handle, the type you could throw over your shoulder if you were going to the gym or swimming. She frowned, trying to think where it had come from. It certainly wasn't hers, and it hadn't been there when she'd left the flat the night before.

Had someone come home with her last night?

'Hello?' She felt stupid saying it as she crept along the hallway that linked every room: the tiny kitchen squeezed into one corner, the living room, a bathroom that had seen better years and two small bedrooms. But she was alone. There wasn't a strapping hunk wearing next to nothing, preparing a bacon buttie before bringing it to her in bed. There wasn't even a fat hungover bloke, which was what she normally woke up next to on mornings like this one.

She went back into the bedroom and crouched on the floor next to the bag. With an overwhelming sense of curiosity, she pulled it nearer and turned it over. There were no indications of who it belonged to. Nothing. She undid the drawstring and looked inside.

'Shit a brick!'

The bag was full of money – twenty-pound notes, fifty-pound notes, bundles and bundles of them. She threw it down on the floor again. Trying to calm her breathing, she willed herself to think. Was she saving it for someone? Had someone given it to her as she'd got home last night – taking advantage of her drunken state to con her into keeping it for them? Surely she hadn't been that stupid?

Think, Leah, think!

A rush of adrenaline tore through her as she remembered her walk home last night, cutting through the grass at the front of the flats and tripping over something.

Suddenly her memory came back fully and she raced to the bathroom, managing to get her head over the toilet and her hair out of the way before she threw up.

A body. She'd tripped over a body.

Leah slumped to the floor, gasping as she struggled for breath, realizing how much trouble she was in. Her prints were all over the bag. Her footprints would be next to him, for Christ's sake. She would be caught in no time – she might even be charged with his murder!

She went back into the hallway and fished her woollen gloves from out of her coat pocket, slipped them on. Then she picked up the bag and tipped the notes onto the floor.

One thousand pounds in each bundle.

Ten bundles.

Leah laughed nervously. What she could do with that. She could pay off the money that she owed to Kenny Webb and still have some left. She could take her mum out for a nice meal, somewhere posh. She could buy a few new clothes.

But she wasn't stupid. It couldn't be coincidence that there was a dead man and a bag of money within yards of each other. The police would probably want to check everyone's flat too.

Still, the money hadn't been near the body. It had been hidden away in the bushes. So maybe the two things weren't connected. It could be a possibility.

In your wildest dreams, Leah. Someone will be looking for it.

There was a knock at the front door. Leah gasped, looking around her in horror. Hurriedly, she shoved the money back inside the bag, removed the gloves and pushed everything under the settee out of view.

Allie took a call from the remaining member of her team, DC Sam Markham. Sam had gone straight to the office that morning rather than come on site when she'd been given the details of the crime. Without asking, Sam always became the officer manager, something that the whole team was grateful for. Allie knew she would have started to set things up for them, log in actions, marry up and tie things together and do the necessary to keep things running smoothly. Everyone took her a little for granted but she was damned good at what she did.

'Hi, Sam. Can you source out a phone number for me for anyone who works at Flynn's nightclub in Hanley? I need to get over there to pick up some CCTV, have a nosy round inside. It's looking possible it was the last place that Jordan Johnson was seen alive.'

'Will do.'

As she spoke, Allie sensed someone nearby. She turned around, expecting to see someone waiting for her, but she was alone.

'Erm . . . can you run a check on Johnson's phone for me, please?' she added. 'Get the usual, but in particular the number from which a text message was received at eight oh one a.m.'

'Did you say *eight* oh one?' Sam sounded confused.

'Yes, Dave Barnett found the phone on the ground nearby, heard the ringtone. He rang the number. A woman hung up when he asked who he was speaking to.'

'Right. I'll get on to that. I've begun doing checks on other numbers from the family too. And also I'm checking on the residents nearby – see if any of them have been in trouble lately. Maybe with it being one of the Johnson brothers, it could be gang-related.'

'Thanks.' Allie nodded into the phone. 'I'll get Perry to have a word with the Granger brothers too.'

'Oh, and there's Craig Elliott. He's in flat –'

'Two oh nine,' she interrupted. 'Yes, I'm off there soon.' Perry had sent her a text message to say that Elliott had returned and gone up to his flat. Oh, how much fun they would have interviewing him. Whether he knew anything or not, he was bound to keep it to himself. She and Perry weren't his favourite people.

When Allie disconnected the call, she looked around again but couldn't see anything out of the ordinary. She was being ridiculous. Surely he wasn't here? She pulled her coat closer and, head down, made her way over to Perry.

10.15 A.M.

There was another knock at Leah's door and a voice shouted out.

'Are you in there, Leah? What the hell are you doing?'

Leah sighed with relief as she went to answer the door.

'You took your time.' Stella marched past her and into the living room. She glanced around before nodding her head in the direction of the bedroom. 'What's up? Aren't you alone?'

'Of course I'm alone,' Leah replied. 'I was on the loo.'

Stella seemed to be pacified. 'You're missing the best thing ever. There's a bloke been murdered on the pathway. Rita Pritchard found him this morning. He's been stabbed and beaten up. She's lording it up down there telling everyone what she saw.'

'No way!' Leah feigned shock, her stomach still churning.

'I know! Can you believe it? Practically right outside our door.'

Leah went into her bedroom.

'Where did you get to last night?' Stella shouted through to her.

'I didn't go out in the end.' The lie rolled off her tongue as she pulled on a pair of jeans. 'Couldn't be bothered.'

'But it smells like you did!' Stella said.

'I was tired so I bought some cans and watched TV.'

'That's not like you – did you work late?'

'Only until eight. Like I said, I couldn't be bothered.'

'Did you hear anything outside then?'

'At quarter past three in the morning? Why would I?' Leah snapped.

'How do you know it happened at quarter past three?'

'I don't!' She swore under her breath. 'It was just a figure of speech, that's all.'

Stella's head popped around the bedroom door. 'The police are going to be talking to everyone, they told me.'

'But I didn't hear anything. Did you?'

'No, I was at work until half ten. As soon as I got in, I fell asleep on the sofa until Craig came in about midnight.' Stella dropped her eyes for a moment. She sat down on the unmade bed. 'I wish you'd said you weren't going out. I would have changed my shift and come along to see you.'

'It was a last-minute thing. I was in a foul mood after another bollocking at work.'

'The police woman keeping guard told me that they interview whoever is in and then come back until everyone is accounted for.' Stella clapped her hands like a four-year-old. 'How exciting.'

'Someone died!' cried Leah. 'It isn't a freak show!'

'I know, but . . . What's got in to you? The first bit of excitement around here and you go all flaky.'

'By excitement, you mean that someone lost their life?'

Stella wouldn't be put off. 'Oh come on, Leah, we don't know the bloke from Adam! And there are some fit men in those uniforms. We could have a giggle.'

Leah shook her head in exasperation.

'Okay, don't get your knickers in a twist. Go and put the kettle on. And then we can stand on the walkway and have a nosy.'

Leah tried to stop her hands from shaking as she added tea bags to two mugs. What should she do? The problem wasn't going to go away: she could almost hear it calling her name from the next room. Could she trust Stella to keep quiet? She desperately needed advice.

She and Stella had been friends from the age of five, ever since Diane Minton had pulled Stella's hair and Leah had punched her in the thigh, giving her a bruise and landing herself in trouble. But despite her penchant for lashing out with her fists, Leah had never had a go at Stella, though they'd had their share of spats. It seemed their friendship worked because Stella was there for her, no matter whether she agreed with what she was up to or not. So what was stopping Leah from confiding in her friend this time?

Once the water was added, Leah stirred the liquid absent-mindedly. Of course she knew the reason why she hadn't said anything. She wasn't sure that she could trust Stella with this one. If that arsehole husband of hers got wind of anything, he'd want a cut of the money. Not that she was planning on keeping it herself but, for now, she wanted to hold on to it. Once it went dark, she'd slip out and hide it somewhere. Then if anyone did search the place, she'd be in the clear. It would give her some breathing space, time to think with no pressure.

Trying not to let the drinks slosh, Leah joined Stella outside.

'I wonder when the police will give out his name,' Stella said as she took a mug from her.

'I'm not sure I want to know who he is.' Leah stood next to her, hoping the blush spreading across her cheeks wouldn't give her away.

Stella looked at her like she was mad. 'Everyone wants to know, you silly mare. It's – what's that saying?' Stella searched through her mind. 'It's too close for comfort, that's the one.'

They both peered down on the scene below. A line of police had begun to walk along the green. They were taking tiny steps, searching for evidence. Leah gulped: she couldn't have dropped anything, could she?

Stella held up her finger as her phone rang. 'Hi, hon.'

Leah watched as Stella's face dropped. She could hear someone shouting down the phone from where she was.

'Yes. No, I haven't told anyone! I'm coming.' Stella moved the phone back from her ear and looked at the screen. 'Bloody bastard's cut me off mid-sentence.' She handed her drink to Leah. 'I have to go. Craig's doing his nut because he wants me back at the flat again.'

'Why?'

Stella paused for a nanosecond, looking around to see that the nearest neighbour was two doors away. Leah looked, too.

'Promise not to tell anyone if I tell you what I know?' Stella kept her voice low. 'The dead man out there? It's Jordan Johnson. You know – he runs Flynn's nightclub in Hanley.'

Leah knew exactly who he was. She felt herself sway slightly. 'Jordan Johnson. Is he sure?'

'Yes, he's sure. And from what he tells me, the Johnson family are bloody mental. I wouldn't like to be in the killer's shoes. Can you imagine what . . . what's up?'

Despite her earlier prep talk to herself about keeping quiet, Leah found she couldn't breathe and her cries came out as big rasping sobs.

'What's the matter?' Stella's eyes narrowed. 'Ohmigod, you know something about it, don't you?'

Leah nodded. 'You have to promise now, not to tell anyone.'

'I swear.' Stella crossed her finger across her heart and pushed her back into the flat. 'You and me, we go back forever. Of course, you can trust me to keep a secret.'

———

Craig's phone rang, bringing him back to reality with a thump. He gulped when he saw who it was. Pressed the answer button with dread.

'You fucking killed my brother!' Ryan yelled.

'I didn't.' Craig stood up and paced the room. 'I swear to God it wasn't me.'

'You were told to rough him up enough to put him in hospital for a couple of weeks.'

'I only –'

'Whose idea was it to kill him? Was it Burgess's?'

'No, I –'

'Was it Ryder then? Did he set us up?'

'I don't know!' Craig ran a hand over his head and down his neck. 'Do you really think I'd kill your brother after knowing you both for so long? And anyway, everyone knew I was the one roughing him up! Do you think I'd be so stupid as to kill him and not expect to be prime suspect?'

'I think you'd do anything for money, you fucking scrote – and you were the last person to see him.'

'I can't have been. I did what I was told and grabbed the money.'

'So how did he end up dead?'

'It wasn't down to me!'

There was silence down the line. Craig took the opportunity to put his point of view across again.

'I didn't stab him, mate. I couldn't do that.'

'Did you see anyone else?'

'No. Steve thinks I've kept some of the money for myself. I suppose he told you that it wasn't the full quota I delivered?'

'Yeah, I want the ten grand back too.'

'But I don't have it!'

'Find it then. And when you do, I want it bringing here. You do not give it to Steve.'

'But –' Craig screwed up his face. 'Fuck. I don't know what to do. I don't want to be on the wrong side of Ryder.'

'Forget Ryder. I'll be worse than him if you fuck with me, Elliott. I want that money and I want it in my hands by tonight. You got that?'

'What if I can't find it?'

'Then I'm coming after you – and then your wife. And your family. And your wife's family. I'll take them all down if you don't get me the money.'

Craig was left holding the phone as he was cut off. 'Ryan? Ryan? Fuck!'

He needed to find that money, and pretty sharpish. He had a feeling his life was going to depend on it.

10.30 A.M.

Leah knelt down and pulled the bag out from under the settee. She passed it to Stella.

'Holy crap.' Stella's eyes were on stalks when she looked inside. 'Where did you get that from?'

'From him.' Leah pointed to the window. 'Jordan Johnson.'

Stella drew in her breath.

Leah sat down on the settee, her right knee jangling. 'I am in so much trouble. What if they think I killed him for the money?'

'You didn't – did you?'

'No, I did not!'

'Well, how did you get . . .' Stella pointed to the bag, 'that?'

'It was on the path.'

'Just like that?'

'Yes . . . no, well . . . I can't really remember.'

'How much is there?'

'Five thousand pounds.' Leah couldn't look her in the eye as she lied.

Stella sat down next to her. 'Tell me everything.'

'I'd been up to Hanley. On my way home, I cut through the back way and across the grass.'

Stella pouted. 'How many times have I told you not to walk that way when you're on your own? It's dark and you don't know who's around.'

'I was desperate for a pee! I was running over the grass and I didn't see him and I tripped over him . . . Jordan Johnson.'

'I thought you said you didn't know who it was.'

'I didn't know who it was until you told me! He wasn't moving, I swear. I spoke to him but nothing.'

'So you just *left* him there?'

'I must have done. Because the next thing I remember was waking up and seeing . . . that.' Leah pointed at the money.

'But he might still have been alive. If you'd called for help, he might not have died.'

'When I rolled him over, he just flopped.'

'You mean you touched him?' Stella recoiled.

'Yes, but not with my hand, I don't think. I nudged him with my shoe.'

'Are you certain he was dead?'

'He looked like he was.' Leah gasped. 'You don't think they'll trace it back to me, do you? I mean, I hardly touched him.'

'I don't know. I'm not the police. But those women on CSI who prance around in high heels and white vests seem to get a lot of info from clothes.'

Leah burst into tears, her feet bouncing on the edge of the settee. 'What am I going to do?'

'I still can't believe you left him there.'

'I didn't *take* the bag from him. It was lying on the grass by his side.'

'You said it was hidden in the bushes.'

'Well . . . yes, it was.'

'If it was hidden,' Stella paused for a moment, 'maybe whoever killed him was going to come back for it?'

Leah sobbed. 'I hope not.'

Stella shook her head. 'Shit, Leah. What happens if someone saw you and they come after you?'

'I'm a goner, that's what!' Leah wiped her nose on the back of her hand. 'What do you think I should do?'

'I don't know.' Stella shoved her hand in her pocket, pulled out a crumpled tissue and gave it to her.

'But what if the police come searching every flat?'

'The police can't search properties without a warrant and a reason.'

'Are you sure?'

'That's what Craig told me.'

'But surely that's different when there's a dead body outside your house!'

Stella paused. 'Yeah, you're right. It's not worth chancing.' She was quiet for a moment. 'Is there somewhere you can hide it for a while?'

Leah frowned, unsure what Stella was getting at.

'If you hide it in a safe place, then maybe when this blows over, you can keep the money.'

'I could take it to my mum's, I suppose.' Leah shook her head then. 'No, I prefer to keep it where I can see it.'

'If the police find you with it, you could be charged with his murder!'

'I didn't kill him!'

'But you know how they stitch people up if they're short on evidence. You were probably the last person to see him until Rita Pritchard took Maisie for a walk this morning. It only takes one sneaky bastard in Harrison House to get wind of that and someone will start talking. And even if the police don't know anything, the Johnson family will want to know where it is. They'll be looking for whoever killed Jordan too. You need to get rid of it.'

'I can't.'

'I think you should take it to your mum's.'

Leah took a deep breath. 'It seems a little dodgy to move it while the police are around.'

'A little . . .' Stella stared at her, wide-eyed. 'The whole frigging thing is dodgy!'

'I can't undo what I've done!' Leah stood up. 'Should I just throw it out of the window? Let the search party find it?'

'Don't be stupid. Someone will see it fall. There're neighbours everywhere, never mind the police.' Stella thought for a second. 'Shall I have a word with Craig? He might know what to –'

'No!' Leah shook her head vehemently. 'You can't tell anyone!'

'But the police are practically metres away from you!' Stella jerked her thumb in the direction of the door.

'Do you think I don't know that?' She looked down at Stella with pleading eyes. 'I need to think things through. Just give me a bit of time.'

'Okay.'

'You have to promise that you won't tell anyone I have it.'

'I promise,' Stella replied.

'I mean it, Stel. Especially not Craig.'

'I won't tell a soul.' Stella stood up and drew Leah into her arms. 'I'm scared for you, hun, but we'll sort this out.' She glanced at her watch. 'Look, I'd better go and see what he wants me for. You never know, he might have some useful information.'

'You promise not to tell him?'

'I promise. I'll be back as soon as I can.'

10.45 A.M.

Stella left Leah's flat in a state of nervous excitement. As she made her way back to her own flat, her mind was in turmoil with gossip overload. She could see the police had moved along to her side of the first floor. Officers were knocking on doors three away from hers. Once she had seen what Craig wanted her for, she was going back downstairs. The stakes had been raised dramatically. She needed to find out as much as she could now.

She steeled herself for Craig's onslaught. Even she knew she'd have a tough time keeping everything that he and Leah had told her to herself. Jordan Johnson had been murdered and her best friend had stolen a load of money from him. It just didn't get any better than that.

Was she right to feel so excited? The money wasn't Leah's. She had broken the law. But still, she couldn't help the wave of euphoria that kept ripping through her.

Outside their door, Craig stood on the walkway looking down on the commotion. Deciding to keep her promise and not tell him about the money, she rested a hand on his back.

'Where the fuck have you been?' he snarled.

'What's the big rush? I've only been along to see Leah.'

'The pigs are going to be at the door soon. We need to get straight on our story.'

'What do you mean?'

Craig looked behind and grabbed her arm. 'They'll want to know what time I came home last night.'

'You told me to say twelve. I don't understand why I need to lie for you, though.'

He pushed her inside the flat and closed the door. 'You know what the police are like. They only need a reason to lock me up. I'm always the main target for anything going on, just because I have a record.'

'That's usually because you've done something wrong.' She paused. 'You haven't touched Jordan so I don't see why I should –'

'Just do as you're fucking told!'

'Okay, okay,' she cried, flouncing into the living room. 'What do you want me to say?'

'That I got in just after midnight.' He followed her.

'Yes, you told me that already.'

'Just say I bought a takeaway in or something.'

'What takeaway?'

'What does it matter?'

'It matters a lot. They could catch you out if they want to know which one you visited, what you had. What if you say somewhere that is closed now? Or somewhere that has CCTV? You need to think things through.'

'For fuck's sake, this isn't *Law & Order UK*.'

'I'm just saying, that's all.' Stella shrugged her shoulders. 'Anyway, weren't you at Flynn's last night?'

'Yeah, I told you I was at the party.'

'So there'll be CCTV of you leaving, right? You'll be in the clear so you don't need to lie.'

'No, there was no CCTV working.' Craig planted an unexpected kiss on her lips. 'I hadn't thought of that.'

'Why? What's going on? Either you were at Flynn's until you got home at half past three or you weren't.'

'Mind your own business, Stella.'

There was a knock at the door.

Craig pushed her towards it. 'Remember what I said and keep your fucking trap shut.'

Allie flashed her warrant card at Stella. 'Mind if we come in and have a word?'

Stella held the door open and Allie and Perry walked in.

Allie could walk the layout of the flats in her sleep now. Every one in Harrison House was the same. Long hallway. On the left, two small bedrooms. To her right, a kitchen and bathroom, in between them an airing cupboard. To the far end, the living room.

Craig Elliott was sitting on the settee. He glanced at them warily.

'I can't believe someone has been murdered outside here,' he said. 'Do you know who it is yet?'

'Yes,' said Allie, 'but we're not releasing a name until formal identification has taken place.'

'Right.'

Allie was already on alert. There was none of the usual cocksure attitude that they normally got from Elliott. And something wasn't right with Stella, who had quickly turned the colour of an overripe tomato. Blushing before she had started to ask questions wasn't a good sign.

'We're just checking on a few details,' she told them as Perry got out his notepad. 'Can you both tell me your whereabouts this morning between the hours of one a.m. and four a.m., please?'

'That's easy,' said Craig. 'We were both in bed, weren't we, Stella?'

'Yes, that's right.' Stella wouldn't look at either of them. She sat down, seeming more interested in a spot on the wall behind Perry's head. 'We went to bed at midnight, just after Craig came in.'

'Where had you been?' Allie addressed Craig.

'To a party at Flynn's nightclub. I work there but it was my night off.'

'What do you do?'

'Bouncer on the doors.'

'So I suppose people can vouch for you being there?'

'Of course.'

'So they must be able to vouch for what time you left, too?'

'I guess.'

'They have cameras at Flynn's, Mr Elliott?'

'Yes, but they don't always work, though. I think they were down last night. Some problem with the machine, I was told.'

'Ah, that's a pity. How about you?' Allie turned her attention to Stella next. 'Is there anyone who can vouch for you?'

'You've already asked me that.' Stella's face reddened even further. She stood up and then sat down again next to Craig and folded her arms. 'Craig's just said he was at home with me from midnight, so I was with him.'

'You didn't go out at all last night?'

'I was at work until half past ten, The Golden Plaice chippie in Goldenhill.'

'And you got home at . . . ?'

'Eleven. My friend gave me a lift.'

'Name and address of your friend?'

'Sylvia Minor. She lives on Highgate Road, number one four seven.'

Allied nodded. She paused to see if anything more would be forthcoming but she was met with silence. 'A woman fitting your description was seen coming into the building shortly after the body was found in the early hours,' she said after a few moments. 'You don't happen to know anything about that, do you?'

Stella gulped. 'I told you, I was in bed.'

'Just need to hear it from you. It's a process of elimination.'

'Wait a minute! You're not suspecting I had anything to do with the incident outside, are you?'

Allie stayed stoic. 'We've been told she had long dark hair so I'm checking on lots of women in the flats. I'm just establishing the facts.'

'Do you think –'

'Stel, let the good people do their job and be on their way,' Craig tried to pacify her. 'We're not involved so there's nothing to worry about, is there, Sergeant?'

Allie held his gaze. 'Not at the moment, no.' She nodded at Perry and he closed his notebook. As they both turned to the door, she smiled. 'We'll see ourselves out.'

Once outside on the walkway, Allie looked at Perry and shook her head. They moved away for a moment. Then Allie grabbed his arm and they stepped back and listened. Sure enough, she couldn't make out what was being said but there were definitely loud voices.

'Something heated being discussed, boss?' Perry raised his eyebrows and smirked.

Allie nodded. 'It's just like Stella to land herself in it because she says too much. She was so defensive when I asked where she was.'

'Sounds like she knows more than she's letting on.'

'And it seems that Elliott is none too pleased about it as well.'

They walked away, Allie looking back over her shoulder, half expecting Craig to come storming out of the flat.

'One of them, or both, are keeping something from us,' she said. 'We'll wheedle it out of them soon.'

———

'So do you want to tell me where you were for the three hours you're wanting me to lie about?' Stella stood in the living room with her arms folded.

'Just doing some business.'

'I hope that wasn't the female type of business that you were doing last year. Because you told me that was all over.'

'It's business,' he reiterated. 'I need to go to Flynn's later.'

'Is that to do with Jordan?'

She heard him sigh. 'Why do you say that?'

'Maybe because your boss has died and I thought that you'd be consoling Ryan and the others.' Her voice dripped with sarcasm but then she relented. 'I know Jordan was a big part of everything.'

'Jordan was a piece of shit who didn't mind who he trod on to get his own way.'

Shocked by his hostility, Stella said nothing.

Craig glared at her, enough to make her skin redden again. 'You haven't told anyone who it is, have you?' he asked, his tone accusatory.

'Of course not.' She dropped her eyes for a moment. 'Craig, what's wrong? You're so tetchy today.'

'Nothing.' His phone rang. He glanced at it and groaned. 'I have to go.' He checked his jacket pocket for his keys before answering the call.

'When will you be . . . ?' Stella sighed as he walked off. She stood for a while watching everything below but she couldn't stop thinking about Leah.

Inside the flat, she grabbed her purse again. She'd go downstairs, see if she could find anything else out. Then she'd go to the shops, grab some sandwiches and head on back to see Leah. No doubt she'd be too scared to show her face yet. Then they could work out what to do about the money. If she played her cards right, some of it could be hers by the end of the day.

And if not, there might be a finder's fee in it somewhere along the line.

11.30 A.M.

It had been over three years since Allie had been to Royal Avenue, yet just pulling up outside The Gables had her covered from head to toe in goosebumps. A flood of memories rushed to her mind, things she thought she'd buried long ago. Even now she couldn't believe her own stupidity – the danger she'd put herself in. And still she felt mortified at having been attracted to Terry. Him, of all people – a criminal and a murderer. She knew she'd gone too far to get at the truth, and it still haunted her.

The Gables was a five-bedroomed property with a three-car garage attached to it and a specially commissioned stained-glass window above the entrance depicting the emblem of the local premier football team.

Allie wondered if there were more secrets behind the oak-panelled double doors now than the first time she had called. Back then, she'd been visiting and interviewing local businessman Terry Ryder after his wife had been murdered. Their daughter Kirstie had been almost eighteen. After her father had been sent down, Kirstie had stayed in the house, taking over things. But as much as she liked lording it up while he was in prison, and thought she had the freedom of the city because no one dared touch the daughter of Terry Ryder, she had kept her nose fairly clean.

She wondered, too, if having a Johnson brother nearby had worked out well for Kirstie. It must have given her confidence, and Allie wondered whether that would be knocked with his death, or whether she'd still be as bolshie as she had been at seventeen.

When Nick arrived a couple of minutes later, he briefed her on his findings. Jordan's mother, Betty Johnson, hadn't seen Jordan for three days but had spoken to him on the phone a few times.

'She doesn't have an alibi as she was in the house alone last night,' he told Allie as they walked up the driveway of The Gables. 'But at this stage in the enquiry, there's no reason to think that she was in any way involved.'

'Thanks, sir. Did you hear that we found his mobile phone? It went off while we were on scene. It was in the grass: it might have been slung there so we're looking for prints, too. Someone sent a text message. Dave heard the alert and then rang the number back. A woman answered but she hung up when he asked who he was speaking to.'

'Interesting.'

'I tasked Sam with getting on to Single Point of Contact and they're working on the call log now.'

'Thanks. Right, let's get this over with.'

Allie could easily see why Kirstie Ryder would fall for the bad-boy looks of either Johnson brother when Ryan opened the door. At thirty-seven, he was very much a version of his younger brother – tall, dark hair and skin, slim and healthy. His clothes looked expensive, as was, she assumed, the cologne she could smell wafting her way. She breathed it in, enjoying its fresh, clean aroma compared to the vile odours she'd smelt coming from some of the flats that morning.

'Mr Johnson, Detective Inspector Carter. This is Detective Sergeant Shenton,' Nick introduced them both.

'Yes,' Ryan looked at Allie in particular, 'we've met before.'

Nick raised his eyebrows.

'I was talking to Joe Tranter not long before he died. Terrible news about him.' Ryan held the door open and met Allie's stare. It made her feel uncomfortable but she didn't let it show.

Inside, the hall was exactly the same as Allie remembered it from three years ago too. Cream textured wall, a light oak parquet floor and a ridiculously over-the-top chandelier. To her left, a large oak cabinet claimed most of one wall, glass doors protecting a collection of Wedgwood pieces and Royal Doulton figurines. Up above, a lofty ceiling and a galleried landing. Downstairs, double doors to their right.

'We're sorry for your loss,' said Nick.

Allie noticed Ryan's eyes welling up as he showed them through to the living room.

'So you've been staying here too?' Nick asked.

Ryan cleared his throat. 'Yes, I separated from my wife a few months back.'

It took all of Allie's will to stop from giggling at the sight of the huge portrait of Kirstie and Jordan on the back wall. They were sitting on a red sofa, wearing jeans and white shirts. Both had bare feet and cheesy grins, artfully posed but dreadfully tasteless, in her opinion. The image must have been at least six foot by four. She laughed inwardly, thinking how Terry Ryder would have responded if he'd known it was there. Such trash in his oh-so-orderly house.

She looked around, anywhere but at that awful picture, and felt a blush rising sharply across her cheeks as she tried not to picture herself sitting on the settee with Terry. The decor in this room was as it had been before, too, which surprised her a little. Kirstie obviously hadn't felt the need to make her mark in her father's absence. There were two large black leather settees, a coffee table in the middle of the vast floor area, and violent slashes of red added here and there in stark contrast to the pale cream walls. The room led onto a large dining area and state-of-the-art kitchen, glazed doors framing a lawn large enough to hold a marquee.

A young woman with long dark hair walked into the room. She was small and slim. Her eyes were red from crying but they still had the steely, determined look in them that reminded Allie of her father. Allie swallowed.

'Oh, for Christ's sake, anyone but you,' Kirstie muttered. She pointed to the door. 'I do not want you in my house!'

'We won't keep you long, Kirstie,' Nick spoke matter-of-factly. 'We're sorry for your loss but, as you can imagine, we need to get to the bottom of this as quickly as possible.'

'Like you did when you stitched my dad up?'

Allie straightened up with a frown. Nick ignored Kirstie's jibe altogether.

'Can you tell me when you last saw Jordan?' he asked her.

'Why should you care?' Kirstie looked pointedly at Allie. 'Especially you. You should leave, before I have you removed.'

'I'll have you arrested if you don't stop with the threats,' Nick warned.

Kirstie lowered her eyes for a fraction of a second.

Allie was shocked to find that the girl was still as immature as ever. Obviously fending for herself for the last three years had done nothing to help her grow up.

'Can you tell me when you last saw Jordan?' Nick repeated.

This time Kirstie answered. 'Last night. We had a row.'

'Do you often argue?'

'We're a couple – of course we do.'

'What were you arguing about?'

Allie tried not to smirk at Nick's bluntness. She saw Kirstie bristle but at least she didn't retaliate too much.

'That's none of your business.' Kirstie glared at Nick.

'Please cooperate, Kirstie,' Allie couldn't help but snap. 'I'm sure you have things to be doing.'

'I wasn't talking to you!' Kirstie snapped back. 'And yes, we have a funeral to sort out. I'm . . .'

Finally, they saw some grief, some atom of emotion hinting that Kirstie might have cared for Jordan, as she began to cry.

'Jordan had been coming home late at night a lot recently,' Kirstie spoke after she had composed herself again. 'He was at the party –'

'The party?'

'It was for the bar manager's wife,' Ryan explained. 'It was held at our club, Flynn's. I was there, too.'

'Yeah, and I wasn't.' Kirstie's top lip curled into a snarl. 'I wasn't lowering myself to go. Can't stand the woman. But I was so bored and pissed off being alone so I rang Jordan to check when he would be back.'

'What time would that have been?'

'Around ten, I guess.'

'Was Jordan at the party when you spoke to him?' asked Nick.

'Yes, he said he was coming home soon, but when I rang him again at eleven, he told me he had some business to sort out and he might not be home at all.'

'Does he often stay out at night?'

'There's a stay-over room at Flynn's,' said Ryan. 'It isn't used much though.'

'I stormed over to Flynn's and had it out with him anyway,' added Kirstie.

'Why?'

'I put the money up for it and he takes the piss by thinking it's his. I own that place, not him.' Kirstie glanced at Ryan. 'Nor you, either.'

Ryan threw her a warning look that didn't go unnoticed by either Allie or Nick.

'So, this row?' Nick tried to move things along.

'Rowing was an understatement,' muttered Ryan.

'I lashed out at him, okay?' Kirstie retorted. 'I was convinced he'd been having it away with some stuck-up tart behind the bar. I had a go at her, too, but she denied anything was going on. Well, she would, wouldn't she?'

'What time would that be?' asked Nick.

'About half past eleven, I guess.'

'And what did you do afterwards?'

'I came home. Jordan didn't. I thought he was at Flynn's until I heard this morning.'

'You didn't call him later to see where he was?' asked Allie.

'No, I was too mad with him.' Kirstie shook her head. 'Not that it's any of your business.'

Allie kept her sigh to herself. 'Were you on your own here?'

'No, I came back, too,' said Ryan.

Allie and Nick turned to him at the same time.

Ryan raised his hands and then dropped them by his side. 'She'd more or less ruined the atmosphere by then.'

'Thanks for that,' said Kirstie.

Ryan rolled his eyes.

'And you were both here for the rest of the night?'

'Yes,' Ryan nodded. 'Kirstie was still up when I got in so we had a coffee and then she went to bed. I stayed up, had a couple of whiskeys and went to bed myself about an hour later.'

'You didn't check up on Jordan?' queried Nick.

'Why should we?' retorted Kirstie.

Ryan stiffened. '*I* gave him a call, about half past one I think, but he didn't pick up.'

'You wouldn't think anything of him not coming home?'

'I'm not my brother's keeper, Inspector.' Ryan look bemused. 'It's a long time since I've looked out for him. He's – he was thirty-one.'

'What about his car?'

'I hadn't given that a thought.' Ryan frowned.

'Does he still drive a Land Rover Discovery?' Allie had received details back from the PNC check, although she hadn't been informed as to whether it had been found on the car park or surrounding streets yet. She made a note to see if Sam was checking any cameras in the area too.

'Yes. Black, mark four,' said Ryan. 'Nice beast.'

'A status symbol, if you ask –' said Kirstie.

'No one was asking you,' Ryan responded.

'Don't you have *any* idea as to who it is yet?' Kirstie turned on Nick next.

'We're following a few leads,' Nick informed her.

'I hope they're the right ones after the fiasco when my mother died.'

Allie saw Nick tense as Kirstie rose tall. God, the girl really was more obnoxious now than when they had first met her three years ago.

'I'm not sure I recall any *fiasco*, Ms Ryder,' Nick replied.

'She fitted him up.' Kirstie pointed at Allie before looking away.

'Shut up, Kirstie,' said Ryan.

'Don't tell me what to do!'

Another awkward silence followed.

'We'll be in touch when we know more,' Nick said eventually.

'I hope you have something concrete soon,' Ryan said as he showed them out.

'I hope so too, Mr Johnson.' Nick nodded, making eye contact for a fraction longer than was necessary. 'We'll be seeing you soon, no doubt.'

'What do you reckon?' Nick asked Allie as they walked back down the drive towards their cars.

'The last time we saw Kirstie Ryder, every other word was a curse. At least she's grown up in that respect.' Allie raised her eyebrows. 'Her manners are still atrocious though.'

'Couldn't agree more.' Nick smirked. 'We have a whole bunch of people at that party to interview, and we need to get CCTV footage from Flynn's nightclub to look at that fight.'

'I can collect it – get it gone through ASAP. I want to have a look around too – that okay with you?'

'Yes. I'm going back to the station.' He paused for a moment. 'I trust you can handle this one on your own?'

Allie knew he was referring to what had happened during the Steph Ryder investigation. He wasn't the only one who thought she had stepped over the mark.

'Yes, sir, thanks.'

'I don't mean *alone* when I say that.'

'Yes, sir.' She jerked a thumb over her shoulder. 'And I'm not sure about all that back there. Did it seem obvious to you that they were trying too hard to make us think they couldn't stand each other?'

'Who, Kirstie and Jordan or Kirstie and Ryan?'

'Kirstie and Ryan. Didn't you see the furtive glances passing between them? That conversation had definitely been rehearsed.'

Nick paused with a hand on the roof of his car. 'I think Jordan Johnson was put in there to keep an eye on Kirstie and maybe when it all went sour, Ryan was moved in, too.'

Allie nodded in agreement. 'Although it does seem a weird choice, given his age.'

'That's Terry Ryder for you. I'm sure he'll have some strange reason for it. And remember what you said to me the last time we had to deliver bad news?'

'Yes, sir.'

'How do you feel about this visit?'

'I feel exactly the same.' Allie sighed. 'They're crocodile tears, aren't they?'

As soon as the police had left, Ryan raced back through to the living room.

'What the hell was all that?' he seethed. 'Don't you think you laid the sarcasm on a bit thick?'

'That woman ruined my family!' Kirstie stood with folded arms. 'I do not fucking want her in this house again!'

'Watch your language.'

'Oh, so now you think you're my father as well as my lover?'

'No, but I might slap your legs just the same.'

Kirstie flinched but stayed where she was as he stepped closer. 'You wanted me to throw them off the scent, didn't you?'

'With a bit of believability, yes. Not by playing stupid games. They could see right through that. You sounded suspicious.'

'I don't know how I could because I didn't have anything to do with his death. And you're supposed to be grieving – I didn't see much of that.'

Ryan clenched his hands into fists. 'Just because I'm not bursting into tears every five minutes doesn't mean I'm not grieving. I'm just trying to get us out of this mess in one piece. I do things at my own pace, Kirstie, you know that, and that includes taking revenge on the bastard who did this to my brother.'

Kirstie relented. 'We'll be off the radar in no time. The police will be clueless as to what really happened.'

Ryan shook his head. 'But even we don't know what happened! Nothing should have gone wrong.'

Kirstie walked slowly towards him and cupped his face in her hands. 'I know you'll miss him; so will I. But he was in the way, you have to admit. And once this is all sorted we can get on with *our* life together. You and me – just think how powerful we'll be.'

Ryan smirked. 'You are one shrewd bitch.'

'I'll take that as a compliment, Mr Johnson. The detail is always in the small things – the surname Ryder give it away to you?'

'You really think you're untouchable, don't you?'

She clasped her hands together around the back of his neck and licked her lip in anticipation. 'Oh, I'm definitely touchable, as you well know.'

He released her hands, pushing her to one side. 'My brother is dead and I want to know who the hell killed him.'

'Don't go overboard with the family thing,' Kirstie huffed, folding her arms. 'You were happy enough to put him in a hospital bed.'

Ryan shook his head in exasperation. 'You might think that you're indispensable because you're a Ryder, but look at you now, alone in this big house. Someone needs to look after you or else who knows what could happen to you . . .'

'Oh, grow up, Ryan. You can't threaten me.'

He grabbed her arm as she tried to push past him. 'Really, Kirstie,' he warned, 'don't fuck with me. I'm nowhere near as nice as my little brother.'

Ryan tried to contain his temper as he stormed into the garden to the mini-gym he and Jordan had installed the previous summer. He began to lift some weights, trying to get rid of his aggression. It would be much better than cracking Kirstie one, despite his yearning to punch away that smug grin from her face. She was still such a child at times. But at least she hadn't guessed the exact reason why he was here.

Jordan moving in with Kirstie had been Ryder's idea but it couldn't have worked out better for Ryan. When Terry had gone to jail, he'd asked Ryan to step in to look after a couple of branches of Car Wash City. But it hadn't been enough. He'd wanted to be more in the know, find out how Ryder made his money. Eventually, he'd come up with a plan to wheedle his way into the house, maybe get Kirstie on side. So far that had led to nothing. Ryder obviously kept his cards close to his chest, not even trusting his daughter with much of his business.

Still, he'd had some great sex. It hadn't taken long to get Kirstie into his bed. It had been fun to feel young legs wrapped around him, see firm breasts hanging down as she'd straddled him, feel ribs and hips instead of rolls of fat, see smooth lines instead of wrinkles. Like her mother by all accounts, Kirstie was a goer and her appetite for sex made up for the obligatory once-a-fortnight missionary position he'd got, if he was lucky, after being married to Nicole for so long. Not that he'd ever gone without in between, but that was nothing to do with anyone.

Yet, even though he was still in shock over his brother's death, Kirstie was right. There was no love lost between him and Jordan. And now that his brother had gone, it seemed he might possibly be in a better place. He could even take over things from Jordan. By the time Terry got wind of anything going wrong, it would be too late. He couldn't do much while he was locked up, especially now that Steve Burgess was on side with Ryan. Two powerful men against Ryder. Terry might think he was in control but he was running out of enemies on the outside who would keep his empire going.

What he needed to do now was to keep Kirstie sweet – no matter how hard it would be to hear her constant whinging and complaining and keep up with her insatiable appetite for sex. But first he needed to find out who had killed his brother and get the missing money back. And he knew just where to start.

Kirstie slumped on the settee, trying to take it all in. Ryan was an aggressive bastard, but she wasn't going to let him intimidate her. She'd been through too much over the last few years to let that happen. Three years ago, Kirstie had had to grow up fast. Although there was no love lost between her and Steph, Kirstie had always looked towards her late mother for money. Finding herself alone a few weeks later when her father had been remanded in prison for the murder of several people, she had gone into a mad panic.

She'd been slightly crazy, she thought now. She'd even fallen out with her best friend Ashleigh, for no good reason. Alone in this big house with no real friends, just people looking to take advantage of a Ryder. There had been a few wild parties, the police being called out to their tiny respectable avenue of individually designed houses on numerous occasions, until she had been summoned to see her father. Terry had told her in no uncertain terms that if she didn't grow up and stop making him look like an idiot, he would cut her off and she would be out on her ass. And then he'd dropped the bombshell that he was putting in someone to look after her. No matter how she had protested, it hadn't made a scrap of difference.

Three days later, Jordan had knocked on the door.

She'd been bowled over by him in the beginning. Jordan had been twenty-eight then, and everything she might want in a man if he hadn't been shoehorned in to look after her. He kept himself fit too, something that she loved. A toned and firm body to tempt her. She'd been horny from the moment she saw him. She'd thought it would be one of her father's old cronies – her money had been on Steve Burgess. But he had a wife and children and although he was there to help her out regardless, he had a family home to run. But Jordan wasn't married. He had a child with another woman but the relationship between them had fizzled out way before he'd come to live with her.

It hadn't taken long before they'd started sleeping together, but they'd argued almost immediately and eventually they'd agreed to see other people discreetly, although to the outside world they would be a loving couple so that Terry wouldn't get mad that they were not getting along as planned. Both of them wanted to keep him happy. Jordan had moved out of her bed and into a spare room.

When Ryan had turned up on the doorstep a few months ago, the story that he'd fallen out with his wife and needed somewhere to stay for a while had fallen flat with Kirstie. She wasn't stupid, knew it was her father interfering.

Eventually she'd realised the advantages of having the older brother onside, so she'd made it a goal to seduce Ryan, too. It had taken her a bit longer than with Jordan, but after a month, she had had him. And he wasn't bad either.

But, still, at least she had an alibi for where she was when Jordan was murdered. And that was all she wanted Ryan for. All she needed to do now was keep him sweet until this was all over and then she would be on her own again.

12.00 P.M.

Time was ticking on and Craig was no closer to finding the money. He'd rung a few contacts but no one knew anything about Jordan's murder, so he decided to look closer to home. Craig went up two flights of stairs and banged on the door of flat 404. The police hadn't got up to the top floor yet and he was more or less out of view of the woman who was standing guard at the foot of the path leading to the crime scene.

A woman in a well-lived face appeared. She had egg yolk down the front of her grey jumper, an inch of blonde hair at the bottom of a mass of wiry-straw grey hair, and a large mole on her upper lip that Craig remembered from when they had gone to school together. She was the same age as him but looked ten years older. He'd go so far as to say that she had let herself go more than Stella had.

'Your boys in, Sand?'

Sandra Granger didn't bother to open the door further, just turned and walked back the way she had come. He stepped into the hallway. Stale cigarette smoke, body odour and something he couldn't quite put his finger on but didn't want to think too much about stung his eyes. He blinked profusely.

He followed her into a living room, stark and grubby, the curtains still closed even though it was nearing midday, the television showing one of the home makeover shows that seemed always to be on a loop. A coffee table sat in the middle of a chequered red and white rug, stacked with mugs, plates and an overfilled ashtray.

A young lad lay on the sofa but he sat up as soon as he saw Craig in the doorway. In his late teens, he was thin to the point of being gangly, as if he hadn't grown into his body yet. His hair was shaved quite close to his head, his skin covered in spots. On the right side of his neck, he had a tattoo of the Staffordshire knot. He wore a black tracksuit.

'Jacob?'

'I might be.'

Craig pulled him to his feet and flung him up against the wall. A picture of a kitten and a bull terrier began to wobble but hung on to its hook for dear life. The coffee table upended, the contents of the ashtray spewing over the carpet.

'Hey, be careful!' Sandra complained. 'I'm the one who'll have to clean it all up afterwards.' She flounced off into the kitchen, slamming the door behind her.

'Do you want to tell me what happened last night?' Craig's face was an inch from Jacob's.

'I didn't do anything!' He pushed at Craig's hands. 'I swear.'

'He's telling the truth!' His twin brother, Tommy, appeared in the doorway. 'I was with him.'

'I'm warning you. If you had anything –' Craig drew back his fist.

Tommy grabbed it but Craig shrugged him off.

'I swear, we had nothing to do with it,' said Jacob.

Craig loosened his grip on Jacob, his eyes flitting from one to the other. It was a really strange experience, making him feel a little giddy. Tommy and Jacob were identical twins. They'd even had the same tattoo inked in the same place so that no one could tell them apart.

'Where did you go last night?' Craig kept his eyes on Jacob.

'We walked in to Burslem – to The Leopard for a few pints,' said Tommy. 'Then we went for a kebab before piling in our mate's place off Moorland Road for a couple more drinks.'

'What time were you back?'

'About half one, I think?' Tommy looked to his brother for confirmation.

Jacob nodded, still looking at Craig.

Craig looked from one to the other again. He didn't trust Jacob at all but decided to use the opportunity to get a bit more information from him. He dropped his guard.

'Do either of you want to earn some cash?' he asked them.

'Doing what?' asked Jacob.

'Someone in these flats knows something. I need a pair of eyes and ears.'

'Not me.' Tommy held up his hands. 'I'm in enough trouble with my lady already. If I end up inside again, she'll swing for me.'

Jacob was quiet for a moment. Then, 'How much?'

'Fifty quid.'

'That's less than minimum wage,' he protested.

'Take it or leave it.' Craig shrugged.

'Seventy-five sounds better to me.'

'Don't push your luck.'

'Okay.' Jacob grinned.

Craig pushed him towards the door. 'If you see anything, come and give me the information as you get it.'

'Wait!' Jacob shouted after him. 'What time do you want me here until?'

'All day and night if necessary.'

'But . . . When will I get paid?'

Craig raised a hand. 'Don't worry about that. You just find out what you can.'

———

As soon as Craig had disappeared out of sight, Jacob went out onto the walkway. He lit a cigarette and took a puff, waited for the hit to get him and sighed as he blew out the smoke.

He glanced at the media van that was parked in the background next to a Ford Fiesta with the local BBC radio motif across its door. A cluster of people were chatting, holding mugs of tea that had been brought out on a tray by some woman. A camera had been set up on a tripod by their side.

He wondered if it would be better to go downstairs and sniff things out in the heart of the action, but then again he could see everything from here. He didn't have to hear everything to get his cash. Craig couldn't have it both ways – or else he'd have to pay him double.

Tommy came out to join him a few minutes later. 'Do you know who it is?'

Jacob nodded, watched his brother's face lose its colour.

'Yeah,' he said. 'It's Jordan Johnson.'

'Fuck, no way!' Tommy gasped. Then his eyes narrowed. 'How the hell do you know?'

'It's not what you think. I heard someone say downstairs.'

'You've been out first thing?' Tommy's tone was dubious.

'Yeah, went to fetch some cigs. I ran out last night.' Jacob rested his chin on his arms, watching what was going on below. 'Someone is looking sick when they find out who did it.'

'I don't think anyone round here has the bottle. Do you?'

'Naw. It'll be someone come from outside. It'll be a setup or something.'

'You mean a hit?'

Jacob nodded.

'Shit.' Tommy ran a hand over his chin. 'Are you sure he won't think we had anything to do with it?'

Jacob shook his head. 'Why would he?'

'Oh, maybe the fact that I didn't go out with you last night, so I was lying.'

Jacob grinned. 'Yeah, cheers for covering for me.'

'Landing myself in the shit, more like it.' Tommy looked down onto the ground for a moment too. 'So where were you?'

'Stayed over at Diane's.'

'Yeah, right.'

'I was – you can ask her. Where were you?'

'Over at Kayleigh's.'

'Cool. At least I know.'

'How about Flynn's? Have you been there lately?'

Jacob looked sheepish. 'I was thrown out of there last week.'

'For fuck's sake.' Tommy sighed. 'What for this time?'

'Someone knocked their pint over me and wouldn't say sorry. So I lamped him one.'

Tommy shook his head in disbelief.

'I was tanked up! Bouncers threw me out. I told one of them that I'd have him if I saw him on his own too. And I would. He thinks he's hard but he's an old-timer. I could take him down easy.'

'What if they have it on camera or something? The police are bound to check out all CCTV there. When exactly was it last week?'

'Last Saturday night. But they won't link it to this, will they?'

'I don't know how far they'll look back!'

'I was drunk!'

'You were fucking stupid.'

They were quiet for a moment.

'It will blow over,' Jacob tried to reassure his brother.

'What if the bouncer grasses you up when they find out where Jordan was murdered?'

'Why would he do that? It's nothing to do with what's going on down there.' He pointed to the ground. 'Besides, they probably won't remember me. They must be knocking back punches all the time in their job.'

'They might!' Tommy prodded him in the chest. 'Have you any idea what will happen to you – to us – if Ryan Johnson does think you're involved? He'll be after your fucking blood.'

'I'm telling the truth!'

'Yeah.' Tommy wouldn't meet his eye. 'Look, we just need to get our story straight, that's all.'

'But I didn't do anything.' Jacob stared at his brother. 'We have to look out for each other, bro. You're either with me or I'll do this on my own.'

Steve didn't know how he'd managed to keep his temper under control when he'd first seen Craig that morning. He'd wanted to rip out his eyes for losing some of the money. But he had a bigger problem on his hands now that Jordan was dead. He needed to figure out a way of keeping the truth from the police.

If everyone kept their mouth shut, things would be fine, but he knew only too well that the more people were involved, the more risky the operation would be, and the harder it would be for everyone to keep quiet. Unless he was a good actor, Craig didn't seem to know anything about there being less money. But Steve knew him from old and he wasn't going to trust him. If Craig was fearful of what could happen, he might do a runner before even attempting to locate the money. He had to take a chance.

More importantly, though, he needed to figure out for himself who was likely to have their money. He had to have it back in his hands by the end of the day. He didn't want to disappoint Terry now, not after all this time waiting for a chance to prove that he was trustworthy.

His phone went. 'Yes?' he barked down it.

'Mr Burgess. My name is DS Shenton from Staffordshire Police.'

Steve sat up straight in his chair. 'What can I do for you, Sergeant?' he asked.

'I'm at a crime scene at the moment and wondered if there was anyone I could talk to at Flynn's.'

'Crime scene?'

'There's been a suspicious death this morning. We believe the victim was at the club last night.'

'Oh, right. I see.' Steve played ignorant. 'I could meet you there in, say, an hour, if I leave now?'

'That would be great. Thanks.'

Steve disconnected the call and grabbed his jacket. He made his way across the city from Longton to Hanley, parked his car and unlocked the doors to Flynn's. After a quick look around to see whether any staff had come in early, he went upstairs to his office and closed the door. Sitting down at his desk, he pressed play on the cameras. He wanted to check what was on the camera footage, see exactly what it showed on the screen. See if he needed to bury anything before the police turned up or whether he was home and dry.

He'd been lying when he'd told Craig that the machine wasn't working but he wasn't going to let on why.

12.15 P.M.

'Where were you last night?' Sandra asked Tommy as he sat glued to the television. She'd made them both a sandwich for lunch and had eaten most of hers but he still hadn't stopped playing the video game he was engrossed in.

'I was out with Jacob,' he said, eyes not leaving the screen as he shot another round of bullets. He held up his hand. 'You made me lose my concentration. I'd only just got to level four!'

'You'll lose more than that if you're lying to cover up for your brother again.' Sandra had his attention then. 'I know you stayed over at Kayleigh's house last night so why did you say you were out with him?'

'Because we're always the first to get the blame for anything around here. He'd do the same for me.'

Sandra scoffed. 'You sure about that?'

'Yeah.'

'Is that why he's let you do time for him?'

Tommy scowled at his mother. Just because she was right didn't mean that he wanted to hear it again. It was like a broken record, brought up every time someone came after them. Jacob often landed himself in trouble and because they were identical twins, there were many occasions when he hadn't taken the rap, saying he'd been mistaken for Tommy. It had been his word against his brother's and no matter how close they were, there had always been an underlying threat that Jacob would hurt him if he didn't do as he was told.

On several occasions, he'd pulled out a knife if Tommy had threatened not to lie for him.

Because he hadn't been able to handle a beating, Tommy had also admitted to things he hadn't done. Only eight months ago, he'd served six weeks as half of a three-month sentence for theft, yet he hadn't done anything wrong. Jacob had denied everything. DNA – it was the same for identical twins. They had unique fingerprints but blood, saliva, sperm, anything that could be tested, Tommy would match to Jacob. It worked to Jacob's advantage, not to his, and he wasn't about to go through it all again, not now he had a girlfriend.

Jacob was the braver twin, the one who would take all the risks. He was better with his fists and used to talking his way out of things. That's why Tommy had always pleaded guilty despite never being involved in anything.

But was Jacob involved with this? Surely he hadn't had anything to do with a murder? What the hell would he be covering for this time – or worse, trying to get out of?

'That's what family do,' he said to his mother.

'That's only loyal when it's done both ways.' Sandra sat forward, placed a hand tentatively on Tommy's forearm. 'Look, son, our Jacob is a bad one, but it doesn't mean that you have to do his dirty work for him. If he's involved in any way, don't take the blame. He needs to be responsible for his own actions.'

'What do you mean?' Tommy turned sharply towards her. 'Do you think he had something to do with that lot outside?'

Sandra shrugged her shoulders. 'I just have a feeling, that's all.'

Tommy went cold.

At Harrison House, Allie located Perry on the ground floor and pointed upwards. 'Uniform knocked on both flats where the women live but no one answered at either. We need to go to Flynn's for one p.m. but shall we try them again first?'

The woman who answered the door to flat 210 certainly fitted the description of the woman who might have been seen earlier that morning. She was of slim build and had long dark hair. Her eyes and face were swollen and blotchy. Allie noticed a tissue in her hand.

'Hello. DS Shenton and DC Wright, Staffordshire Police. We're going door-to-door at the moment about the incident that happened last night. Mind if we ask you a few questions?'

Sophie nodded but didn't move aside. 'I'm not sure I'll be able to help.'

'Let me be the judge of that. May we come in for a moment, please?' Allie smiled at her.

They were shown in to another living room, this one more orderly, homely and fragranced better than some they had visited over the past few hours. Perry drew out his notebook again.

'Are you okay?' Allie asked, noticing how ill she looked close up. 'You don't look very well.'

'I've got a rotten cold at the moment.' Sophie held up a hand. 'I wouldn't get too close to me, if I were you.'

'Just got rid of one myself,' said Perry with a smile. 'Nasty bugger too. Man-flu, probably.'

Sophie gave a faint smile in return as Allie rolled her eyes in jest.

'Do you live alone, Miss . . . ?'

'Adams . . . Rebecca Adams. And, yes, there's only me here.'

'Thanks. Can you tell me where you were last night, particularly between the hours of one and four a.m., please?' she asked.

'I was in bed.'

'Were you in all evening, too?'

'Yes. With the Night Nurse.'

Allie grimaced. 'Nasty medicine but it does the job. No husband or boyfriend looking after you? No friends?'

Sophie drew her cardigan around her middle. 'No, I live alone.'

'I assume you've heard about the incident last night?'

'A little on the radio – and from what my neighbour told me. Do you know who it is?'

'We're still making enquiries. But you didn't see or hear anything out of the ordinary? Anything – anything at all?'

'No.' Sophie shook her head. 'Sorry, I was out like a light.'

'Only the victim was found by one of your neighbours. She was out walking her dog and she said she saw someone with long dark hair going into the flats around three thirty a.m. this morning. It wasn't you, was it?' Allie's hand went up before she could reply. 'Don't worry; we only need to rule people out at this stage.'

She shook her head. 'I don't go out on my own around here at night, even when I'm feeling okay.'

'And you didn't hear anything unusual, any noise?'

'No, sorry.'

Allie nodded. 'Thank you for your time, Miss Adams.'

Perry wrote in his notebook before looking up. 'We'll be in touch if we need to speak to you again.'

'Thoughts, Perry?' Allie asked once they were out on the walkway again.

'Hmm, not sure she has a cold. She wasn't nasal. When I have a cold –'

'You're ten times worse than that?' she teased. 'You're right, though. It was her eyes that were puffed. She looked like she'd been crying to me.'

They walked along to where Leah Matthews lived at flat 203. Allie held up her warrant card as she opened the door. No need for introductions: Leah was known to them both.

'Yes.' Leah cleared her throat. 'Yes,' she repeated in a lower tone.

'We're investigating a suspicious death that happened in the early hours of this morning. Can we come in for a moment?'

'I suppose.'

'I bet it came as quite a shock, something so close to where you live,' said Allie, as they went through to the living room.

'Yes,' said Leah, sitting down.

'We're going round checking people's whereabouts last night, to see if anyone saw or heard anything unusual. Can you tell me where you were between one a.m. and four a.m. this morning?'

'I was here.'

'Do you live alone?'

'Yes.'

'And were you alone last night?'

'Yes. Why?'

'A woman matching your description was seen coming into the flats last night around three thirty a.m. and we wanted to talk to her, to eliminate her from our enquiries.'

'Oh,' Leah shrugged. 'Well, it wasn't me. I fell asleep on the sofa.'

'Can you remember about what time?'

Leah's eyes darted everywhere. 'It must have been about half nine, I think.'

'And you went to bed at . . .'

'I didn't. I woke on the sofa.' She rubbed at her neck. 'Still aching from it.'

Allie paused for a moment. As the silence became loaded, she saw Leah sit on her hands. She looked at her pointedly.

'You been keeping out of trouble lately, Leah?' she asked.

'Yes.' Leah swallowed.

'No thieving and shoplifting. Nothing like that?'

'No!'

'That's good to hear.' Perry eyed her warily.

'So you're sure you didn't hear anything out of the ordinary?' Allie asked one more time.

'Sorry.' Leah bit down on the inside of her lip. 'I wish I could help more but I can't.'

Back on the walkway after nothing else was forthcoming, Allie shook her head. 'I don't know if she's hiding something or is just too drunk to remember. The place smelt like a brewery.'

'Exactly,' said Perry. 'She'd obviously had a skinful last night.'

'She was a bit shifty though, wasn't she?'

'Yes. I know she seemed to have a hangover but her eyes wouldn't rest for one minute.'

'Hmm. And a woman with dark hair is our priority now to rule out.' Allie paused. 'I think I'll get uniform to take statements from them both. See if the details match. Something just doesn't sit right with me.'

12.30 P.M.

Leah dropped the card on the coffee table and paced up and down. She'd been thinking of handing herself in until the police had brought up all that nonsense about her past. Maybe she still could? She thought about running after them, but neither officer would have believed that she had just found the money. They'd assume she had something to do with Jordan's death.

Ten thousand pounds. She had never seen so much money in her life. She had certainly never had any more than a few hundred pounds in her savings account.

But she had stolen it.

She was in too deep: once whoever was after the money found out it was her, she would be dead too. Knowing her luck, the money had to be dodgy; she could be pissing off someone far worse than Kenny Webb.

She had to get out of the flat. If she could get out of Stoke, she could start afresh somewhere else. She could leave all her debts behind, maybe change her name and reinvent herself.

But then reality came crashing down. There was no way she could leave her mother to fend for herself, and ten thousand pounds wouldn't be enough for them both to up and leave – even if she could persuade Mum to go away for a while.

She'd counted it again after Stella had gone. There was something compelling about seeing it all piled up. But she'd put it away sharpish when she'd heard a noise outside. Would this be what her life would be like if she didn't give it back? Looking over her shoulder all the time? She couldn't handle that.

She didn't know what to do long-term but she knew she couldn't keep the money here – it would have to go. Finally, she decided on moving it. She'd have to chance going tonight. The police wouldn't be there forever – and although they were covering the front entrance to the building, they couldn't keep an eye on everyone who might jump over the walkway, climb down and do a runner in the dark. And even if they did, surely they weren't allowed to conduct random bag checks unless they had prime suspects?

Leah wondered how long it would be before the police found out that she was the mystery woman. It was her, she was sure, but she wasn't going to admit it. She thought of all the tenants that she knew in the flats, going through them floor by floor, wondering if there was anyone else who looked similar to her living in the block.

Then she stopped. There was another woman she could think of who fitted the description too. Someone who looked like her and was more or less the same age. Someone who lived on the same floor.

Someone who could possibly be set up to look like it was her if need be.

Stella's stuck-up friend, Sophie.

———～———

Jacob lit another cigarette as he stood watching the scene below. It was the first time he'd felt the advantage of being on the top floor. He could see everything that was going on. He watched the police working away, and he watched as Craig's missus went back and forth to her friend Leah's flat, with a very worried look on her face. He'd store that up to use later. Made a change to get something useful out of the flat. Usually he hated it here. The lift hardly ever worked and he'd have to haul himself and his push bike up the stairs, stinking of sweat as he reached the top.

He hated living at home with his mum and brother, too. It was too cramped sharing a bedroom with Tommy, and at eighteen they both needed their own space. As soon as his girlfriend Diane got a flat from the council, he was moving in with her. She reckoned she'd go to the top of the list now that she was pregnant. He'd only been going out with her for a few months – his mum would do her nut when she found out, especially as he already had a son with mad Malory Victor.

His mum couldn't say much really. She'd had him and Tommy when she was eighteen. Their father had stuck around for three years until he'd pissed off with some slag from the council estate down the road. She never stopped going on about how she had been deserted by him, but everyone knew why. She used to look after herself but now she was more interested in her next drink.

Dragged up – that's what everyone said about the Granger brothers. The police, social services, even the neighbours. It had pissed him off for years, hearing them all make out their mum was a waste of space. She wasn't that bad. She'd been great before alcohol had become her only friend.

Having to rely on each other, fend for themselves from an early age, had made them both harden up, and with hardly any money coming in, they'd had to go out and find some from somewhere. Thieving had become their trade from an early age. If anyone wanted anything, they would ask the Granger twins to get it for them. Mum used to have a go at them about it but when she realised they could bring in enough for her to get drunk on, she'd relented. Not that she would have been able to do anything about it anyway. She'd lost control of them way before they hit puberty.

They weren't all bad, however. Only last month, they'd been involved in a sponsored darts match down the pub to raise funds for some local kid who was dying of leukaemia. They'd raised over a grand and none of them had nicked a penny – now that was good in his eyes.

Even as young as he was, Jacob's criminal record was a mile long – something he was more proud of than ashamed. He'd been sent to juvenile detention twice already for thieving and wasn't afraid to do time again if it meant getting in with the big boys.

He rested his chin on his hands on the wall and glanced around. Along the walkway, he spotted uniformed officers now on their floor. They were only a few doors away – they'd be questioning him and Tommy soon. Behind them, he could see Martha Sterling. Jacob made a mental note to go and speak to her later. She always had her head in the window gawping out or was sitting on the walkway, as she was doing now. She might have seen something he could report back to Elliott.

He could see Philip Derricott, too: he was a decent bloke but his wife was a bit of a nutcase. Next door to him, Tracy Weston was talking to her mum: now she was a bitch if ever he knew one. She was a right slag too, sleeping with anyone if she could use them to her advantage.

Tommy came out onto the walkway.

'See anything?' he asked Jacob.

'Nothing interesting enough.' Jacob jerked his head to the right. 'You've come just in time though.'

Tommy swore under his breath when he saw DC Wright walking towards them.

12.45 P.M.

Perry wasn't sure if he was looking forward more to seeing what lies the Granger twins concocted between them or seeing if he could rattle their cages a little. If truth were known, he didn't have much time for either of them, the trouble they caused on a regular basis – and that was just fighting between the two of them.

He'd first come across the boys when he'd still been in uniform. There had been a milk lorry doing the rounds back then and they'd been caught taking milk and bread from the back of it. Both had blamed the other so both had received a caution. The milk lorry had then been vandalised three weeks on the trot but with no evidence to link the boys, it had been up to Perry to take the wrath of the milkman for not doing his job properly and nailing the thieving little bastards.

Several times, he'd tried to speak sense to their layabout mother, to no avail. Now, nine years on, the crimes had become increasingly worse, although for the moment it was still petty crime, nothing too major. But for how long? They were trouble, especially that Jacob, and Perry wouldn't put it past him to be involved here, or at least to know something.

'All right, boys,' Perry nodded a greeting as he approached them. 'You heard what's gone on downstairs, I take it?'

'We'd be stupid not to have,' Jacob lipped him. 'And you know we're not stupid.'

'Pipe down,' Perry chastised. 'We need to check where you were last night and then we can get on with things. Catch the big boys at work. So . . .' he looked from Jacob to Tommy and back. 'Where were you both in between the hours of one a.m. and four a.m. this morning?'

'That's not fair!' Jacob protested. 'I bet you haven't asked all the neighbours where they were. Always the same if you're a Granger.'

Tommy nudged his brother sharply, glared at him before speaking.

'If you weren't doing anything wrong, you have nothing to lose by telling me.' Perry raised his hands. 'So what's it to be? Here or at the station?'

'You don't have anything to arrest us on, do you?'

Perry said nothing.

'We were in Burslem.' Jacob let out a sigh. 'We had a few pints in The Leopard. Then we went for a kebab and then we went for a few more drinks at a mate's house.'

'Mate's name?'

No one spoke. Jacob looked down to the ground as if disinterested.

'Mate's name?' Perry repeated.

'Denton Harlow,' said Tommy eventually.

Perry wrote the details down in his notebook, not knowing of a Denton Harlow off the top of his head.

'What time were you back?'

'About half one, I think?'

Jacob nodded. 'About that, I suppose.'

'You suppose?'

'Yeah, well, Tommy did stop on the way home to see his girl. And then we went to his mate's house,' Jacob clarified.

Perry watched as their eyes flitted to each other and back to him. 'And the girlfriend's name?'

'Kayleigh Smith.'

'Address?'

He took down the details as Tommy relayed it reluctantly. 'Anything else?' he tried one more time but was met with a stare from Jacob and the shake of his head from Tommy.

Tommy waited for Perry to be out of hearing range. Then he grabbed Jacob's arm, dragged him into the flat, closed the door behind them.

'What the fuck did you say that for?' he turned on his brother.

'What?'

'That I stopped off at Kayleigh's.'

'I was covering for you.' Jacob shrugged. 'They'll probably find out you weren't here. So, as I knew you *were* there . . .'

Tommy gritted his teeth as he spoke. 'But you landed me in it by saying we went to a mate's house as well!'

'I wasn't the one who gave him Denton Harlow's name'

'I had to say I was with someone!'

'He knew we were lying anyway.'

Tommy shook his head. Jacob didn't give a stuff that he might have landed him in trouble again. He'd have to go and see Kayleigh, see if she would bend the truth a little.

Tommy went to speak but Jacob walked off. He grabbed his shoulder. 'What aren't you telling me about last night, Jay?' He pointed a finger in his brother's face. 'If you're involved in that lot downstairs, I'm not covering for you, do you hear?'

Jacob pushed him away. 'Mind your own business.'

'You make it my business if you're involved.' Tommy spat. 'He's been fucking murdered!'

'Chill out, will you?' Jacob sighed. 'Look, just keep your mouth shut and your wits about you and it will all blow over soon.'

Tommy kicked at the wall in temper as Jacob left him there.

1.00 P.M.

Flynn's nightclub was at the bottom of Hanley City Centre and, thanks to the hard work of the Johnson brothers, it had done well over the last two years. It had been completely refurbished before re-opening, now boasting two floors of sophistication with a further private members-only area upstairs. Known as Freddie's before, it had been cleaned out of riff-raff since then, too, if the reduced number of call-outs were anything to go by.

'Wonder what we'll find in here,' said Perry as he knocked on one of four front doors across the entrance.

'Oh, I bet there'll be a murder weapon or two. It has a killer atmosphere apparently.'

Perry groaned at Allie's lame joke.

The door was opened by someone they both recognised. At forty-seven, Steve Burgess could pass for late thirties easily with his whitened teeth, tall physique and full head of dark brown hair, although it was greying at the roots. Allie would say one thing about the criminal fraternity – the men were mostly lean, exuding power and magnetism by keeping themselves in good shape. To her, it showed hard work, commitment and a healthy ego. Although, she laughed inwardly as she thought of Craig Elliott, there were always exceptions to the rules. He was more of a bulldog than an offspring of the breed itself.

Steve showed them through the entrance and into the nightclub. The vast open area seemed eerie in its silence as they followed him across the empty dance floor. Booths fitted with low lighting were set around the edge; there was a stage at the far end where a DJ or live entertainment would be set up. Despite her joking earlier, Allie knew that the club did have a reputation for a good night out.

'Do you work for Mr Johnson or Ms Ryder?' Allie asked Steve Burgess.

'I don't work for either,' Steve glared at her. 'I keep an eye on things. They're both young and inexperienced. I'm a father figure to look up to – someone in the business who knows the business.' They came to a door and he pressed down the handle. 'Of course they are the glamour couple who run and own the club but it's me who does all the legwork. I dread to think how long it would have been before their egos ruined the business. And I know Mr Ryder wouldn't have been at all happy with that.'

Allie struggled to control her reaction to Ryder's name, aware of Burgess's intense stare.

'You were the one who arrested Terry, weren't you?' he pushed.

'I don't see how that has any relevance to what we're doing now,' she replied curtly.

Steve shrugged and opened the door with a wry smile. 'He still speaks about the one that got away.'

Allie couldn't look at Perry. She refused to be drawn into Steve's game.

Down a long corridor at the back of the building, they were shown into a small office.

'Here it is.' Steve opened the drawer of a desk, took out several discs and handed them to Allie. 'Last night's security footage.'

'I need a list of all the staff who were working. Their addresses, too.' Allie switched into investigation mode. 'Were you here last night, Mr Burgess? I believe there was a party?'

'Yes, my wife's. We celebrated in the members-only area.'

'What time did it finish?'

'I left around half past two – most people had gone around one a.m. There were a few stragglers around still saying goodbye until then.'

'How many were in the room?'

'Over a hundred, I should say.'

'Were you witness to the fracas between Kirstie Ryder and Jordan Johnson?'

'We all were.' Steve sat down at the desk. 'Jordan was sitting at the bar with a few of us when she stormed in, making a fool of herself as usual.'

'Does this happen on a regular basis?'

'Afraid so. Kirstie hated Jordan spending too much time here. She was always accusing him of having an affair with some woman or other.'

Allie frowned. 'Was there ever any truth in her accusations?'

Steve shrugged his shoulders. 'I think there might have been someone. I wasn't interested in finding out. It was none of my business.'

'So what happened after she'd started shouting?'

'She wanted him to go home with her and when he wouldn't, she started lashing out at him. It took three of the lads to drag her off him. They went downstairs with her to try and calm her down but she stormed off, so I heard.'

'And how did Jordan react to that? It must have been embarrassing?'

'He laughed it off but I could see he was annoyed. He left shortly afterwards. I think Ryan left at the same time.' He shook his head. 'I can't believe he's dead. Such a shock.'

'Can you recall what time they left?' Perry asked.

'It was just after midnight, I reckon. The recording will confirm times, I'm sure.'

'Do you have any idea who would have wanted to kill Jordan?' said Allie.

'Half the men in Stoke wanted to have a go at him, no doubt. He made this club very popular by getting rid of some of the layabouts and dealers who were running it down in the first place. Before Jordan came along, Freddie's, as you know, was a dump, full of parasites. I have to give credit to the lad and his brother – they certainly turned it around. Jordan made a fair few enemies because he stopped people's livelihoods, I suppose, but I'm not sure how many of them would be up to murdering him.'

'Do you have any names for us to check out? Anyone who would have been at the party, for instance?'

'Not off the top of my head, no. I'll be sure to let you know if I think of anyone.' He pointed to his computer. 'I'll get that list sorted out for you, shall I?'

Afterwards, Allie and Perry called in at a sandwich shop on Piccadilly.

'I don't like Burgess,' said Perry as they joined the small queue in front of the counter. 'Something about him, not sure what.'

'Your gut reaction is the same as mine.' Allie grabbed a bottle of water from an open fridge. 'As well as that, if Kirstie Ryder is strong enough to lash out at Jordan and it takes three men to pull her off him, maybe she could have followed him to Harrison House, taken him by surprise?'

'With a bat and a knife?' Perry grimaced.

Allie shrugged. 'Like father, like daughter?'

'But her alibi checks out so it can't be that.'

'Her alibi is the victim's brother. They could easily be covering for each other.' Allie nodded. 'As far as I'm concerned, I wouldn't trust her any more than I trusted her father.'

As soon as the words 'Rebecca Adams' had fallen from her lips, Sophie had been kicking herself. What on earth had possessed her to lie? The police were bound to find out and then they'd want to know why she'd said it. She might even be arrested for obstructing their enquiries! But it had been the only thing she could think of to stop them from linking her to Kirstie Ryder. If she found out, Jordan's reputation could be in ruins. She seemed the type to want revenge.

Who would kill him? Had Kirstie found out and attacked him in revenge? Surely not. Maybe someone else had been waiting for him because they knew he was coming to visit her? Even if it were a random attack, she would never forgive herself for causing his death. Not only had she lost the man she loved, but he had been killed – murdered – right outside where she lived. It would be too painful to see that every day.

She pressed a button on her phone. Tears pricked her eyes as the selfie Jordan had taken of them flashed up. She ran a finger over the image. Jordan had taken it when they'd been sitting up in bed. Nothing sultry: they were naked but only their shoulders were showing. She was tucked underneath his arm; he had a look on his face that made her heart burn with love. Her long hair was bed-messy, falling over the chest that she'd loved to run her hand over, feeling coarse hairs prickling against her palm.

Just as quickly, she turned it off. She couldn't look at his face right now. It was too raw. Instead, she took her place behind the curtain again, looking down across the car park. People were still milling around. A group of photographers had set up in a huddle in the far background. Sophie could make out the logos of the local newspaper and radio stations on the sides of vehicles. There were police everywhere, too. Over the past couple of hours she had seen more and more officers arrive and knew it would only be a matter of time before they questioned her again, put two and two together as to who she really was.

In amongst a group of people, she could still see Stella flitting around. Now if anyone could get the gossip to confirm it was Jordan, it would be her. Stella would be the one to go to, to see what was going on. But she couldn't bring herself to go down *there*. She didn't want to be anywhere near the police. And what if Stella said her name and they heard it and realised she wasn't Rebecca Adams after all?

But then her thoughts turned to Jordan again. She didn't want to go downstairs because she would see where it had happened, be closer to the gossip about his death. And while she was here, in her flat, she could live in denial.

She cast her mind back to what the police had asked her about. She hadn't seen anyone coming into the building when she'd been watching earlier that morning. They couldn't suspect her, though. She wasn't the only one with dark hair. There was Stella, for instance. She wondered if the police had questioned her yet.

And then there was Stella's horrible friend, Leah. Sophie doubted it would be Stella getting back in alone at that time of morning because Jordan had said that her husband wasn't very nice and would probably go mad. She wouldn't put it past Leah, though. She was always going out and coming home drunk, making lots of noise. Jordan used to bump into her all the time.

Would it be her? Could Leah have something to do with Jordan's death?

Feeling like her heart would break, she hugged herself, trying to stop the shivering panic building up again. Tears poured down her face and neck and she did nothing to wipe them away.

She would have to move. She'd never be able to look out of the window, go out of her front door, walk down that pathway ever again without imagining him lying on the grass, bleeding to death, looking over at her flat where she slept, oblivious.

Once Stella had gone downstairs, she'd been caught up in the goings-on and it had been an hour before she'd managed to nip back upstairs. She went to check on Leah, but she was stopped in her tracks by a phone call from her friend Sophie, saying she needed to see her urgently. She hot-footed back the way she had come and knocked on the door of the flat next to hers.

When Sophie answered, Stella stared at her in surprise. Used to seeing her made up and always looking smart, she was shocked to see that Sophie was still in her pyjamas. Her hair wasn't a mess but it hadn't been straightened as usual, and her face was devoid of makeup, a ball of red blotches and swollen eyes.

'Jeez, Soph, what's wrong? You look like death warmed up.'

Sophie burst into tears. 'I . . . I –'

Stella bustled them both inside. 'What's the matter?' she asked once they were sitting down on the settee.

Sophie composed herself enough to speak. 'That man – that man who was attacked last night.' Her face crumpled again as she looked at Stella. 'If it's who I think it is, I was having an affair with him.'

'You mean Jordan Johnson?'

Stella saw Sophie freeze.

'How do you know his name?' Sophie asked.

Stella raised her eyebrows. 'I make it my job to find out. How long have you been seeing him?'

'Six months.'

Stella gasped. 'But he's seeing Kirstie Ryder!'

'It's not what you think. He isn't one of those men who tells me he's going to leave his wife and never will. I knew what I was getting into from the beginning.'

'Did you meet him at Flynn's?'

Sophie nodded. 'He comes to see me when Flynn's closes – always late at night. No one knows we're seeing each other.' She glanced at Stella. 'You can't tell anyone. Anyone. Do you hear?'

'Oh, I won't tell a soul.' Stella mentally crossed her fingers behind her back. This information was too valuable to keep to herself.

1.30 P.M.

'Where the hell have you been?' Leah grabbed Stella and pulled her into the flat, shutting the door behind her quickly. 'You've been gone for ages.'

'I've been trying to find things out for you,' Stella fibbed. 'And we've been interviewed by the police. Have they been to see you yet?'

'Yes.'

'Did they mention seeing a woman with dark hair coming in to Harrison House this morning?'

Leah nodded.

'They did to us too. I can't for a moment understand why they would think it might have been me.'

'It could have been.'

'I know that, but I also know that it wasn't. It was you.'

'You didn't land me in it, did you?' Leah's shoulders drooped.

Stella put up a hand. 'Don't worry, I steered them well clear. You do still have the money, though?'

'What do you think I'm going to do with it? Give it away to the Red Cross? Hide it up my jumper?'

'There's no need to be sarcastic.'

'I don't know what else to do with it but keep it here.' Leah sat down with a thump. 'I have to give it back, don't I?'

'No, you can't! Not now. They'll want to know why you didn't do it straightaway. It will look more dishonest.'

'But what if they come and search the flat?'

'I told you, they can't do that without a reason or a warrant.'

'I bet they have ways and means.'

Stella moved over to the kitchen area. 'Tea?'

'No, I don't want bloody tea!' Leah exclaimed. 'Did you find anything else out?'

'Not much more than we already know.'

'And it's definitely him – one of the Johnson brothers?'

'Yes, but you mustn't tell Craig that I told you his name. You promised.'

'I know.'

Stella paused. 'He was with Jordan last night. He went to a party at Flynn's.'

Leah wasn't listening. 'It could have been anyone.'

'At that time in the morning?'

Leah stopped for a moment, wondering whether to say what was on her mind. She blurted it out anyway.

'It could be your friend, Sophie.'

'Why do you say that? She hardly ever goes out.' Stella stopped short.

'She's the same build as me and she has long dark hair.' Leah paused again. 'We could make out that it was her.'

Stella recoiled. 'To get the police off your back, you mean?'

'No! But we could at least *talk* to her.'

'I already have.' Stella's eyes darted around the room before landing on hers again. 'I know it wasn't her.'

'When? And why couldn't it have been her?'

Stella stared at her pointedly. 'Promise you won't tell anyone I've told you this.'

Leah looked at her blankly. 'Who the hell would I tell?'

Stella relayed her conversation with Sophie.

Leah shook her head in incredulity. 'I thought she was a right goody two-shoes. Never had it down for her being a home-wrecker.'

'Well, ordinarily yes, but messing with Kirstie Ryder?' Stella gave a shudder.

'Come to think of it, I've seen him here a few times.'

'I haven't.'

'You're not out as late as I am. It's when I've been coming home.' Leah sat with her head in her hands. 'I should have just handed the money in.'

Stella sat down beside her and put an arm around her shoulder. 'I think the best thing is to keep quiet and act normal for now.'

'But you don't have a bag of money! And –'

'If we stay one step ahead of everyone, then we can sort this out.'

'We?'

'You do want my help to keep it quiet, don't you?'

Leah laughed inwardly so as not to annoy her friend. Stella had never kept quiet about anything in her life. But she did need to trust her with this.

'If you say anything to the police, you know what people are like,' Stella added. 'They'll point their fingers at you regardless, and then everyone will know you're a thief. Mud sticks around here.'

'Well, Sophie's in the wrong, too.' Leah knew she sounded like a spoilt child but she hated that Stella seemed excited.

'That's completely different from what you've done!'

'You see!' Leah stood up quickly. 'I'm giving it back.'

'No!' Stella stood up too. 'Just hide it and then we'll see what happens later.'

'Okay. I suppose I could take it to my mum's.'

At the station, Allie was walking up the stairs with Perry to their office when her phone rang.

'It's Mark,' she told him. 'I'll catch you in a moment.' When he'd gone ahead, she answered the phone. 'Hey.'

'Hey.'

'How is she?'

'No change. They said the results of the tests should definitely be back tomorrow though.'

'And how's work?' Allie didn't want to hear anything about the tests yet. Oblivion was her best option at the moment.

'It's not as hectic as yours. No one has committed a murder – well, not yet, anyway.'

Allie smiled as she pushed on the door to her office. An open plan space was crammed with desks in twos and threes, officers at some of the computers. At the far end she could see Sam over at the whiteboard.

'I have to go. I'll catch you later.'

'Okay, I'd better go too – they're calling me to a meeting. Stay safe. You're still with your bodyguard?'

Allie laughed and said goodbye to him. Then just as quickly, she sighed. She had disconnected the phone before she'd told him that she had been at Ryder's house again. She knew he wasn't going to be happy. If she mentioned his name at home, Mark's shoulders always rose and his face darkened. But she had to tell him before the press conference that afternoon. After all that had happened last time with Ryder, he'd be angry if he thought she was holding it back from him.

Sam was writing in black marker pen on the board as she got to her. She handed her the disc.

'Thanks.' Sam turned to her. 'How are you?'

'Good.' Allie smiled at her friend. 'Everything's good at the moment. Steady. Stable. Holding on.'

'Good,' Sam repeated and gave her arm a squeeze. 'What have you got?'

'CCTV from Flynn's nightclub last night. Can you check it from nine p.m. onwards, please? Log who goes in and out of the private room for me?'

'Will do. Coffee?'

'Gagging for one.'

Allie sat down at her desk, keen to grab a bite to eat. Perry was already tucking into his sandwich.

Minutes later, Sam plonked a mug down next to her.

'You're an angel.' Allie pointed to a small package. 'Cheese and onion bap for you.'

'Ooh, thanks. So how did your big reunion with Kirstie Ryder go?'

'She was very welcoming. Said she didn't want me in her fucking house.'

Sam smirked. 'Was it weird being there again?'

Sam and Perry had worked with Allie on the investigation into the murder of Steph Ryder and knew a bit about her demons around Terry Ryder. They'd both been at the funeral when Ryder had been arrested and had seen how Kirstie had reacted to her afterwards, screeching in front of everyone that it was all Allie's fault, that she had it in for her family. That she had been out to get her father for years and that it was common knowledge.

She'd blamed Allie for stitching up her boyfriend too, reassuring everyone who would listen that he was a loving, charming man and not the murderer he had been made out to be. All lies, of course – the said boyfriend, Lee Kennedy, had kidnapped Kirstie and tied her up for a short while.

'Yes, it felt as if Ryder was about to come back through the door again,' she said. 'As if he was still there, you know?'

'He practically thinks he still is. Lots of people seem to be working for him on the outside. Did you learn anything new?'

'Yeah, there are too many bloody flats at Harrison House,' Perry joined in. 'Glad I'm not in uniform and having to collate all the actions afterwards.'

'That'll be me here until midnight then,' Sam sighed.

'We'll get help if necessary,' Allie soothed.

'Speaking of which, uniform have found Jordan's car,' she added. 'It was parked in Sparrow Street, a few minutes' walk from the flats. Residents questioned there say that it was a regular sighting.' Sam clicked her mouse a few times. 'Oh, Jordan's phone records are just back.'

'Who was the last person to contact him?' asked Allie, wiping crumbs from her mouth with a napkin.

'Miss Sophie Nicklin, flat 210, Harrison House. A text message.'

'Flat 210?' Allie looked at Perry. 'That's where Rebecca Adams lives. We went to see her earlier.'

'She was one of the women with dark hair who we spoke to,' confirmed Perry.

'There are tons of calls and text messages to that number, mostly in the early hours of the mornings,' Sam continued, eyes flicking over the screen. 'All late at night, and text messages during the day.'

'Did she say she lived alone or did she have a flatmate?'

Perry looked through his notebook. 'I thought she lived alone.'

'Me too.' Allie took a gulp of her drink. 'We'll go to see her next, find out why she gave us a false name. Sam, let Nick know, will you?'

2.00 P.M.

As Ryan turned his car into Malcolm Parade, Kirstie was reminded of where she used to live on the Marshall Estate. Uniform semi-detached houses lined up in a row, postage-stamp sized front gardens, drives for one car, hardly room for any garages. Miserable-looking at this time of year with its dark nights and mornings, dreary grey days and winter weather.

She'd been a teenager when she'd left all her friends behind to live in The Gables. The property had wowed her, especially the size of her bedroom, but in some ways life had been much simpler before. For starters, Mum hadn't been drinking as much and they had got on fairly well. Maybe if they had stayed on the estate, Mum might still be alive today.

She spotted a tabby cat sitting on a windowsill as they drove along to number 46, Ryan's family home. Already she was dreading the game playing. So far, the brothers' mum, Betty, had not cottoned on that she and Jordan hadn't really been able to stand the sight of each other for the past year or so. Kirstie had been rehearsing what to say all morning: how she was going to miss Jordan, how much she loved him, how she would never get over losing him this way, blah, blah, blah. It was all about keeping up appearances; she hoped she could still convince Betty that she and Jordan had been very much in love. What would happen if she slipped up now that it came to it?

Ryan and Jordan were Betty's only children. Ryan's father, Clive, had died several years back now so Kirstie had never met him. She found his mother suffocating, to say the least, and she seemed so old. But even though she would never admit it to anyone, she did enjoy their family get-togethers, although it did make it awkward when Ryan and Nicole had separated. Ryan's children had been annoyed at the separation too – both were teenagers who threw more tantrums than she did. Kirstie hoped they wouldn't be there now.

Betty made the best Sunday roast dinners and always made a fuss of everyone, regardless of their ages. There was always a sit-down meal, presents on birthdays and a stocking filled with delightful goodies hanging from the back of everyone's chair on Christmas day. Family and tradition were very important to her. She'd even taken Kirstie under her wing. They got on really well, often sharing memories over numerous mugs of tea. Kirstie hardly made time to call to see her but when she did she always wondered why she didn't make more of an effort. It was usually fun.

Ryan had told her that Betty had been devastated when he'd separated from Nicole, too. Betty had thought they had staying power; she'd been certain they would last out. Not like Jordan. He'd married Leoni when he was twenty, despite his parents' wishes for them to wait a while. He'd known her for only six months before marriage had been suggested. News came soon after that she was pregnant. Betty had shown Kirstie umpteen photographs of her grandson, Liam. She'd complained to her often that she never saw enough of him, not in a bitter way, but regretfully.

As they drew level with the house, she pointed to a Toyota Arius parked in the driveway. 'Oh, for fuck's sake, that's Nicole's car! What the hell is she doing here?'

'She knew Jordan for far longer than you.' Ryan parked next to it. 'She's entitled to be here as much as you are. And besides, it means you won't have to comfort Mum. I'm sure you'd find that hard to do, you being the grieving girlfriend.'

'Well, she'd better not open her mouth and say something she shouldn't. If she says one more bitchy thing about me, I'll close the bloody thing for her with one punch.'

'Just keep a civil tongue in your mouth for a few hours,' Ryan warned. 'This is about my mum. She doesn't need anything else to worry about.'

'Don't tell me what to do!' Kirstie snapped indignantly as she got out of the car.

A woman she didn't recognise opened the door. She wore a blouse tied at the neck, a pencil skirt and court shoes. Kirstie thought she looked like a secretary, wondered if she was with the funeral director, although she hadn't seen a car outside.

'Mr Jordan,' she addressed Ryan first. 'I'm PC Maria Temple. I'm a police family liaison officer.'

Kirstie tutted her annoyance as Ryan shook her hand. Maria held it out to her afterwards but she ignored it and went into the house.

'I hope you can look after my mum,' she heard Ryan say, his tone one of politeness rather than contempt. She rolled her eyes.

'Of course.' Maria touched his arm. 'I'm really sorry for your loss. I'll make this as comfortable as I can for you all.'

All of a sudden Kirstie felt an almost irresistible urge to shout out that he was a hypocrite. Let everyone know how much of a doting brother he really was. How would his mum feel if she found out the truth? Instead she took a deep breath and held her tongue. Shoulders back, she went into the living room. It was a room she loved and hated in equal measures. According to Jordan, its decor had been the same for over twenty years until their father died. Clive had painted over the same wallpaper every twelve months with magnolia paint to freshen it up. Now that the walls were plastered with large flowers and the settee covered in chintzy fabric, it was much brighter but still it seemed claustrophobic to her.

Nicole was sitting on the settee next to Betty, all teary eyes and streaked makeup. Her nails had been manicured, her long blonde hair freshly washed and straightened. Her clothes were black but stylish, high heels finishing the outfit. Kirstie had to admit that she always tried to keep herself smart and trendy but all she could see was mutton trying to dress as lamb.

As soon as Ryan came into the room, Nicole ran into his arms and burst into tears.

'You know he was like my little brother,' she sobbed, burying her face in his chest. 'I can't believe he's gone. Have the police said anything else yet?'

'It's too early,' said Ryan, comforting her.

Kirstie watched the scene unfolding with disbelief. Her eyes on Ryan made him turn his head for a moment and she glared at him. She folded her arms.

'Surely they should know something by now?' Nicole wiped her eyes with a tissue. 'Don't you have any ideas at all?' she asked Maria, who had come in behind Ryan.

Maria shook her head. 'I'll tell you as soon as I know anything.'

'At least it's stopped raining,' Kirstie said for want of something to add. 'It means evidence might not get washed away easily.'

'What are you – *CSI Miami*?' Ryan barked. 'Horatio Cain would be proud of you.'

'Ryan,' Betty cried. 'There's no need to attack poor Kirstie like that. She's grieving as much as you.'

'Sorry, Mum.' Ryan bent down to kiss his mother's cheek.

'It's unbearable. How could someone just take him away from us like that? Leave him to die on a pathway. Why would anyone want to do that? He never did anyone any harm. Why, why . . .'

As she burst into tears, too, Kirstie couldn't take any more.

'I'll make a drink,' she said.

In the kitchen, she sighed. She'd hoped that she could visit in peace and disappear as quickly as possible. She needed to get geared up for a call from the police, rehearse what she had been repeating to herself over the past few days.

Behind her, the door opened and Ryan came in. As he stood looking out of the window on to the garden, she reached for his shoulder, turned him towards her and pressed herself into his chest. For a moment she felt him give in as he hugged her tightly.

'I'm sorry about earlier,' he said. 'I was upset.'

'It's understandable,' she soothed. 'But we can get through this. No one really knows what happened.'

Ryan gave her hand a squeeze. 'Once this is sorted, then we can come out in the open about things. Okay?'

Kirstie nodded. 'We just need to keep our cool, get our stories straight at the end of every day and we'll be in the clear before you know.'

'I hope so. I don't need the police sniffing around at every opportunity. They'll want to know everything – the less they find out the better.'

'Let's just forget for now and look after each other.' She smiled up at him.

The door opened and they moved apart. When Ryan saw it was Nicole, he left the room.

As she filled the kettle with water, Kirstie turned her back to Nicole, hoping that the woman would take a hint. They hadn't liked each other since they'd met, when Jordan had first introduced her to the family as his girlfriend. She reckoned Nicole was jealous of her age and her power. Her father's reputation preceded her.

Nicole marched across the room, her heels clicking on the tiled floor. 'Need a hand?' her tone was snide. 'I'm sure the other one has spent far too long down my husband's trousers.'

Kirstie turned sharply. 'I beg your pardon?'

'Oh, come off it.' Nicole folded her arms as she stood in front of her. 'You might fool Betty but it's clear to me that you're sleeping with Ryan.' She laughed harshly. 'Never had him down for the guy who'd want a youngster though. Still, I suppose even he would make an exception for Terry Ryder's daughter.'

Kirstie snarled at her. 'Keep your mouth shut and your opinions to yourself or I'll make sure you regret it.'

'Don't threaten me.' Nicole wasn't afraid to look her in the eye. 'I know how much Ryan wanted to get in with you. This is just a business proposition to him. He's using you like he used Jordan.'

Kirstie took hold of Nicole's forearm and squeezed it tightly, relishing the look on her face when she could see the pain she was causing.

'You seem to have a smart head on your shoulders,' she told her. 'Just make sure it stays that way or else I'll ensure that you're cut off and you won't have a penny.' She sneered. 'Now go back and comfort the old dear, there's a love.'

'Don't patronise me,' Nicole seethed. 'I know too much about you.'

'I might be younger than you but please don't make the mistake of taking me for a fool,' Kirstie countered. 'I'll do too much to seek my revenge, starting with the bloke who's sharing *your* bed with you at the moment.'

Nicole paled.

'You think I don't know what you're getting up to?' Kirstie shook her head slowly. 'Just remember, I have people everywhere. There's nothing about you that I don't know. So like I said,' she touched her lips with an index finger, 'keep your mouth shut. Otherwise, I'll make sure he's forced to take everything from you.' Her smile was cruel. 'You know I'd do that, don't you?'

'I'd be very careful, if I were you,' Nicole hit back. 'You might think you're okay because Ryan is under your roof, perhaps in your bed, but you are nothing but expendable. I know him far better than you. Once he's had what it is he's after, he won't give you another thought. So don't come threatening me, little miss. I'm too old and too experienced to suffer fools gladly.'

'You're too old to keep your husband happy. From what I heard, it was hard for him to get it up once a month with you. Whereas me, I –'

'You cheeky bitch.' Nicole raised a hand.

Kirstie grabbed it before it reached its target. 'Don't even think about it. I'll have –'

'What the hell's going on in here?' Ryan whispered loudly as he came into the room. 'We can hear you in the living room. Pipe down and show some respect.'

Kirstie glared at Nicole, making sure she looked away first.

'She started it.' Nicole's words seemed childish.

Ryan shook his head and went back into the other room.

Kirstie smirked. That was one thing she'd learned from her mother. She'd never let any woman get the upper hand.

2.30 P.M.

Back at Harrison House, Allie followed Perry as he marched up the stairs.

'How are we playing this?' he asked.

'There's no point in taking her down to the station just yet.' Allie went through the door as he held it open for her. 'For starters, I'd rather not bring her to the attention of the media scrum unless we have to arrest her. Let's see why she gave us a different name and assess the situation then. We can get uniform to take a statement again afterwards.'

'Interesting, though. Maybe you were right about the cold.'

Allie nodded. 'Let's check it out with her first.' She knocked on the door. 'Hello . . . Sophie,' she said when it was opened. 'It's Sophie Nicklin, isn't it?'

Sophie nodded, bursting into tears as she let them in.

When they were all seated in the living room, Allie looked at the younger woman. She had that wide-eyed look of an animal about to be mowed down with nothing to do but accept her fate.

'Am I in a lot of trouble?' Sophie asked. 'I'm so sorry.'

'Why did you tell us your name was Rebecca Adams?'

'It was the first thing that came into my head. I – I panicked. I was shocked that Jordan was dead and I wasn't thinking straight. It is Jordan, isn't it?'

'We've yet to release a formal statement but we believe so.'

More tears fell.

'Why did you think it was him?' Allie asked after giving Sophie a moment to compose herself.

'I didn't – I just assumed. And then when I called him, I saw someone pick up his phone near to the path and I . . .'

'You do know that you're not stored under his phone as Sophie?'

'I didn't know for sure.' She started to pick at the skin around her nails. 'He lives with Kirstie Ryder. Everyone knows how powerful she is.'

'She isn't.' Allie bristled at the remark.

'Well, that's what everyone around here thinks.'

'Everyone?'

'My friend Stella says that Kirstie is a law unto herself, and she can do anything because of who her father is. They also say that if you go after her fella, she'll scar you for life.'

'Who's *they*, Sophie?'

'Stella. Her husband knows her too. He works at Flynn's, I think, although I'm not sure what he does.'

'How long have you known Stella?'

'Eight months, since I moved in. I –' She looked up with tears in her eyes. 'I don't know anyone else.'

'Not even from work?'

'No, I work from home now. I did a bit of temping when I first arrived, for Holdcroft's Motors on Leek Road. I made a few friends in the office while I was there and went out a couple of times. That was when I met Jordan at Flynn's. But I was only there for six weeks and when I left, no one kept in touch. They were just work colleagues, really. That's why when Jordan took my phone number . . . Well, I was lonely.'

'How long had you been seeing him?'

'About six months. He'd come here after he'd finished work, early in the mornings. It suited me. With being self-employed now, I sometimes work late into the early hours.'

'What do you do?'

'I design book covers. There's a huge market for it online.'

'We can see from the phone records that he often called you late at night. Were you worried when he didn't ring?'

'Yes, that's why I sent him a message.' She looked up, fresh tears forming.

Although she had to keep an open mind, Allie suddenly felt sympathy for the woman sitting across from her. She knew from experience that people do stupid things when they're in shock and Sophie Nicklin' tears seemed genuine to her, unlike Kirstie Ryder's earlier that morning. The young woman sitting by her side was raw with grief. She'd also confessed as soon as she had seen them. Maybe she had given a false name because she was scared of repercussions. She didn't seem to be hiding anything.

'Do you think anyone knew about the affair?' asked Perry.

'Jordan never said.' Sophie paused to wipe tears from her face. 'We thought we'd kept it quiet, but can't you see? He was murdered because of me.'

'What makes you say that?' Allie glanced at Perry, saw that he was frowning too.

'If he hadn't been coming to see me, he wouldn't have been on that path.' Sophie's breath caught. 'And if he wasn't on that path, then no one . . . no one would have . . . do you have any idea who did it?'

'Nothing we can release yet, I'm afraid,' Allie continued. 'Did he always cut through from the main road?'

'Yes, he parked his car in one of the streets off Ford Green Road. He'd use the path and walk along the side of the building to the main entrance. Less chance of being seen, I suppose.' Sophie looked at them both in turn. 'Did he suffer?'

Allie shook her head. 'I can't be certain but he would most probably have been unconscious within a minute or so.' She chewed on her lip. 'Sophie, when we asked you earlier if you had been to the scene of the crime last night, and you said no, did you lie about that, too?'

'No, that wasn't me. I waited up for Jordan but I fell asleep on the sofa. I woke up just before half past three and then I went to bed. I – I must have just missed him because I saw Rita out walking her dog just as I closed my curtains. I only lied about my name because I was scared.'

'Of what?'

'Being attacked by Kirstie Ryder. Jordan and I might have loved each other, but he was hers.'

Once out on the walkway when they had finished with their questions, Allie sighed loudly. 'Those weren't crocodile tears,' she said to Perry. 'I wish we could tell her it was more than likely nothing at all to do with her.'

'We don't know that for certain,' said Perry.

'I know. But it's possible that if someone knew Jordan would be there, they might have figured it was the perfect place to carry out the murder.'

'Which means it could be someone local? Someone in these flats?'

'Yes,' said Allie. 'We need to rule out who *couldn't* have been in the vicinity because they were elsewhere.' She looked down to the ground, could see that Nick had arrived to address the press later at the news conference. She glanced along the walkway and on the walkways overhead. Lots of people still hanging around, despite the drizzle in the air and the dark drawing in.

But Allie had another black cloud hanging over her head right now. She needed to ring Mark before it was too late.

3.00 P.M.

Allie felt a sharp stab of apprehension as she heard Mark's voice again.

'You're there for a late one, aren't you?' he said.

His annoyance was clear in his tone. And, although she knew he wouldn't be happy when he found out that she was going to be here for the night, she was more unsure of what she was about to say next. 'I'm afraid so. We're just gathering everything together for the press conference.'

She heard him sigh. 'I might go out for a pint with Chris.'

'Great.' Her tone was fun. 'Have one for me.'

'Are you going to be on the TV?'

'I'll probably be in the background. Look, there's something I need to tell you.'

'Christ, you don't know him as well, do you?'

'No, this is nothing like before!'

'Good! I know Stoke is a small city but it was getting a bit ridiculous.'

Allie relented when she heard his tone soften. Well, in for a penny . . .

'You will have heard of him. Or more, to the point, you will have heard of the nightclub that he runs. It's Jordan Johnson, from Flynn's.'

'That super cool young dude who was in *The Sentinel* about a month ago? Sitting on some flash car as he talked about a new wing opening?'

'Yes. He was in a terrible way. Most neighbours have been pretty friendly with us today but there is a growing atmosphere of . . . something. There's more I need to tell you.' She paused for the briefest of moments before blurting it out. 'He was living with Kirstie Ryder.'

There was a long pause from him. Allie didn't know what to fill it with.

'What goes around comes around, hmm?'

'Sorry?' She didn't quite catch his meaning.

'Well, her father was a nasty piece of shit who deserved to be locked up. I suppose I shouldn't complain that my wife is dealing with him again if it means solving a murder. Do you have to visit his house?'

'You know he isn't going to be there!'

'But the memories . . .'

Allie closed her eyes for a moment. What was she supposed to do? Tell her DI that she couldn't work the case anymore because her husband was annoyed that she could be in Terry Ryder's clutches again?

'I wish I could tell you to stay away, but I know you won't,' he added.

'I can't do that. I have to do my job. It's not like I want to –'

'So you're not going to be back in time for tea this evening?' he broke in.

'No.' She held back a sob. 'I'll definitely make time to call in and see Karen though, even if it's really late.'

'Okay. Priorities and all that.'

'And you'll call me the minute anything changes?' She hated to sound so needy.

'Of course I will.'

A small pause. 'Mark?'

'If it isn't some maniac coming after you that I'm worried shit-less about, it's another one that nearly wrecked our marriage. Just be careful, Allie. I want you for myself – is that too much to ask?'

'Of course it isn't!'

Another pause. The noise around her came back into focus. People talking, machinery clanking, doors banging, lenses clicking. Life was going on while hers was suspended in time. And there was still a murder to solve.

'I'm sorry,' was all she could think of to say.

'I'm not happy, but I'm not about to have a strop like a teenager and hang up either.'

'I know. But, thanks.'

She disconnected the phone after another long silence between them. 'I just need something from the car,' she told Perry as she rushed off. Ignoring the people on the ground, she almost ran across the car park. The car had been reversed into a space with its boot up against the wall to the flats. She flicked up the boot lid, went to the back of the vehicle and dipped her head behind it, out of sight. She breathed in deeply, pressing her hand across her mouth. Squeezing her eyes tight, she gasped as she tried to contain her emotions. Why did this murder have to happen now? Why couldn't it have happened next week or the week after, when she had said goodbye to her sister?

But she knew it wasn't all to do with Karen. It was the guilt of everything rushing at her. She had let Karen down all those years ago but she had let Mark down too. Why hadn't she been honest with him, shared her fears as well as her hopes?

If the man who had attacked her sister was watching her now, hiding while she broke down, he would think he had won. He'd done this to her. What a way to live her life.

No.

She wouldn't let him win. She wouldn't let Ryder win either.

'Allie?' Perry appeared gingerly by her side.

She wiped at her eyes quickly. 'Be with you in a moment,' she said, turning her back to him.

'Okay.'

She heard him step away and then stop. 'I'm not Sam so I can't do the girlie thing but Lisa tells me I give her a mean hug that always cheers her up. Let me now if you need one.'

'Piss off, you soppy sod. You'll have me crying more.' Allie looked at him through watery eyes, before batting him away with a hand. 'I'll be fine in a minute.'

3.45 P.M.

The press conference was due to start shortly. As senior investigating officer, Nick was running through some final preparations before it was time to speak. Even though Allie wouldn't have to be in front of the camera, she could still feel her stomach flipping over at the thought of the footage going out live. She prayed that the residents in the flats didn't start swearing loudly or pulling faces, do anything vulgar or disrespectful while they looked over from the walkways. She could just imagine the rumours that had been circulating around the flats during the day about who the man was and why the police wouldn't give out his name yet. Jordan's body had been removed from the crime scene half an hour ago now and formal identification would take place once they'd been briefed for the evening. Jordan's name would most probably be given out formally later that night. Local press and radio had speculated as much as they could and she'd informed Simon Cole that she couldn't give any definite answers yet, although he would still be the first to know.

Perry came over to her. 'It couldn't have happened in a worse place for privacy, could it?'

'I know. Everyone seems to be taking a look.' Allie glanced up through the drizzle that had started again in the last hour. 'Bloody mobile phones – all the photos being taken no matter how many times we tell them not to or remove them, videos being made. They'll be all over YouTube and we can't police that as well.'

'And we can hardly cordon off every home either.' Perry shook the rain from his hair. 'I'm sick of people complaining about us taking over the car park. I had someone have a go at me earlier, annoyed at being routinely questioned. They've got no respect for the fact that someone has died.'

'Always the same, Perry. Murder's okay as long as it's not on your doorstep. Selfish, that's what I call it.'

'I just hope they show some respect for our vic's family.'

'Mrs Johnson has asked if she can lay flowers at the scene after seeing Jordan.'

Social media was the one thing Allie had mixed feelings about. Over the past few years, everything had become so open. She disliked the public's penchant for watching another's sorrow, seeing if they could pick out any suspects. She could almost hear the whispers above. *He hasn't shed a tear. He must be guilty.* '*She doesn't look upset. I bet it's her.*' Everyone had their own thoughts. Luckily most kept them to themselves.

Nick beckoned them over. 'We have enough cover at the office for when the number goes out,' he told Allie. 'For a few hours at least. It will be interesting to see if anyone talks.'

A short, stocky cameraman who looked better placed to be at home with his grandkids came across to them. 'We'll be going live as soon as you're ready,' he told Nick.

Allie watched Nick quickly flick over his notes for one final time and then walk towards where the microphones were set up. She followed, positioning herself to his left behind him, not directly on camera.

Nick cleared his throat and ran through the details they had so far. Then he took a few questions from the waiting press.

'Can you say what the exact cause of death was?' Simon Cole asked. Allie noted his confident stance, not deterred by the rabble of reporters jostling him for room.

'We don't have those details yet. Once the post-mortem has been carried out, I'll be able to tell you more.'

Nick answered a few more questions and when there was a natural lull, looked into the camera again. 'Anyone who has any information can contact us at the station or on the national crime line telephone. The numbers are coming up on your television screens. I have handouts for press.' He turned to leave.

'Speculation is that it's Jordan Johnson. Can you confirm if this is true or not?'

All heads turned to see who had spoken. Allie groaned inwardly when she saw it was Pete Simpson from *The Staffordshire Times*.

Nick turned back to the camera. 'That's speculation. I can confirm nothing at this present moment. You all must understand that this is a sensitive issue and until we have formal identification for the family, we cannot give out a name.' He walked away quickly. Allie followed, too.

'They knew his name,' said Nick as she joined them. 'I know it's hard to keep it at bay but any idea how they got it?'

'Just speculation, like you said,' said Allie, 'although there will be lots of staff from Flynn's who know about it now.'

'Let's hope the press conference jogs someone's memory.' Nick glanced at his watch. 'I'll head back to the station, check in with the DCI and leave you to it here.'

'Okay, sir.'

Once Nick had gone, Allie took out her phone to see if there were any new messages or emails for her to deal with. As she looked at the screen, she had the distinct feeling that someone was watching her. Her head shot up, her eyes skimming the small crowd who were rubbernecking. Was someone after her attention?

She watched for a little longer, but she couldn't see anything in particular, just faces, people intrigued by what was happening. It still caused her to shiver.

'You okay, boss?' asked Perry.

Distracted, Allie looked up at him. 'Hmm? Oh, yes, I'm fine. Just thinking what to tackle next.'

She smiled to appease him. There was no way she was telling him that. He'd never leave her side. Besides, she glanced around the area one more time, the feeling had gone now. It was probably something and nothing.

'That stupid bitch!' Craig flung down the TV remote control and grabbed his jacket. He left the flat and flew down the stairs, keeping his head bowed as he strode over to Stella.

'Phone call for you.' He grabbed her by the arm.

'But I have my mobile with me and –'

'I told you to keep your mouth shut,' he seethed as he marched back up the stairs with her.

'I haven't said a thing!'

He kept his eyes peeled as he led her along the walkway. When they got to their front door, he pushed her inside and kicked it shut behind them.

Stella ran into the living room.

'Who did you tell?' He came in after her, slamming that door too.

'No one!' Stella held up her hands. 'I swear I told no one.'

'You must have. No one else knew.'

'That reporter said people have been speculating all day. I've heard his name mentioned quite a few times.'

'You do realise that the police will know someone in these flats knows something?'

'You're not listening to me! Whoever it was didn't find out from me. Besides, people everywhere must know by now.'

Craig's eyes narrowed. Of course it was possible. He'd received lots of messages from people asking if he'd heard what had happened.

'Did you tell Leah?' he asked.

Stella wouldn't look at him.

'What aren't you telling me?' Grabbing a handful of her hair, Craig dragged her through to the hall. 'Was she the woman seen last night going into the flats at the same time Jordan was found. Was it Leah?'

'No, I don't think so.'

Craig raised his fist and pulled it back. 'My fucking life might depend on this!'

'Don't hit me! Please!' Stella began to cry. 'She saw Jordan last night.'

Craig released his grip a little. 'Go on.'

'She was drunk. She can't remember why but she knew it was Jordan. I didn't tell her anything.'

Craig went out onto the balcony and marched towards Leah's flat.

'Hello?' Leah answered her phone.

'Leah!' cried Stella. 'Where are you?'

'I'm in my flat. What's –?'

'Craig's coming along. Make sure your door is locked.'

Leah ran to the door and locked it immediately. 'What's going on?'

'He knows.'

'You promised you wouldn't say anything! Why the –'

There was a bang on the door. Leah jumped and ran into the kitchen. She peeped around the corner of the door frame. 'He's here,' she whispered.

'Did you lock the front door?'

'Yes.'

'Stay where you are and I'll come to you when he's gone.'

'But –' Leah heard the letterbox being lifted and pulled her head back sharpish.

'Open the fucking door!' Craig banged with his fist again. 'I know you're in there, Leah. Me and you need to have a little chat.'

Leah clamped a hand to her mouth to stop him from hearing her frantic breathing, a gasp, a sigh, anything that would give her away. Finally, she heard the letterbox snap shut, a kick at the bottom of the door and then silence.

'Are you there, Leah?' Stella was still on the phone.

'Yes, I'm here,' she said. 'I can't believe you grassed me up.'

'I had to tell him. He was going to hit me, I swear. He wanted to know who I had told about Jordan's name after it got out at the press conference.'

'But I didn't tell anyone!' Leah's voice came out high-pitched. 'Don't you dare go around spreading that rumour.'

'I know it wasn't you. Everyone was talking about Jordan Johnson. But Craig was so mad that he wouldn't listen. You know how violent he can be. I panicked. I'm sorry.'

Leah dropped to the floor and pulled her knees into her chest. 'What am I going to do now? Everyone will be after me if he says anything.'

'I didn't tell him about the money. I just told him that you came across Jordan last night and –'

'It's the same thing. He'll work it out.'

'Look, let me check from here where Craig goes. If he leaves, I'll come to you.'

'No, I don't know if it's safe.' Leah stood up.

'It's me, Leah. You can trust me!'

'I did trust you and look what's happened!'

'He just caught me unawares and scared the truth out of me. I never sold you out.'

Leah disconnected the phone and paced the room. Shit, she was in for it now. She had no choice but to move the money as soon as possible.

If she didn't, she might lose more than ten thousand pounds.

4.15 P.M.

Jacob sighed when he heard the door to the communal stairs bang open and Craig appeared.

'A word in your ear.' Craig drew level with him and pushed him into the hallway of his flat.

'What's up?' Jacob sensed this wasn't going to go his way.

Craig punched him in the stomach. 'Did you know it was Jordan Johnson?' He was in his face again.

Jacob tried to push him off. 'No!'

'Don't fucking lie to me!' Craig shouted.

'I'm not –'

Sandra came from out of the living room. 'What the hell is going on now?' she cried. 'Can't I have a minute's peace around here today?'

'Go back inside and shut the door,' Craig told her.

'No! This is my bloody –'

He pushed her away with his free hand. 'I said go back inside!'

The door slammed and she was gone.

Craig punched Jacob in the stomach again.

He groaned, coughed, held up a hand. 'I'm your eyes and ears, you said. That's what I've been doing. Watching and listening – I haven't spoken to anyone because I didn't know anything.'

'So who was it that told that fat reporter?'

'It wasn't me! I was just doing as you asked.'

'Find out who it was.' He pushed him to one side and headed for the door.

'But – '

'I'll be back in half an hour and you'd better have some answers!'

Jacob stooped, holding his stomach as he caught his breath again. He wished he could have lashed out at Craig. He was strong enough to take him, fight back and defend himself, but he hadn't wanted to rouse suspicion. But what the hell was Craig talking about, that no one would know Jordan's name? He'd already had numerous text messages telling him who it was. News of that kind always travelled fast.

Craig must be losing it. The pressure was obviously getting to him.

Sandra ventured back into the hallway. 'What the hell have you got into, Jacob?' she cried.

'What have *I* got into?' Jacob's face creased with anger. 'It's always me, isn't it? Not your precious Tommy. He's a troublemaker too but I never see you having a go at him.'

'It *is* always you!'

'Leave me alone.'

'Jacob, wait!'

Jacob stepped back out onto the walkway. It was a good job Harrison House was known for everyone minding their own business. If anything was reported, the police would be on to it. All this coming and going, someone would see something.

He stood up tall, holding onto his stomach. How the hell had he thought this was going to be easy money?

5.00 P.M.

Leah sat on the armchair. She was dressed ready to go out, her jacket and gloves on against the cold and rain that was now settling in for the night, her hair bundled up inside a black woollen hat. Her right knee jiggled as she watched Sky News for further updates on Jordan Johnson before she plucked up the courage to go out.

It was dark enough to be pretty safe to risk it. Letting out the breath she'd been holding, she knew it was now or never. She had to chance it and hope that Craig wasn't lying in wait for her. Her hands shook, sweating under the thick layer of wool as she picked up the bag of money, slipped it inside her jacket and zipped up. Sliding back the bolts at the top and bottom of the front door, she opened it slowly. She popped her head out enough to see that the walkway was empty. She stepped out and looked over the wall. Most people had gone in now, the wind and rain as unwelcome as the police intrusion.

Time to make her move. She pulled the collar to her jacket in closer to her face and, with head down but keeping a look out, she walked towards the communal stairs. There was no way she could chance climbing down a floor to stay out of sight.

Her shoes hardly made a noise but the sound of her heart beating in her ears intensified. It made her feel breathless. She pushed on the door to the stairwell, grimacing as it squeaked, glancing around before closing it quietly behind her, not letting it bang like she usually would have done. Then she jogged down the stairs to ground level.

In the entrance hall, there was no one around. She took a look through the window at the side of the door and moved away from it immediately. That sergeant and her sidekick were outside. Oh, God, what happened if they saw her and guessed that she had something under her jacket? She'd be in for it if she told them where the money was from. And she could hardly say that she carried her life savings around with her, could she? What fool in their right mind would do that?

Before she was seen, Leah ran back upstairs to her flat. There was no way she could risk moving the money yet. She'd have to try later that night.

5.30 P.M.

Allie had gone back to the station. She was at her desk when Sam waved her over to the big screen television.

'I took a call from The Genting Club after the press conference went out. Jordan Johnson was at the casino last night. He arrived there alone at quarter past midnight and he left alone at just after two thirty. I spoke to the manager, who said that he'd played a couple of tables and drank coffee with a few of the regulars. Johnson then went to his car and left Hanley a few minutes later. The manager sent me footage, which I've gone through, and everything looks satisfactory.' She held up a finger as Allie was about to speak. 'I followed Jordan and Ryan into the car park after they left Flynn's. Both went to their cars. Ryan drove off and Jordan stayed for a couple of minutes and then left too. So he must have gone straight to the casino.'

'Well, at least we know that he didn't go back home to The Gables,' said Allie. 'Thanks, Sam.'

'I also watched CCTV from inside Flynn's last night.' Sam pointed the remote control at the television monitor. 'There's Jordan sitting at the bar at 23.03. Then in comes Kirstie.'

They both watched as she flung out a hand and caught him on his chin. Pandemonium broke out before she was pulled off him by three men.

'She's such a nasty piece,' remarked Perry as he joined them. 'She's bloody fearless.'

They watched again as she left the VIP area. Sam fast-forwarded until Jordan and Ryan got up and left. The time on the recording was 00.05. 'There you go. And . . . wait for it.'

Allie watched as another man left the party, too. She recognised him immediately.

'Craig Elliott! Interesting, because he and Stella told us that he was home and in bed for midnight.'

'Most people leave around one a.m.,' Sam continued, pressing the remote to fast forward, 'exactly as Steve Burgess said. The party wound up around two thirty.'

Allie pointed at the screen. 'Please tell me there are cameras situated on the entrances too?'

'Yes.' Sam quickly swapped the DVDs over. 'Here you go.'

Allie felt the adrenaline building up inside her, that feeling that they might be on to something. First, they witnessed Kirstie being escorted outside by two bouncers.

Sam pressed fast forward again, stopping forty minutes later. She pointed to the screen. 'There's Jordan leaving. Ryan, too.' Fast forward again. Finally, out onto Marsh Street came Craig.

'Ryan told us he left around midnight, which we now know is correct. Do we know if he came back?'

'Not according to this but I'm only at two thirty. I'm just going through the rest of it now.'

'Good work, Sam. After team brief, I'll check out why the delightful Elliotts are lying.'

5.45 P.M.

Craig took a call from Jacob as he was on the walkway. He stopped in front of his front door.

'You'd better have something for me,' he barked.

'You might want to look closer to home. Your bird's been to see the posh cow who lives next door to you.'

Craig looked up. Jacob was leaning on the wall outside his flat.

'When was this?' he asked.

'This afternoon. About oneish.'

'And you're just telling me?'

'You wouldn't listen to what I had to say when I last saw you,' Jacob defended himself. 'You just laid into me.'

Craig wasn't interested in that. 'What time did she leave?'

'About half an hour later, and then she went to see Leah.'

'Leah?' Craig frowned.

'Yeah. Your Stella's been flitting around all day here and there.'

'Has she now? Anything else you didn't tell me?'

'It all went quiet for a bit and then as soon as it was dark, Leah went out, too.'

'Was she carrying anything?'

'What?'

'A bag.' Craig rubbed at his temple. 'Was she carrying a bag?'

'A handbag, do you mean?'

'I don't know – any type of fucking bag!'

'I didn't see.'

Craig stared up at him. 'What time did she come back?'

'A few minutes ago.'

'You sure now?'

A pause. 'Yeah. Looked a bit shifty, if you ask me.'

Craig disconnected the call. Stupid bitches! Were they all playing him? And why had Stella been to see the posh totty? Had she picked up something and given it to Leah to move? He needed to talk to her, figure out what she was up to. Because if she was double-crossing him too, then she'd be getting much more than her usual slap.

He was certain now more than ever that Leah had something to do with the money. Once he caught up with her, she was in for it. No one put his life in danger by making a fool of him.

———

When a knock came at the door, Sophie answered it, thinking if it wasn't the police, it could have been Stella. She was surprised to see Stella's husband there instead.

'I want a word with you,' Craig said, pushing on the door.

Sophie tried to close it but his foot was in and he had the upper hand in no time.

'Just having a look around, darling,' he told her. 'Don't mind me. I won't be long.'

He pushed her into the living room so hard that she fell to the floor with the force.

'What do you want?' Paralysed with fear, she found her voice at last.

'Steve Burgess wants to know if you have something of his.'

'I don't know anyone named Steve Burgess.'

Craig went over to her desk and began to rifle through her drawers.

'Hey, that's private!'

'Nothing's private as far as money is concerned.'

'Money?' Sophie frowned. 'What are you talking about?'

'Cut the crap. I know about you and Jordan. All about your midnight rendezvous.'

Sophie froze. 'He didn't visit me last night.'

'Like I believe that.'

'It's true. You can ask the police. He was supposed to be coming but he never turned up.'

Craig had moved to her bookcase now.

'Stop it!' she cried as he threw some of the books down to the floor. 'There's nothing here.'

'There's lots of places you can hide money.' Craig glanced around again.

'But he didn't come here last night!' Sophie burst into tears. 'He's never going to come here again.'

———

Stella was in the living room when she heard the front door slam.

'What the fuck were you doing next door at that posh woman's flat earlier today?' Craig wanted to know.

'You mean Sophie?' Stella cursed under her breath. 'I was just seeing if she was okay. She's been a little under the weather recently with a cold, so I asked her if she wanted anything bringing in from the shops.'

'Don't take me for a fool. Was she the one who was screwing Jordan?'

Stella laughed nervously. 'Whatever gave you that idea?'

'Because I've just been to see her.'

Stella swallowed.

'Why are you lying to me?' Craig sneered.

'I'm not! She's never said anything to me.' She tried to move past him but he blocked her way.

'And Leah? Are you looking after that sneaky bitch, too?'

'Leah's my friend.' Stella folded her arms. 'You don't have to like her but I –'

Craig backhanded her before she had time to react.

She fell to the floor, holding her face. 'What the hell was that for?' she cried.

'I know you have the money.'

'I know that you're a bully!'

He stood over her. 'Where is it?'

'I don't have it!' she screamed. 'Why won't you believe me?'

'You three – you're all in this together, aren't you?' Craig grabbed her hair, pulling her to standing again. 'Jordan must have given it to her, then she gave it to you and you gave it to Leah. Where has she stashed it?'

'I don't know!'

'Wrong fucking answer!' He brought his fist up.

'Don't hit me again!' Stella raised her hands too, her pluckiness disappearing in an instant. 'Leah said she was taking it to her mum's!'

Craig pushed her away. Before he left the flat, he picked up her mobile phone and put it in his pocket.

In the silence afterwards, Stella gasped as she caught her breath. She put a hand to her lip. There was definitely blood, the bastard. And now he'd taken her phone, she wouldn't be able to contact Leah discreetly. She didn't want the police to see her flitting about too much or else she might slip up if they questioned her.

Embarrassed because she had let him scare her rather than stand up for herself, she vowed to change her ways. Once all this mess was sorted, she wanted him out of the flat. And if he wouldn't go, then she would.

She couldn't let him get away with it again.

6.00 P.M.

Craig had just parked up his car in Fegg Hayes Road when his phone rang. He picked it up. Shit. Steve Burgess.

'You got anything for me, yet?'

'Still working on it.'

'You're taking your fucking time!'

'I'll get it to you! I'm nearly there.'

'You'd better. If I don't have the money by the end of the day, you're a fucking goner, do you understand?'

Before he could say yes, Steve had hung up. Craig cursed. Did Steve think a reminder like that was going to help him? The thick prick. He was scared enough anyway without him breathing down his neck. And it was a sorry state of affairs when he had to give his wife a slap to get the truth out of her. He couldn't get it into her thick scull that she should be sticking by *him*, not any of her stupid friends.

He looked across at the block of four flats to his right, psyched himself up for what was to come. Owned by the city council, from the outside they all had tidy, pristine gardens as opposed to the flats opposite them that looked like they were being squatted in. They were also home to Mary Matthews, Leah's old dear of a mum. She'd had their cast-off table and chairs last year. He remembered cramming them into the back of his car to deliver them.

He jogged over, pushed open the gate and strode down the path. Number 27 was the first door, a downstairs flat. There was a light on in one room. He knocked and waited. No reply. He knocked again and when no one came to the door, he lifted the letterbox. There could definitely be someone in as the television was blaring away.

He went around the back. The garden was surrounded by a six-foot hedge on all sides, hard to see through for privacy but hard to escape through if he had to make a fast getaway. Although it was dark, it was early so he would have to be quick.

There were three windows in a row downstairs. The small one nearest to him was covered in opaque glass so he assumed it was the bathroom. The next one had a large window and two smaller panels. One of them was on the catch. He stretched up to open it and pushed his arm in. After a few seconds, he opened the larger window underneath and scrambled in.

Craig had always done a bit of thieving but since he'd started to work at Flynn's, his days of breaking and entering were over: there were more lucrative ways of getting money. He crept over to the door and opened it quietly. The sound of the television rose. He moved along a dark hallway, made his way to a door that was ajar. He peered through the gap between it and the frame, where a tiny sliver of light shone through, and found himself looking into the living room. Mary Matthews was fast asleep, curled up on the sofa. The fire was on full; she had a coat draped over her. He moved forward into the room, looking around quickly. Inside an old sideboard and behind the settee were the only two places anything could be concealed. He opened the door to the sideboard but it was full of magazines, knitting wool and a few old photos. Moving swiftly on all fours, he looked behind the settee but found nothing there.

Mary was still asleep. She hadn't moved at all. Craig stood over her for a few seconds. He ought to do her some damage, to teach Leah a lesson, but even though he was wearing gloves, he didn't want to draw attention to himself. Turning away, he went through to her kitchen, opening drawers and doors as quietly as he could. After a few minutes, he could find nothing in there. He went through to the bathroom. There was no bath panel to hide anything behind, just a walk-in shower cubicle. He checked out the airing cupboard, pulling down towels and sheets onto the floor.

Nothing.

That bitch Stella must have been lying to him all the time. Wait until he got his hands on her.

He was just leaving the house through the bedroom window when he noticed something tucked in at the side of the wardrobe. He chanced putting a light on. Could it be? It was. A black bag.

He heard a rap on the window and looked up into the face of an elderly man.

'Oy, what are you doing in there?' he shouted.

Craig picked the bag up, hoisted it over his shoulder and jumped up onto the windowsill again.

'I'm the electric man. Don't worry yourself, pops,' he smiled, climbing through the window.

'You're not the bloody electric man.'

Craig jumped to the ground and the man prodded a walking stick at him.

'Mary! Mary! I'm going to call the police.'

'Keep the noise down or I'll —'

'But you can't just take that bag. I —'

Craig pushed the man on the shoulder, sending him hurtling into the garden. He lost his footing and fell backwards, his head banging on the lawn.

'Fuck!' Without a second thought, Craig shrugged the bag onto his shoulder again and ran back to his car. He was gone before a light went on anywhere.

Allie's head went up from her computer as she spotted DCI Trevor Barrow walking into the office. It was a few minutes before the evening's team brief was due to start. He stopped at her desk and she felt his presence, looked up.

'I've barely had a chance to ask you today, it's been that busy. How're you bearing up, Allie?' he asked.

'I'm okay, sir.'

'Let me know if things are too much for you, or if you need a break. We'd understand.'

She nodded. She felt unable to meet his eye as the tears welled up again but, fearing it would be disrespectful if she didn't, gave him a quick smile. She breathed a sigh of relief once he had gone.

'Big sigh, that,' said Sam, sitting down across from her.

Allie gave her a faint smile too. 'Honestly, it's so nice of everyone to show concern and I suppose I'd be pissed off if they didn't. But constantly being asked, being reminded of what's to come all the time wears me down. I feel like I'm going to burst into tears if someone mentions Karen's name.' She bit her lip.

Sam moved her chair closer and gave Allie a sympathetic smile.

'But I also feel guilty for being here, doing my job, getting on with my life when she . . . when she's about to end hers.'

'Don't give yourself a hard time. You're doing what you do best. You've spent so much time with her, supporting her. She'd want you to get on with your life.'

'I know – but it's only to keep my mind off the inevitable. It doesn't seem right.'

They both turned to listen when Trevor addressed the room.

'Okay, everyone.' He turned to the whiteboard behind him. 'Nick, can you run through the events of the day and then everyone can update us with what they know before we crack on.'

Nick moved to stand next to Trevor. He pointed to a photo in the middle of the board and tapped a finger on it.

'Our victim, Jordan Johnson, thirty-one. Blunt force trauma to the head and face with what looks like a baseball bat, plus one incision to the chest. Neither weapon has been located on site. Cause of death is looking likely to be the knife in the chest. He was killed in the early hours of this morning on the pathway next to Harrison House in the dip of Ford Green Road. Found shortly after by a woman walking her dog. Time of death was estimated between one and three thirty a.m., but new evidence shows that Johnson was at the The Genting Club until two thirty, so that narrows the time down. Allie?'

'Our witness, Rita Pritchard, was ringing for an ambulance when she says she saw a woman with long dark hair going into the flats. She heard the electronic door buzzer and caught the back of a female but can't be sure who she was. There are three women in the block who match that description. One name she mentioned was Leah Matthews in flat number,' she checked back over her notebook and nodded, '203 and another woman she thought lived on the same floor as Leah, but she didn't know her name or flat number. The third woman was Stella Elliott at flat 209. She's known to us thanks to her delightful husband Craig, whom I think we've all met at one point or another.'

'They should put a bomb on that place,' joked Perry.

'We'd all be out of a job then,' said Sam.

'Perry and I spoke to all three women,' Allie continued. 'First up, Rebecca Adams in flat 210. She was in all evening, went to bed around eleven and didn't know anything had happened until she saw the police the next morning and asked a neighbour what was going on. But when Jordan Johnson's phone records came back from SPOC, it turned out that the last person to send him a message was a woman called Sophie Nicklin, living at flat 210, Harrison House.'

Nick ran a hand over his chin. 'A false name? Why do you think she did that?'

'Turns out she'd been seeing Jordan on the quiet for a few months, and panicked because she didn't want the wrath of girlfriend, Kirstie Ryder.'

Another murmur spread round the room.

'Well, there's the reason why Johnson was at Harrison House last night,' said Nick.

'Maybe Johnson told Sophie Nicklin that he was leaving Kirstie and then didn't follow through?' suggested Sam. 'She could be attacking him in revenge, then.'

'It's possible, I suppose,' said Allie. 'Although I have a feeling that she isn't involved, it's worth thinking about.'

'Or,' Nick continued, 'did someone know he was going to be there, arrange to meet him? Did someone follow him there? Or was it just a random attack?' He addressed Allie again. 'Leah Matthews – did you get any sense out of her?'

'There was something nervy about her, she wasn't her usual bolshie self. She didn't make much eye contact and was trying to put on a couldn't-care-less attitude. She too said she was home alone, fell asleep on the sofa and also heard about it the next morning.'

'And Stella Elliott?'

'We spoke to her and her husband, Craig. She was in from work at eleven – that checks out with her finishing time, as well as her friend saying she dropped her off afterwards. Craig said he came in about midnight. Sam, do you want to pick up from here?'

'CCTV footage from Flynn's shows him leaving around that time,' said Sam, 'but it would take another twenty minutes for him to get to Harrison House if he went straight home in a taxi or car. Walking, I'd say about an hour. I can try and follow him if necessary to see where he goes, but either way it puts him at home much later than midnight.'

'I'm going to talk to him once the brief is over,' Allie added.

'There's going to be a formal identification taking place straight after this briefing,' said Nick. 'I might need you there.'

Allie looked at the floor. So much for thinking of her feelings. That was the last place she wanted to be. When she looked up, Sam was looking at her. She mouthed 'Are you okay?' and Allie nodded quickly.

Nick turned back to the board and pointed to another photograph of a woman. 'This is Kirstie Ryder. She's twenty-one now and though we don't have any proof of illegal activity, we've been keeping an eye on her for a while and we believe she is helping her father to keep on top of the family business. Even though they now technically belong to Kirstie, Terry Ryder still runs the six branches of Car Wash City, located here and there around the area. We believe he controls his business through making her do some of the running around, and Ryan and Jordan have been doing the rest. I doubt it's a coincidence that Kirstie and Jordan were an item.'

'She also has long dark hair,' Perry pointed out.

'Indeed, so she too could be our mystery woman. Allie and I saw her at home this morning. Ryan was there, too. She says she and Jordan were arguing last night. She'd gone round to Flynn's and they ended up fighting. Kirstie says she went home afterwards, claims to have not seen Jordan alive after that.'

'We saw all that on screen,' said Sam. 'She packs a mean punch.'

'Allie,' said Nick, 'can you have a word with the bouncers when you visit Flynn's to talk to the staff? See if they can add anything. More importantly, see if they close ranks and remember nothing. Take Perry with you.'

'But, sir, I thought I'd go and see Craig Elliott. Perry was going to go to Flynn's.'

Nick gave her a meaningful look. 'I'd rather you didn't go alone.'

'I'll be fine at the flats and I think –'

'If you and Perry are quick at Flynn's, you can be over at Elliott's in no time.'

'There're lots of officers at Harrison House. I'll keep in their sight and –'

'For God's sake, Allie, this isn't open to discussion. This is a basic command. You will stay with Perry.'

Allie stared at the whiteboard behind him, quietly fuming, realising it would do no good to complain any further. Instead, she tried not to show her annoyance that she wasn't being listened to. Even when it concerned her own health and safety, she would never get used to it. Damn that bastard for stirring things up again. Now she wasn't even in control of her job.

Nick looked around the room; if he noticed Allie's belligerence, she couldn't tell. 'Follow up any leads that have or will come in from the press conference too. Sam, have all tenants been spoken to door-to-door now?'

'Most but not all – I'd say ninety per cent.'

'If they're not all done this evening, Perry, can you finish off in the morning? We can get all we have so far checked on HOLMES then. Ideally, I'd like a good presence around those flats in case someone wants to tell us anything.'

'What about the area around – anything found of significance?' asked Perry.

'Nothing on camera yet,' said Sam. 'But lots to look through and lots to come in yet. And a few things we're waiting for on the ground search. I also started checking around after we found Jordan Johnson's car and I came across Craig Elliott's car – parked in Regina Street, one along from Sparrow Street. Not sure why it wasn't in the car park of Harrison House. I'm still checking CCTV images from local shops and houses.'

'Yes, why didn't he park his car nearer to his home? There are plenty of spaces available before we commandeered it. Allie, check that out with Elliott, too.'

Allie sighed loudly. He should make his mind up when it was and wasn't okay for her to go and see Elliott.

Nick and Trevor stared at her long enough to make her feel uncomfortable again before turning back to the team. They exchanged a quick look and then Trevor spoke next.

'Right, let's go to it,' he said. 'Someone in those flats will have seen something. Anything, no matter how small, may lead us on to something else. Or, if we get really lucky, someone will open his or her mouth. Gossip will have been ripe today – who knows what will come in once Jordan Johnson's name is formally released. We'll move back on site first thing after the briefing in the morning, unless we're needed anywhere tonight. In the meantime, people, let's crack on.'

Mark sat next to the bed in the hospital, holding Karen's hand. It was swollen, her fingers the size of sausages because of the steroids. Gently, he rubbed his thumb across the back of it. She looked flushed again. When she had first been taken ill, almost three weeks ago now, both he and Allie had been granted compassionate leave. But as the days had dragged on, they'd both had to return to work. Now they were visiting as much as they could.

It was hard for him to look at Karen without thinking of how much danger Allie could be in if the man who attacked her sister ever got close enough to harm her, too. He knew every precaution had been put into place to keep her safe but still he worried that she might not come home to him one day. This made it raw seeing Karen slipping away, and very real, intensifying his discomfort at the situation.

He looked up as a nurse came into the room. It was Sharon.

'Hi, Mark, how are you?' she asked, the pallor of her skin accentuated in the artificial lighting.

'I'm good. How are you?'

'I'm fine, thanks. How's Allie doing?'

'Bearing up. People don't stop committing crimes, though, just to suit the police.'

'You mean that man who was found dead in Smallthorne? Yes, I heard on the news. Such a shame to go like that. Does she have to go in to deal with it? It's terrible timing for her.'

'I think she copes better when she blocks it out.' Mark shrugged. 'I can't say I blame her, to be honest.'

'It's easier for some people to do that.' The nurse checked a chart at the end of the bed.

Mark sighed as he loosened his tie. Karen was slowly taking in less of the things that kept her alive. She could die within hours if she had another bleed to the brain. It could be weeks if she didn't. It was a sad and cruel way to go but they'd been reassured that Karen wouldn't know any pain. She would eventually slip away – or if things got too bad, he and Allie would have to make the heart-breaking decision to switch off the life support when the time came. He knew that would destroy Allie.

Last weekend, he and Allie had chatted again about what their lives would have been like if Karen had never been attacked. Karen would perhaps have got married, started a family even. It was the one thing he regretted not doing with Allie. They would have made good parents but each time the subject had come up, Allie hadn't been able to face it. For her, there didn't seem to be any room – it had nothing to do with her career. In the back of his mind, he thought it was the guilt of what had happened to Karen, punishment even.

But Karen hadn't died. Did he hate her for it? He couldn't help but wonder how different things would have been if she hadn't been attacked. If catching the attacker hadn't remained at the forefront of Allie's mind for the past seventeen years. If there had been room to spare for the two of them to become a family with a child or two. He'd never voiced this to her, wasn't sure he ever would. He loved her too much to hurt her by saying it, but this niggling feeling that he would have made a good father wouldn't go away. Allie was nearly forty now – he was forty-four. Neither of them was too old by today's standards, but he wasn't sure if he wanted to be in his sixties when his child was leaving high school. For him, they had left it too late.

He looked at Karen now, sad that she hadn't had a chance to become a parent either. It had been hard to visit her over the years at Riverdale Residential Home but he hated to see her like this even more. And he knew how hard it was for Allie to keep her grief inside her. Since her last case had involved the man who had attacked Karen, twice over the past week she'd broken down as she'd come home from work, tired and emotionally exhausted with keeping up the pretence that it wasn't getting to her. He'd found her in the shower one night, water on full, sitting cowering in the corner, her arms wrapped around her knees. He'd taken her out and enveloped her in his arms, sat on the bathroom floor with her while she had cried.

He'd cried with her too, his buried feelings of inadequacy suddenly overwhelming him. His distress, how scared he was of her leaving the house and never coming back to it. His angst at not being there for her when she needed him most. His panic, which only intensified when she wasn't with him.

Worst was the feeling that he couldn't protect her all the time. But he couldn't let her see that. Allie would see her independence being threatened if he worried too much. He couldn't bear it if it broke them, if his feelings made her despise him enough to call it quits.

He would never tell her that either.

6.30 P.M.

Craig drove a few streets away from Mary Matthews's flat and parked up at the back of a row of shops. He reached for the bag that he had thrown into the well of the passenger seat, picked it up and unzipped it. His relief at getting away from Fegg Hayes Road soon turned to frustration and then anger as he clapped eyes on its contents.

He pulled out a pair of curtains, bright frilly fancy things. He threw them to the floor of the car, his hands falling upon netting folded into neat squares, followed by several cushion covers. When his hands hit the bottom of the bag, he clenched them into fists before flinging everything to the floor.

Frantically, he unzipped the two side pockets. There wasn't enough room to store all the money there but Leah might have had the sense to hide it in a few places rather than keep it altogether. Maybe there were a few bundles stashed there.

The side pockets were empty too.

'Stupid fucking bitch!' He slammed the palm of his hand on the steering wheel.

Leah Matthews was going to be in for the hiding of her life.

Leah sat on her sofa, without a clue what to do next. She hadn't even taken off her jacket. Shivering as the nerves took over, she wished she had never laid eyes on Jordan Johnson and the money that morning. It was all well and good being an opportunist thief but getting into this much trouble wasn't worth it. If she didn't owe money to Kenny Webb, if she wasn't so desperate to pay him back, if she had been able to walk away, she would have left it there, wouldn't she?

Now, all she could picture was the image of Jordan's face, beaten, bloody, bruised. What a cruel way for anyone to die. And if the murder had been set up, the perpetrator would most probably be a cruel bastard anyway. She shuddered.

Her phone rang; the caller display screen on her mobile flashed up Stella.

'You lying bitch!' Craig yelled. 'There was no fucking money at your mother's.'

'Where's Stella?' Leah's heart skipped a beat. 'You've been to see my mum?'

'You should never have crossed me, you idiot. I want that money.'

'But I never said –'

'I'm going to tear every fucking bone from your body if you don't tell me where it is.'

Leah disconnected the phone and dialled her mum's number. If he *had* killed her, it would be her fault.

'Pick up, pick up, pick up!'

It rang several times, and then 'Hello?'

'Mum!' Leah cried, relief flooding through her. 'Are you okay?'

'Oh, I'm fine, duck, but I've had a break-in. I was about to ring you but the police have just arrived.'

Leah sat down before her legs gave way.

'Someone got in through the back. I only left the top window open on the catch. The flat is a bit of a mess but I can't see anything missing at the moment. The police said I might remember later.'

'So you didn't hear anything,' she shuddered, 'or see anyone?'

'No, I'd had one of those sleeping pills that the doctor gave me last week.'

'You were in?' Leah gasped.

'Yes. I was awake all night thinking they weren't going to work, got up at six this morning and then I must have dozed off this afternoon. Apparently he came in here and then out again while I was asleep.'

'Oh, Mum.' Leah could hear the tremble in her voice.

'I got off lightly, duck. Bernard from next door was found on the back lawn. He fell and hit his head. The police say I had a lucky escape. Bernard was most probably hurt by the intruder, maybe not on purpose, but perhaps pushed to one side because he was disturbed. It was lucky his head didn't crash on the concrete path instead of the grass. Poor Bernard. This is all my fault.'

'It isn't your fault,' Leah tried to appease her.

'But if I'd closed my window properly, or been awake, I might –'

'You might have been attacked, too.' Leah didn't want to think about it. 'I'm so glad that you're safe.'

'Well, I don't think I'll be venturing out into the back garden for a very long time. I don't want to be reminded of what might have happened to me if I hadn't been asleep.' Leah heard her catch her breath. 'You don't think whoever did this will come back?'

'No, mum. I'm sure they won't.'

Leah said goodbye and disconnected the call. Elliott, that bastard. Tears of anger pricked at her eyes. How could he do that to her mother? What would have happened if she hadn't been asleep? If he'd got into the flat and she had seen him?

He must have thought she had hidden the money there. Which meant that now he knew she hadn't, he'd be coming after her again. Well, he wasn't going to get the better of her. If he wanted a war, then he would get one.

6.45 P.M.

Allie and Perry walked across to Flynn's nightclub, fastening their coats against the wind that was building up. The drizzle had stopped for the past half hour. Allie wore a woollen hat to stop her hair from blowing in her face: Perry wouldn't flatten his hair with a hat but he would get it wet.

'Are you okay, boss?' Perry asked as Allie's strides matched his own. Usually she had to walk fast to keep up with him.

'Oh, I'm fine,' her voice was raised. 'I'm just sick of being told what I can and can't do. It's as if I haven't got a bloody mind of my own.'

'You haven't when it comes to your own safety.'

'Thanks for the vote of confidence,' she snapped.

'You know what I mean.' Perry pulled her back as she nearly stepped out in front of a car that was going too fast. 'I'm sorry that I'm the one who gets to babysit you but I have to agree with Nick for once. We're all concerned for you.'

Allie sighed. Of course they were, and if she weren't so pig-headed she would see it for herself.

'Sorry,' she relented. 'It's just hard for me at the moment.'

They walked in silence past Sentinel House and on to Marsh Street.

'Who's meeting us there?' Perry asked over the noise of a bus going past.

'Flynn's isn't opening this evening so I asked Burgess to gather as many of the staff as he could for us to chat to. He emailed a list to Sam earlier on and she's been checking through it. I've got a couple of uniform coming now too. If we need any more, we'll go back to individual people tomorrow.' Allie had put a call out for officers at Harrison House to bring Craig Elliott in but he hadn't been at his address. 'For now, you and I can do a quick sweep around and if Elliott shows up, we can nip over there as quick as.'

At the door to Flynn's nightclub, they were let in by one of the bar staff. He was late teens at a push, straw-thin as well as tall, with layered black hair, a range of tattoos and what seemed to be eyeliner underneath his eyes.

'Were you working last night, Mr . . . ?' asked Allie.

'Baker. Will Baker.' He pointed to the stairs in front of them and led them up. 'I was in from eight until about two,' he said over his shoulder.

'Did you see Jordan Johnson?'

'Yeah, I was on the bar. It was pretty busy for a Wednesday because of the party.'

They were at the top of the stairs now and Will showed them into a large room with burgundy velvet seating and matching draped curtains, a floor for dancing in the middle and a bar the length of the left wall. Dotted around the comfy chairs and sofas were about fifteen people. Allie assumed glass collectors and washer-uppers. Bar staff. As Perry started questioning, she went over to Steve Burgess.

'Do you know if Ryan Johnson came back to the party again after he'd left at midnight?' she asked.

'Not as far as I know.' Steve shook his head. 'The CCTV footage I gave you should tell you for certain.'

'Thanks.' Although Allie already had her suspicions that this was right, she wanted to hear it from him too. Of course Ryan could have gone back home to The Gables – there had been enough time. And if Ryan and Kirstie were at home, they could give each other an alibi. They'd have to question them both again. Out of the two of them, Kirstie was bound to slip up with that mouth of hers.

The door by her side opened and a slight woman with blonde hair tied back in a ponytail came in. As she hung up her coat, Allie made her way over to her. She was certain she was the girl from the footage that Kirstie Ryder was arguing with.

'You were at the party last night,' she said.

'Yes, I was working the bar.' The girl burst into tears. 'I can't believe Jordan's dead.'

'Did you get on well with him – sorry, what's your name?'

'Lauren Michaels. He was great fun if he liked you, not so much if he didn't. I got on well with him, though. Although nothing like what she was accusing me of.'

'Who?'

'Kirstie Ryder, his girlfriend. She had a right go at Jordan and then she had a go at me. She's bloody mental! Jordan is off limits to anyone – we know that. But I'm not sure why she's so possessive with him, as it's obvious that they can't stand the sight of each other.'

'What makes you think that?'

'On the outside they put up a good appearance, but up here in the VIP club, they're often arguing. She turns up unannounced all the time and it always ends up in a fight.'

'Do you think he was seeing anyone else?'

The girl shrugged. 'Not that I know of.'

'Would anyone else know?'

'They could but I think they might deny it. They look after their own here.'

Allie's phone rang. 'I have to answer this,' she told Lauren when she saw that it was Nick. 'Thanks for your help.'

After taking the call, Allie disconnected it with a sigh. When she'd left the station, she'd thought she'd got away with not going to the morgue, but he did want her there now. It was going to take all night to interview the staff at Flynn's at this rate if they trickled in so she radioed through for the uniform backup. Still, one thing seemed to be coming through loud and clear: Jordan and Kirstie had not been the loving couple that Kirstie would have them believe.

And if that was the case, why had they been keeping up a united front?

⌣

Steve would be glad when the police had gone from Flynn's. Even though they weren't opening so there was no rush, he still didn't want them there. Interfering, poking their noses in. It put him on edge that he would slip up, too.

His mobile rang.

'Burgess,' he answered when he saw it was an unavailable number.

'Everything good there?'

Steve sniggered as he recognised the caller. 'It's going okay for now. A slight problem but nothing we can't sort.'

Laughter. 'How's my girl hanging on?'

'She's okay. Played a blinder by causing a commotion last night.'

'And she and Ryan got their story straight?'

'Yes, I think so.'

'Good. Make it happen then, yes?'

Steve nodded. 'Oh, yes, we'll make it happen.'

8.00 P.M.

Allie arrived back at Harrison House with members of the Johnson family. Tired and exhausted with the day's events, she felt even more drained of emotion after they'd visited and identified Jordan's body in the morgue. Even though she'd had to push her thoughts of Karen aside, it was too much of a reminder that she would be doing that soon, saying goodbye to a close family member.

Afterwards, Betty Johnson had wanted to see where her son had been murdered. Perry had also come back to the flats after leaving other officers to interview the remaining staff at Flynn's. Allie wasn't sure whether they'd find anything useful there. The staff had all seemed pretty honest.

Ryan walked behind his mother as she stumbled up the path. Kirstie held on to one arm, and Ryan's ex-wife, Nicole, hung onto the other. Even though it was dark, cold and raining, nets were twitching. A group of teenagers over by the entrance were making a nuisance of themselves, one circling on his bike and screaming. It was so unnecessary.

Allie held back her own tears as she witnessed the family's distress. At the morgue, she'd wanted to ask Ryan and Kirstie about leaving Flynn's nightclub the night before but when she saw his body behind the glass, all emotions had welled up inside her. It seemed inappropriate right then, just as it seemed inappropriate right at this minute. Ryan seemed deeply upset by his brother's death now, far more than this morning when she first saw him. Maybe it was sinking in for him, too.

'I didn't want Mum to come until tomorrow,' he spoke to Allie. 'I wanted to get a proper wreath, not garage forecourt tat. But she wanted to come tonight, as soon as she could.'

'People often need to,' Allie responded. 'Sometimes they won't believe it's happened until they see for themselves. It must be very hard to take in when a family member leaves you in such tragic circumstances.' She swallowed hard and looked away for a moment.

'Have you got the flowers, Ryan?' Betty turned back to them, holding out a shaky hand. She was dressed in a long black coat, a black fake-fur scarf tied tightly around her neck. Her eyes were red but she still took pride with her appearance: a little lipstick, grey hair in a bob curling under almost to perfection.

Ryan handed the cellophane bundles to her. 'I promise to get some better ones in the morning, Mum,' he said, his voice breaking with emotion.

Betty burst into tears as she laid down a bunch of chrysanthemums. Nicole held on to her arm and they cried together. Kirstie stayed just behind them, hands clasped in front. Allie turned when she heard Ryan sob, but he gathered his composure quickly.

They stood in silence. Even though the screams and chants from the group of teens weren't anything to do with what was going on, she hoped the noise didn't carry too much. But a few seconds later it went quiet. One of her colleagues must have gone across to them, she surmised, told them to show some compassion.

A few minutes later, Allie watched again as Ryan stiffened when Betty was led away by Nicole and Kirstie, his face creased into annoyance rather than grief.

'Have you any idea yet who would do this to your brother, Mr Johnson?' Allie asked him again. 'You haven't been able to think of anything else since this morning?'

'I have no idea – isn't that your job?' Ryan bristled. 'I thought you would have had someone in custody by now. It's been nearly twenty-four hours.'

'We're still making enquiries.'

'I hope you find whoever was responsible soon, Sergeant.'

Even though his tone was threatening, Allie chose to say nothing. She wouldn't put it past him to seek revenge given his reputation, but, unless there was evidence to prove that he was somehow involved, even she couldn't retaliate when he'd just seen his brother lying dead in the morgue and was now visiting the place of his death. She might have to be hard to do her job but it was only on the outside. And there was always room for compassion.

As she left them at their car, she sent a quick message to Simon Cole. She wanted to make sure that if the paper did take any photos of the crappy flowers, they could come back and take fresh ones once the family wreath was laid. It was the little things that made the most difference for the families.

'Going up to 209 for a moment,' she shouted to Perry. Before he could follow, she was halfway up the stairs. If Craig Elliott hadn't come home yet, it might work out in her favour if she could get Stella on her own.

8.15 P.M.

Sophie looked through the spy hole and paled to see a man she instantly recognised. She'd never seen Jordan's brother before but they were so alike she knew it had to be him. She slid the chain on the lock and opened the door the inch or two allowed.

'I – I–' She gasped, her hand covering her mouth.

Ryan frowned.

'I'm sorry, you look so much like your brother.'

'You knew him, didn't you?'

'Yes,' she said, a tear already dripping down her cheek. Her hand went to her mouth to hold in a sob as she watched him check up and down the landing.

'I know about you and Jordan.'

Sophie closed her eyes momentarily. She didn't want to see him.

'Please,' Ryan said, 'can I come in for a moment? I won't keep you long. I have my mum downstairs in the car. I just need to talk to you.'

Sophie nodded. In the living room, she stood in the doorway as Ryan moved to the window.

Unsure what to do, she spoke into the uncomfortable silence. 'Would you like a drink? Coffee? Tea?'

He turned to her and shook his head. She could tell he was hurting – red rings around his eyes, drooping shoulders. His stance was sharp and his dress was keen, but holding himself together was a front.

'Were you meeting him last night?' he asked.

She nodded. 'But he didn't show up.'

'When did you find out what had happened?'

'This morning.' Sophie came into the doorway and leaned against the frame with her hands behind her back. 'I never ring him. If he doesn't come, I know something has come up. He can't always keep to our arrangements.'

'I suppose not.'

'Can I ask you something?'

He nodded.

'How long have you known?'

'A few months. He told me.'

'Does she know?'

'Kirstie?' He sat down on the settee. 'I'd hope not, for your sake. She can be a nasty bitch.'

Sophie sat down in the chair.

'Have the police questioned you yet?' he asked.

'Yes. I couldn't tell them anything as I didn't know. I wasn't sure if he was coming or not. I went to bed. He –' She looked down at the carpet, feeling the heat rising in her cheeks. 'I knew he'd wake me up.'

That silence again. Ryan stared straight ahead.

'I'm so sorry,' she said eventually.

'Did you love him?'

She nodded, another tear escaping. 'With all my heart.'

'So you're positive he didn't come here first and then get attacked?'

'Of course. Why would you say that?'

'Something's gone missing.' Ryan shrugged.

'Money?' Sophie guessed.

He looked at her. 'How do you know?'

'I had a visit from Craig Elliott earlier.'

'Did he threaten you?' Ryan's features darkened.

'A little. He left, though, once he realised I didn't have anything.'

'You don't?'

'No.' She wiped away another tear that had dripped down her cheek.

'If you hear anything, will you ring me?' Ryan stood up and took out his wallet. 'If anyone threatens you or intimidates you, if you see anything suspicious going on, call this number any time.' He handed her his business card.

Sophie closed the door behind him and sank down onto the carpet behind the door. She held a hand over her mouth to stop herself from crying so that he would go before she gave herself away.

Jordan was still gone. The police were looking for his killer and she had lost him forever.

She thought she had no more tears left but they came in force again.

Allie knocked on the door to flat 209.

'Might I have a word?' She stepped inside before Stella could protest. 'Is Craig in?' she asked when they were in the living room.

'He's been and gone out.' Stella was looking through the window, keeping her back to Allie.

'Do you know what time he left?'

'No.'

Allie frowned. 'Stella?'

Stella didn't turn around.

'Stella,' she said, 'look at me.'

Reluctantly, Stella turned to face her. Her lip was swollen and bruises were already forming on her chin. It was obvious that she had been crying, too.

'What happened?'

'I walked into a door.'

Allie sighed. 'Did Craig do that to you?'

'No.'

Stella folded her arms so Allie didn't press her anymore.

'It's not just Craig I wanted to see,' she said, spotting an opportunity. 'I wanted to talk to you too.'

'Me?' Stella took a small step back.

'I just wondered what you thought of this whole thing. It's kind of a coincidence, don't you think, that Jordan Johnson was found here?'

'Not really.'

'You don't think Craig had anything to do with his murder? He worked for him, after all – was there ever any friction?'

'No! Why would I think that?' Stella shook her head vehemently.

Allie stared at her. 'You're not covering for him, are you?'

'Of course not.'

'Okay.' Allie made a show of getting out her notebook. 'Only there are some discrepancies in what you told me earlier today. Can you confirm again for me what time Craig got in last night?'

'It was midnight.'

'But we have him on camera leaving Flynn's nightclub just *after* midnight. Which means that even if he came straight home, it would have been more like half past twelve. That's right, wouldn't you agree?'

'I must have got it wrong then.' Stella shuffled on the spot.

'So what time did he come in?'

'It must have been when you said.'

'So if I said he left Flynn's at half past two, would you say that he got home about three?'

'No, it was definitely midnightish.' Stella shook her head.

'Another thing I find strange, Stella, is that we have CCTV footage of his car parked in Regina Street last night. Do you know why it would be parked there and not here on the car park?'

'No.' Stella's shoulders drooped.

'Don't *you* find that strange?'

'He's – he's always running out of petrol. Perhaps he did that last night.'

Allie laughed. 'He could roll down the bank and park it nearer than that. Nice try, Stella. You also know that he'd been drinking last night, so are you telling me he was drink driving?'

'You can't blame me if he was.'

'Is there anyone he knows in Regina Street?'

Stella suddenly found the carpet interesting to study. 'You might be better coming back when he can answer his own questions.'

'Oh, don't worry, I'll be asking him the minute I see him.' Allie put her notebook away. 'You know, if he's involved and we find out that you're covering for him in any way, you'll be in trouble, too. I know we don't always see eye to eye, but I'd hate to see you locked up in prison because you're covering for a toe-rag like Craig.'

Eventually Stella glanced at her fleetingly. 'You don't think it was a random attack on Jordan Johnson, do you?'

'Do you?'

'I – I don't know what to think but Craig can't be involved. He wouldn't do anything like that.'

Allie stayed quiet.

'He wouldn't!'

She left the flat satisfied that she'd put doubt in Stella's mind. As she stepped out onto the walkway, Ryan Johnson was next door, outside Sophie Nicklin's flat. They glanced at each other surreptitiously. She couldn't hear anything untoward as she walked away. They seemed to be having a peaceful discussion. She hoped they'd found comfort in each other's words.

She was walking downstairs to Perry when her phone rang. It was Mark.

'Hey, you!' She felt genuinely calmed to hear his voice.

'You're definitely going to be there all night then?'

'Yes, I think I am.' She tried to stay cheerful.

'I was hoping you'd be home by now.'

'Me too. But you know how these things go on the first day. I have to be here until –'

'I know, I know – until you can do no more. But I've been at work all day and then I've been to see Karen and now I'm back in an empty house. I'd just like to unwind knowing that my wife is safe and –'

'Mark, don't do this to me now, please. I can't think about anything else.'

'You mean you can't think about *anyone* else.'

'Oh, stop being so bloody needy.'

'Thanks a million.'

'Mark?' Allie checked her phone but he'd hung up. 'Shit!'

⌣

Craig ducked behind the hedgerow out of Allie's line of sight, watched her go downstairs again. He smirked after overhearing her conversation. It seemed she wasn't so perfect after all. But it was the sight of Ryan Johnson leaving Sophie's flat that piqued his interest more. What the hell was he visiting her for? That could prove very useful information to use later if necessary.

Once they'd both disappeared, he ran to the side of the building. He waited a few more moments and then climbed up to the first floor.

8.30 P.M.

After the phone call from her mum, Leah had done nothing but think about what to do next. Even though it was risky, as the police would think she was involved if she disappeared, she packed an overnight bag, covering the money with a few of her things. She would go to her mum's for the night and then if Craig was still after her, she could hide for a while. Stuff Kenny Webb. She would keep the money for herself.

Her phone rang. Stella was on the line this time.

'Stella, what the hell am I going to do? Craig has been to see my mum and broke in to her flat!'

'Oh, Leah, I'm so sorry. Craig took my phone. I've borrowed next-door's to ring you. Is your mum okay?'

'Yes, she's fine. But he's assaulted an old man, too. He knocked his head on the ground – he might be dead for all I know now!'

'Jesus Christ.'

'He thought I had the money hidden there. He was searching through her things and then he rang me to say I'm dead when he finds me. Did you tell him –'

'He's . . . he's hit me,' Stella interrupted.

'That bastard! Are you okay?'

'Yes, but I've just had the police here again. They think Craig's involved with Jordan's murder somehow. I can't believe it, though.'

But Leah wasn't listening. She slapped her hand on the wall. 'I should never have kept that money. I should have given it back.'

'It's too late now.'

'But I'm in trouble already so if I say I found it, they –'

'They won't believe you!'

'They can't prove I took it.'

'Your prints will be on the money. And the bag.'

'Yours too, remember? I gave it to you to look inside.' Leah paused. 'I'm going to hand it in. That sergeant gave me a card. I'm going to –'

'No, wait! You can't do that. I'll be in trouble, too.'

'I have to! I can't do this anymore.' Leah paced the room. 'I'm scared of where it's going to end.'

'Don't do anything until tomorrow. Just keep your head down and we'll think of something.'

'I don't know, Stella. It's all got out of control. I can't –'

'Give me five minutes and I'll be along to you.'

There was a bang on Leah's front door.

'What's that?'

'Someone is kicking my door!'

Before she could react, it had crashed against the wall. Craig appeared in her hallway.

Leah dropped the phone and screamed as she ran into the kitchen, Craig following her. She tried to close the door but he was too strong.

'Where's the money?' he cried.

'You're not having it.'

Craig went for her neck. As he squeezed his hands tightly around it, Leah gasped for air and she scrabbled about for anything along the kitchen worktop. Her fingers clasped around something hard – the tea caddy. She grabbed it and smashed it into the side of his face.

Craig stepped back, momentarily stopped in his tracks, and clutched his head.

'You mad bitch!' he cried.

Leah glanced behind him. The bag was behind the door. Would she make it past him before he caught up with her?

She chanced it, grabbing it on the way. Hearing Craig's boots thundering behind her, she screamed again. He pushed her up against the wall and slapped her face.

'Let go of the bag.'

Leah struggled for a few seconds but she realised it was no use. Despite all her fighting in the past, he was too strong for her. The bag slid down her arm and dropped to the floor. Craig bent to retrieve it. She wanted to bring up her knee and catch him full in the face but she was too scared of the consequences. Instead she watched him grab it, shrugging it onto his shoulder.

'That's a good girl.' Craig squeezed her chin then and pressed his face within an inch of hers. 'You'll feel much better now it's out of your hands.'

He let go of her and moved towards the door. But something inside her flicked, and she found that she couldn't let that money go. Why should he have it and not her? She ran after him and grabbed the strap of the bag.

'It's mine!' She pulled at it with all her strength.

Craig came back at her. The bag swung away from him and she clung tighter to it, pulling harder.

'You're not taking it to anyone else, are you?' she said. 'You're going to keep it for yourself and let them think that I've still got it and then they'll come after me.'

'Clever girl.'

'But they'll kill me if they know I have it!'

'I'll fucking kill you if you don't let go of the bag!'

'You're not taking it.'

'You don't have any choice.'

He dragged her onto the walkway. She pulled, her fingers burning as the leather strap slipped through them, but she wasn't going to let go. Craig punched back at her but she continued to cling on. She pulled one more time, then twisted and aimed a kick where she knew it would hurt the most. With a groan, he lost his grip.

The bag came at her. It hit her full in the chest, the force of it sending her hurtling backwards. The base of her back hit the edge of the wall on the walkway, overbalancing and tipping her over the side. Screaming as she felt herself falling, she let go of the bag, her arms and legs flailing. She landed on her back, pain shooting through her as she hit the grass below with a thud.

A second later, the bag dropped to the ground a few feet away from her.

———

'Leah!' Stella shouted in horror as she saw her best friend fall. Her slippers flapped as she ran along the walkway. She looked over and down and then ran towards Craig, who was outside Leah's door. 'What the hell have you done?'

He held up empty hands. 'I had the money and now it's gone.'

'But . . . but how could you have done that to her?' Stella turned wildly back to the edge and looked down at the ground again. 'Leah!'

'I have to have it, Stel.' Craig grabbed both her arms.

'Did you kill Jordan?'

'No!'

'But you're involved somehow, aren't you?'

'Leave it alone. The less you know the better.'

She pushed his hands away and looked at him in disgust. 'You won't get away with this. Not with all the police around.' She turned to leave. 'I'm going down to see if she's okay.'

'No, you don't.' Craig grabbed her again. 'You need to be my alibi. Say I was in the flat with you.' He began to march her along the walkway.

'You've gone too far this time.' She tried to pull her arm away again. 'You could have killed her!'

'I'll be dead myself if I don't get that money back.' Craig pushed her forward. 'Why can't you understand?'

Stella stumbled, nearly falling to the floor. 'Leave me alone. I hate you. You don't think of anyone but yourself, and you don't care who you hurt as long as you're all right. Well, I've had enough of playing second fiddle to you all the time.' She turned back to him. 'And another thing – that police sergeant called again.'

'What?'

'I've had the police after you twice since you left. She told me they'd seen you leaving Flynn's at midnight, and then they found your car on camera. What were you doing in Regina Street last night? Are you screwing someone there? Because if you are and you think for one minute I'm going to cover for you, you have –'

'Will you keep your fucking voice down!'

Craig clenched his fists, stepped towards her and then away again. His eyes were wild, spittle gathering at the corners of his mouth, but Stella couldn't stop herself, fed up with years of his lies.

'Well, if you're not, then you must be involved in all that.' She pointed downstairs. 'You are, aren't you?'

Craig punched her full in the face.

Blood poured from her nose. She stumbled backwards. His fist came at her again. She felt a kick to the stomach and another. Then everything went black.

8.40 P.M.

Leah couldn't believe she was okay when she landed. But then she tried to move. Red hot pain shot through her back and she winced as she moved her head, remembering she had banged it on the grass. She felt clammy almost immediately.

Then she saw the bag two feet away from her. She tried to roll over to her side but her vision blurred.

'Don't move!'

She heard a voice but couldn't turn her neck. Pain was making her feel queasy. She flopped back to the ground, not caring about the implications.

'Are you all right?'

Someone stooped down beside her. Christ, it was that sergeant.

'What happened?'

Leah tried to move again.

'Please, stay where you are.' Allie pushed her gently back down. 'You need to stay still. I've called for an ambulance.'

'No! I'm fine – just a bit winded.'

'Stay where you are. The paramedics need to assess you first.'

Leah kept glancing to her right. She had to keep the bag in her line of sight. Tears welled in her eyes. Oh, God, what happened if they opened it up and saw the money? It would all have been for nothing.

'You're in safe hands.' Allie stooped down. 'But what happened?'

Leah decided playing dumb was going to be the best policy. 'I – I can't remember.'

'Not to worry.' Allie's smile was warm as she picked up the bag and placed it by her side. 'The ambulance staff will make you comfortable, give you pain relief before they move you. You took a nasty fall there.'

Leah blinked back tears. What was the point of going on with the pretence? Even if she had got away with the money, Craig would still come after her. He wouldn't give up until he had it back.

Allie glanced up to Leah's flat. When Leah was in trouble, there would always be a story to cover up the truth but this one seemed an impossibility. How could anyone fall from a balcony like that? They'd have to have been sitting on the wall. What was going on – had she been pushed?

She looked down at her again. 'You're on the first floor, flat 203, right?'

'Yes.'

A small crowd had begun to form around Leah, people asking if she was okay. Two uniformed officers were trying to keep them at bay.

Perry came running over. 'Someone told me she'd fallen?' he said when he reached them.

'Yes, although I'm not sure how.' Allie looked up again with a frown. She lowered her voice. 'Can you keep an eye on her while I go and take a look upstairs? Clearly something isn't right.'

'It's under control down here.' Perry shook his head. 'I'm coming with you.'

They walked across the grass to the entrance.

'She didn't fall, did she, boss?' said Perry.

'I doubt it.' Allie couldn't shake off an image of Leah being pushed over the wall. 'It seems a little too convenient to me.'

At the entrance, they heard a shout. 'Up here!'

A woman stood at the top of the stairs beckoning them up. They jogged up to her and onto the walkway of floor one. Outside Leah's flat, Allie could see a person kneeling down next to someone on the floor. She glanced at Perry and they quickened their step.

'I shouted down to you people,' said a man in a white T-shirt and gaudily patterned jogging bottoms. 'We heard arguing, came out to see and she was lying here.'

'It's Stella Elliott,' said Perry as they reached the top of the stairs.

Allie stooped down over the woman. Blood poured from her facial injuries. She wasn't moving. Perry radioed through for another paramedic while she retrieved latex gloves from her belt and flicked them on quickly.

'Stella, can you hear me? It's DS Shenton. It's okay, we'll get you sorted soon.' She looked at the man who had found her. Two women now stood at his side. 'Did you see what happened?'

'No.'

'What about the woman downstairs? Did you see what happened to her?'

He shook his head. 'I didn't realise anything was going on until I called for help and looked down.'

'You mean you're unwilling to tell me what you really did see?' she barked. She turned to the women and glared at them in turn. 'Any of you two see anything?'

'No, sorry,' said one woman, looking anywhere but at Allie. The other just shook her head.

Allie cursed under her breath. Her initial thoughts were that there must have been some sort of fight. Had Leah beaten Stella up and then tried to get away over the wall and landed wrong? But why wouldn't she have run down the stairs to get away rather than risk injury? And they were supposed to be good friends.

Stella groaned and Allie sighed, glad to hear it, thankful she was still alive. The last thing they needed was another body right now.

9.00 P.M.

Allie rang Nick and updated him as she arrived with Perry at the Royal Stoke University Hospital.

'This can't be a coincidence, sir,' she said. 'Leah Matthews allegedly falling and Stella Elliott being beaten up on the same day that Jordan Johnson is murdered? I know Harrison House is renowned for its trouble but even so, that's a lot of things happening at once.'

'I agree. Can you stay with Leah Matthews and get a statement from her? Gauge her reaction when you tell her how Stella Elliott is, see what she has to say first. Get Perry to stay with Stella, see what he can find out.'

'Yes, sir. I haven't managed to catch Craig Elliott to question him yet about his timing, although I did speak to Stella earlier and she was still adamant he was in around midnight,' she added. 'Her face was a mess then, too; said she'd fallen.'

In A&E, Leah had been transferred onto a hospital trolley. The paramedics at the scene had strapped a padded brace around her neck to support it until she was fully assessed. When the nurse attending to her left to find a blood pressure monitor, Allie leaned on the bed frame.

'How are you feeling?' she asked.

'Like I've fallen and landed on my back,' Leah replied.

'Oh, good. You have a sense of humour.' Allie's smile was full of sarcasm. 'That means you're able to answer me a few questions. Care to explain what's been going on at your flat?'

'I told you – I can't remember. I must have blacked out or something.'

'Cut the bullshit.' Allie leaned in closer. 'We went up to your flat and found Stella outside on the walkway. She's been beaten really badly. She's across the other side of A&E being tended to now. Whoever hurt her is in a lot of trouble. Want to tell me about that?'

Leah's eyes flitted around in confusion. 'I wasn't with Stella!'

'The door to your flat was wide open.' Allie sighed. 'Stop pissing me about.'

'No, Stella wasn't there when I – I fell. Is she okay? What's happened to her? I want to see her.'

Allie took hold of one of Leah's hands.

'You see?' Leah cried. 'No marks. I haven't been fighting.'

'I wouldn't put it past you to hit out with something else. Tell me what happened.'

'It wasn't me! It must have been that bastard. He hit her earlier and –'

'Who did?'

'I – I can't remember.' Tears trickled from Leah's eyes. 'Is Stella okay?'

Allie pointed to the overnight bag placed underneath the seat next to the bed. 'Were you going somewhere, Leah?'

'My mum had a break-in this afternoon and was upset so I thought I'd stay there tonight.'

'Right.' Allie paused. 'Did you jump over the side?'

'No.'

'Is this anything to do with what happened to Jordan Johnson?'

'No!'

'Were you running away from something – someone?'

'I told you – I can't remember!'

'Well, something's not quite right here, is it?' Allie snapped.

'Am I under arrest?'

'Not yet.' Allie stood up to leave but stopped when she heard Leah crying. For a moment, she tried to put herself in Leah's position, understand how scared she'd be if someone had pushed her over the edge.

'Is someone threatening you?' she asked calmly.

'No,' said Leah.

The nurse came back, smiled at them both as she wheeled in the machine. 'Right then, Leah, let's get this done and then we'll get you down for a scan.'

Allie looked at Leah, all compassion suddenly disappearing. 'I'll be here on your return. I suggest you get your story straight by then. I'll keep you updated about Stella's injuries – your friend, Stella, remember? Your best friend.'

Craig had climbed down the side of Harrison House pretty sharpish after he had attacked Stella. A mile away, he parked up and killed the engine, hearing instead the sound of his racing heart. Although his knuckles were cut and swelling, he pounded the steering wheel in frustration.

He was finished if he didn't get that money by the end of the day. And now that stupid bitch had fallen from the balcony with the bag, it was bound to be found by someone in A&E. Someone would look inside. He was well and truly screwed.

With the lesser of two evils in mind, he rang Ryan and told him what had happened.

'For fuck's sake – how the hell are you going to get it back from there?'

'I can't get it back,' he cried. 'I can't go anywhere near the police. They're going to start putting two and two together right about now.'

'I don't give a fuck about that. I want my money and I want it before Burgess gets it, do you hear?'

'But how am I –'

'Just get it, Elliott!'

Craig cursed as the phone went dead. There was nothing for it now but to play one man against the other. He rang Steve and told him what had happened, too.

'Ryan wants me to get the money back and give it to him rather than you,' he concluded. 'And he visited that bird Jordan was knocking off earlier. She lives next door to me. He – he could have been collecting the missing money from her. She might have been saving it for Jordan. It might not ever have been missing – just taken from the bag by Jordan. I've never trusted him.'

There was a pause after he'd finished gabbling.

'I can't go to the hospital,' he added. 'It's too dangerous.'

'Why?'

'Let's just say trying to get the money didn't run quite as smooth as I'd wanted.'

'That's a bit of an understatement.'

'I'll pay you back! I can get the money somehow.'

'From under the nose of the police?'

'No, that's gone. I'll get some more. I – I just need a bit more time.' Craig didn't want to ask but knew he had no choice. 'I – I need somewhere to get my head down for a bit.'

There was a short pause.

'I have to keep away from the pigs. It's best, don't you think?'

'Come over to Flynn's. We're closed tonight so it's doubtful that the police will come again until morning.'

9.10 P.M.

Once home, Ryan took the stairs three at a time and went into his bedroom. Closing the door, he was just about to ring Steve when his number flashed up on the screen of his mobile phone.

'I've just had a call from Elliott,' Steve told him. 'You know he's lost the ten grand? It's fucking gone.'

'He rang me, too,' said Ryan. 'I thought he might be calling my bluff. You think he's telling the truth? The police have it?'

'It looks like it.'

'Fuck! That stupid lowlife piece of shit. What were you thinking, getting him involved? The man's a liability!'

'It wasn't my idea! I was told what to do just as much as you were.'

'Ryder told you to hire Elliott?'

'He told me to hire some loser.'

'Someone we could fucking trust to do the job right would have been better.' Ryan paused for a moment. 'We need to sort him out – take him out if necessary, before he gets us into more trouble. Idiot!'

'You want me to look into it?'

'Yeah, see if he's pulling a fast one or not first.'

'Leave it with me.'

'Talk about a cock-up!' Kirstie said when Ryan joined her in the living room and told her what had happened. 'What the fuck are we supposed to do now?'

Ryan rested his head on the back of the settee. 'They're going to come asking us why Jordan had ten thousand pounds on him. We need to think of another option.' He clenched his fists. 'That stupid fucking Elliott. We had it all planned out.'

Kirstie gnawed at her bottom lip. 'They have no evidence we're involved, do they?'

'Not a thing until they had the money.'

'We could bluff and say we don't think the money has anything to do with Jordan.'

'But they'll dig deeper now.'

'They would have done that anyway, surely?'

'Yes, but around Jordan and not us.'

Kirstie sat back in a panic. 'Shit.'

'So if you have any favours that you can pull with Daddy, now would be the time to call them in.'

'What?'

'You heard. We're going to need all the help we can get to dig ourselves out of the huge hole we're in.'

'In your dreams.' Kirstie stood up to walk out of the room. 'I didn't know he was playing away again so I'm not getting involved.'

Jordan grabbed her wrist as the realisation hit him. 'Terry wanted rid of Jordan all along, didn't he?'

'What?'

'Is this because he didn't want to know you anymore?' Ryan glared at her. 'It is, isn't it?'

'He was a free man, could do what he wanted.' Kirstie could feel her skin getting hot, giving her away. 'I didn't own him.'

'But you were pretty angry when he ended the fling. Is this your way of getting revenge?'

'Don't be stupid.'

He grabbed her again as she walked away.

'Take your hands off me,' she warned. 'And Jordan didn't end the fling. We both did.'

'It's beginning to make sense now,' Ryan sneered. 'Do you think Jordan didn't know that I was fucking you too? Did you think that we didn't laugh about you behind your back? About how pathetic, how easy you were?'

Kirstie laughed, but all the time thought of Nicole's spiteful words earlier. 'Well, you certainly seemed as though you were enjoying it. There are some things a man can't fake . . . whereas a woman can.'

'It passed a bit of time away, but mostly we did it to keep you on side so that we could see what was happening with your father and his businesses.'

'You were spying on us!'

'Got it in one.' Ryan nodded. 'I'd warn him, if you can, to watch his back. He's not so hard to get at when he's locked up in one place with a gang of equally dangerous criminals.'

'You wouldn't dare!' Kirstie challenged. 'If you —'

Ryan swiped his hand across her face.

Kirstie's head reared to the side. She felt the sting of his fingers, but she stared back at him.

'I've wanted to do that to you so many times, but I didn't want to mark Daddy's precious cargo.' Ryan's eyes were dark. 'But now something is amiss with how Jordan died, the rules have changed.'

'And you think things will get better by hitting me?'

'I know your father had something to do with Jordan's death and I'm going to prove it. I hope for your sake that you're not involved, too.'

Kirstie swallowed, praying her nerves wouldn't desert her now. As usual she turned to the most powerful weapon she possessed.

'My father will protect me,' she said. 'He always has and he always will.'

9.30 P.M.

After she had questioned Leah, Allie went to find Stella. A nurse told her she was being x-rayed so she sat down to wait for her. Even though she was a mere five-minute walk away from Karen, she didn't want to go and see her sister just yet. She had to keep her mind clear, focus on the task in hand. She knew she'd get upset if she saw Karen and she couldn't take the risk, not while she was working. God, she hated herself sometimes for not being stronger.

Perry came in, interrupting her thoughts. He was holding two plastic cups.

'Bit of a mess, this case, boss,' he said, handing her a drink of something that resembled coffee. He sat down beside her in the cubicle.

'Tell me about it. We nearly had another murder to solve. And we still haven't caught up with Elliott.'

'Yeah, strange he's gone off radar. Are the control room still on stand-by to let you know if anyone sees him?'

'Yes. He's obviously hiding from us so that makes me doubly suspicious now that he's involved. I can't wait to get to the bottom of it all.'

They both looked up as Stella was wheeled back in on a trolley bed. Once they'd been given the all-clear to talk to her, Allie moved her chair closer.

'How are you feeling?' she asked.

'A little sore. The painkillers are great.' Stella smiled, then winced. 'How's Leah?'

'She's gone for a scan. Are you able to remember what happened?'

'I went along to see her for a cup of coffee.' Stella swallowed. 'When I got there, the door was open. I knocked and went in.'

'Would you normally just walk in?'

'Yes, we're really good friends.'

Allie glanced at Perry. 'What happened next?'

'I went into the living room and there was a man looking through her things. I asked what he was doing but he just ran past me. I followed him, shouting at him and that's when he turned back and attacked me.'

'Did you know him?' asked Perry.

'No.'

'You must have got a good look at him, so close up,' Allie reasoned. 'Can you describe him?'

'He was tall, thin. Had short dark hair.'

'Age?'

'Early twenties.'

'Does he live in the flats, do you know?'

'I'm not sure, but I don't think so.'

'Would you recognise him again if you saw him?'

'I – I'm not sure.'

'Was it anyone you knew associated to Jordan Johnson?'

'I don't know Jordan that well.' Stella looked away.

'Stella, we know you're lying. Because according to Leah, she can't remember seeing you. She can't remember how she ended up falling over the balcony either.'

'I didn't see what happened to Leah.'

'So he just attacked you and then ran?'

'Yes.'

'I'm not buying it.' Allie shook her head. 'If he was in a hurry to leave, he might have hit you once to get you out of his way, but to do all that damage to you would take up his precious time. To me it looks like you were attacked in anger.'

'But why would anyone do that to me?' she asked.

'Indeed. So for that reason, I think you know who it was, Stella, and I think you're either too scared to tell me or you're covering for someone. Which one is it?'

Stella looked down at her hands.

'I'll tell you the same as I've just told Leah,' Allie continued. 'I'll give you twenty minutes while I go back and talk to her, see what she has to say now, and then I'm coming to see you again. Between you, I'm sure we'll get to the truth. And if we don't, I'm going to arrest you both.' She turned to Perry. 'I won't be long.'

She was almost out of the cubicle when Stella spoke again.

'It was Craig.'

Allie turned back.

'I was on my way to Leah's flat when I saw them arguing. They were playing tug of war with a bag. The next thing I knew Leah had fallen backwards over the balcony. It was horrible to see it, like watching something in slow motion.' Stella wiped tears from her eyes, one already swollen so tight it was a wonder a tear could escape. 'I went mad and that's when he attacked me.'

'Was it an overnight bag?' Allie thought back to Leah's story about going to stay with her mum.

'Yes.' Stella looked away for a moment before taking a deep breath. 'Leah found five thousand pounds near Jordan Johnson's body,' she said eventually, 'and Craig wants it.'

Both Allie and Perry were suddenly awake again despite the late hour.

'Do you know why?' said Allie.

'No,' Stella sobbed. 'But I do know he is a dangerous, lying, cheating bastard. And he didn't come in at midnight – or even midnightish. He didn't get in until half past three. I can't find the clothes he was wearing last night either. I've looked everywhere in the flat for them.'

Allie turned to Perry. 'Stay with her.'

She raced back to Leah's cubicle. Leah hadn't come back from her scan yet but the overnight bag was gone from underneath the chair. Allie opened the cabinet beside the bed to see it had been put in there for safekeeping.

9.40 P.M.

Allie waited impatiently until Leah came back and was settled in the cubicle again. Leah was still lying down with the brace keeping her neck secure. Allie lifted up the bag to show her.

'Mind if I have a look in here?' she asked.

'No, you can't!' cried Leah. 'It's private! No.'

'But you know I'll only apply for a warrant and search it anyway, don't you?'

Leah said nothing, just looked up at the ceiling.

Allie moved over her line of sight. 'Stop messing about,' she told her. 'If what I think is inside proves to be right, it would be much better for you to cooperate with us right now.'

Leah still didn't say anything.

'Okay?' Allie prompted.

'Okay.' Leah's eyes brimmed with tears.

Allie unzipped the bag. Inside she could see a jumper and a makeup bag and prayed that Stella Elliott hadn't been lying. She pulled them out to find a T-shirt and a pair of pyjamas. Underneath those was a pack of notes in a red paper band. Underneath that was another bundle and another.

Allie tipped the money out onto Leah's chest. She lifted a bundle up in each hand.

'Red bands around twenty-pound notes? I'd say these were bundles of five hundred pounds each. Quite a few of them. Where did you get them from?'

'It wasn't anywhere near Jordan Johnson, I swear! For all you know, it might not have been his.'

'How much is there?'

'Ten thousand pounds.'

Allie's eyes widened. Stella had said five thousand – was her best friend selling her short?

'I found it in the bushes,' Leah went on. 'I tripped over him when I was running along the grass and when I bent down to see if he was okay, I saw the bag.'

'And you just left him there?'

'I didn't even remember until this morning that I'd seen him at all.'

'So he could have been alive!'

'He wasn't. I swear he wasn't.'

'How would you remember? Selective memory is not an option here.' Allie tried to calm herself before speaking again. 'Were you the woman who was seen going into the entrance of Harrison House, around three thirty a.m.?'

'Yes,' Leah sobbed. 'I'm sorry! Everything just got out of control and –'

'It's called greed. You didn't think of anyone but yourself. Actually, you didn't think of anything apart from the money. That's pretty heartless when a man was dying.'

'He wasn't dying! He was already dead!'

'Save it for the judge. I hope they throw the book at you.' Allie shook her head in disgust. 'Leah Matthews, I'm arresting you on suspicion of theft and perverting the course of justice. You do not have to say anything. But it may harm your defence if you do not mention when questioned something that you later rely on in court. Anything you do say may be given in evidence. Do you understand?'

<hr />

Craig arrived at Flynn's nightclub.

'I parked my car around the back, out of the way,' he told Steve as he let him into the building.

'Good.' Steve closed the door behind him. 'The fewer people to see you the better.'

'Thanks for this, mate. I owe you one.'

'You're not out of the woods yet. Not until I get that money repaid.'

Craig nodded. 'Sure thing. I'll work on it as soon as all this has died down.'

'And I want my five grand back on top.'

'You never said anything about that on the phone!'

'Would you have come if I had?'

Craig's shoulders relaxed. 'I suppose not.' He turned in the direction of the staff room. 'I don't suppose anyone's left any grub? I haven't eaten for hours.'

Steve put an arm around his shoulder and guided him towards the stairs. 'Never mind that, just yet. Let's have a drop of the good stuff while we work out our next plan of action. We need to keep you out of this to stop the police from getting wind of what really happened.'

They went upstairs and along the corridor into his office. Craig sat down opposite Steve at his desk. Steve poured two drinks and slid one across to him.

Craig knocked it back in one. 'Nectar,' he grinned. The door opened and he glanced up to see three men in the doorway. Shit, it was the clean-up crew.

Quickly, he turned to Steve. 'What the –'

Steve held up his hands. 'You don't think I'm going to dirty these on a piece of shit like you, do you, now?'

Craig heard a knife flick out behind him and saw a bat in the hand of the youngest of the three men. Damien Nielson. A new up-and-coming jack-the-lad, always ready to prove himself. Reminded Craig of himself in so many ways.

'Just returning the favour,' Steve smiled.

Craig put up his hands but was dragged to his feet. The wind was taken out of him as Damien administered the first punch to his stomach while the other two men held on to his arms. A cloth bag was put over his head. He struggled but to no avail. He felt another punch to his stomach and then a heavy instrument cracked into his face, bursting his nose.

'Watch the blood!' he heard Steve say. 'I don't want the police finding evidence of his death all over this room. Use the knife when he's in the car and get rid of that after too – and the car. No trace whatsoever.'

———

Steve went out of the office, along the corridor and into the members-only room. Even from behind the bar, he could hear Craig's screams so he put some music on, turned it up. A few minutes later, he watched as they dragged him across the room and out of the building. He checked the screen on the television monitor until both cars were out of view. Then he pressed the erase button.

Only afterwards did he pour himself a whiskey and knock it back with satisfaction. A job well done, even if he did say so himself.

10.00 P.M.

With things becoming clearer in the case, Allie decided after all to go and see Karen. She wouldn't be able to forgive herself if she left without visiting. As she walked to her sister's ward, her mind kept going over the events of the past few hours. Once Leah Matthews was fit to leave the hospital, she would be taken to the station for formal questioning and charging. And then maybe they'd get to the bottom of this mess, find out where the money had come from – if it had been hidden in the hedge, if Leah was telling the truth about it after all her lies.

Had Jordan Johnson put the money there, she wondered? Was it anything to do with him and Sophie Nicklin? Had the money been payment for something else? Someone needed to see Kirstie Ryder and Ryan Johnson again.

After ringing Nick to keep him updated, she texted a quick message to Mark.

'Hope you're not too lonely. I'm just going to see Karen. Love you. X'

Visiting hours were over but due to the circumstances, she hoped they'd let her in. It was good to get a break. She'd been on shift for sixteen hours and still had to go back to the station before she would go home for the night.

She was surprised when Mark rang her back a few seconds later.

'I ordered in a curry,' he told her. 'I still have a belly the size of Mount Everest.'

Allie laughed out loud and it echoed down the empty corridor. She loved him for wanting to make her do that, more so because it was only now she was realising just how much the past few weeks had taken their toll. He too must be close to breaking point with it all, almost as much as she was.

Apart from her, no one saw Mark when he cracked. He was placid until pushed and although it took a lot to get him to that point, once his temper exploded, he would tell her in a few words exactly what he thought. His words would sting, would break her heart in two, and then he'd feel regretful, say he was sorry and ask her if she wanted a cup of tea.

At times she hated him for it, especially when all she wanted was to have a real good slanging match, throw a few things and make up with frantic sex. But most of the time, she loved him for it. Because no matter what he said, she knew he was being honest and whatever he *had* said in temper had been meant to show how hurt *he* was and not to hurt her. Thankfully the arguments didn't happen often because they took days to get over. Afterwards, they tiptoed around each other until they could get past the hurt and then the make-up sex was good. It grounded them again. Made them realise they were good together.

That's what Mark did, Allie knew. In a way, he made her what she was. And she was far too selfish to see exactly what she had in him. Tears welled in her eyes and she sat down in a chair at the side of the corridor. There were only a few people milling around, the lights on dim.

'Do you think I'm being callous, not being here with her constantly during her last days?' she asked him.

'No. I often think you don't get your priorities right, but it's what makes you what you are. You're a stubborn cow at times, just like Karen, but who knows how long this will drag on for.' She heard him groan. 'Sorry, wrong choice of words, but you know what I mean.'

Allie squeezed her eyes shut tightly. 'I think I've been expecting it for so long over the past few weeks that I've accepted it. It'll be a shock when it does happen but we both know it will be a relief.' A lump caught in her throat. 'I want to be with her, Mark, but right at the end, you know? I can't sit with her day after day watching her deteriorate until there is nothing left but skin and bones and a working heart.' She put a hand to her mouth to stop a sob escaping. 'Keeping busy is the only way I can deal with it. And this case is going to run on alongside it anyway.'

'Allie, I –'

'I won't let her down this time though. Come what may, I'll be there for her, no matter what I'm doing.'

She heard him gasp. 'You can't seriously still think that anyone blames you for being late when Karen was attacked that night?'

Allie shrugged. 'You can't seriously think that I won't ever think that?'

'You *are* a stubborn cow.'

———

Tommy had been keeping an eye on what was going on around Harrison House for most of the day, but more so he'd been watching what Jacob was doing. He'd seen Craig Elliott talking to him, seen Jacob on his phone, his eyes flitting around as if he was really important. Kayleigh had been at work so he hadn't managed to speak to her until now. Unable to take or make personal phone calls, he knew a text wouldn't be enough. Feeling better now he had seen her, she'd agreed to bend the truth a little. If questioned, she was going to say that he had been with Denton and gone to her at midnight rather than that he had been with her all night.

When he'd got home, the smell of curry greeted him. Jacob and Sandra were busy tucking into a takeaway.

'Some in there for you, bro,' Jacob said, shoving another mouthful in. 'Chicken Jalfrezi, your favourite.'

'Where did you get the money to pay for this?' Tommy stood in the doorway. 'You told me you were broke until your dole comes through next week.'

Jacob shrugged. 'I have ways and means.'

'What do you mean, Jacob?' Sandra put down her fork.

But Jacob didn't speak. He continued to eat his food, his eyes on the television screen.

'What the fuck aren't you telling me, Jay?' Tommy asked.

'Nothing! Chill out, man.' He glanced up at his brother. 'Did you go to see Kayleigh, get your story straight?'

'There is no story. You were the one telling lies.' Tommy folded his arms. 'First you say you were with Diane, then you tell the police you were with me and then you cock up and tell them I was with Kayleigh and we were with one of my mates, landing us all in it.'

'Leave it,' Jacob warned. 'It's got nothing to do with you.'

'It's got everything to do with me!'

Jacob slammed his fork down on his plate and took it through to the kitchen, pushing past Tommy on the way.

Tommy grabbed his arm once he'd put the plate down. 'I'm not doing jail for you again, do you hear? If you're in trouble this time, you take it like a man and go inside for it.'

'Are you saying you won't stick by me?'

'Tell me what you're trying to cover up and I might feel better about it!'

'But you're my flesh and blood, Tommy.' Jacob glared at him. 'Blood's thicker than water, right?'

'That's not fair. I can't go to prison again!' Tommy tried to plead with his brother. 'I'm not going down for murder.'

'Murder?' Jacob scoffed. 'Whatever gave you that idea?'

'You know too much, man. And you're trying to set everyone else up, keep the scent from you.' Tommy grabbed the back of his brother's neck and pressed his forehead to his own. 'Was it you?' He could feel Jacob's eyes boring in to his, tunnels of hate. 'You have to tell me!' he cried. 'Did you stick a knife in Jordan Johnson?'

Jacob drew back his head and butted Tommy. Tommy staggered back, his hands covered his face as he clutched his nose. Blood poured from it but he was more concerned that Jacob now held a knife in his hand.

'You said you'd stick by me,' he shouted, waving it about in front of his face.

Behind them, Sandra came in to see what the commotion was. She screamed at the sight of the knife.

'Jacob! No, please. Put it down.'

Jacob turned towards her and waved the knife in her direction. 'Stay out of this,' he cried.

'Jay.' Tommy held out one hand as he wiped furiously at his nose with the other. 'I have your back. You know I always will.'

'Liar!' Jacob waved the knife at him again. 'You're trying to trick me.'

'I'm not.' Tommy glanced furtively at his mother. 'Just put down the knife, man.'

'You remember what we said? Where we were?'

Tommy nodded.

'You'll lie for me?'

'Yes.'

'No, he bloody well won't,' said Sandra. 'He's not taking the blame for you again. I won't let –'

Jacob came at her with the knife.

Sandra screamed and covered her face with her hands. Jacob pushed her to the side, into the wall, and ran out of the door.

'Jacob!' The front door slammed behind him.

'He's wrong in the head,' said Tommy. His hands shook as he wiped off the blood.

Sandra put a cloth to his nose and leaned his head back. 'We have to do something,' she said.

Tommy shook his head. 'We can't.'

'You can tell the truth.'

'I have a record. They won't believe me!'

'You can try.'

'No! You saw him, Mum. He'll hurt me. And if he doesn't hurt me, he'll hurt you.'

10.10 P.M.

Allie buzzed to be let into the ward. One of the nurses, Sharon, recognised her and wagged a finger at her as she opened the door.

'Sorry, I know it's late,' Allie spoke quietly. 'Can I come in for a moment? I have two people in A&E I'm waiting to speak to and . . .'

Sharon beckoned her in. 'You don't have to make an excuse. Come on through.'

'How is she doing?'

'Her blood pressure dipped this morning but she's stable again for now.'

Allie sterilised her hands and walked over to the side room where her sister was. Karen's skin was so pale it almost looked transparent, yet it was flushed, too. Her eyes were closed, and it seemed like she'd lost even more weight in the past twenty-four hours. She looked like a skeleton lying in the bed.

Despite what she had said to Mark, Allie did wonder if she would be strong enough to be there when the time came. A tiny part of her, a part she could barely even admit to herself, was hoping that Karen would slip away while she wasn't there, so that she wouldn't have to deal with it.

Tears rolled down her cheeks. She didn't want to remember her sister like this – fragile, lost, a shell. Even though she had been unable to communicate with them for years, she still couldn't bring herself to wish it was all over. Karen had been a part of her life for so long that she wondered how she would get by without her visits to see her. Would her life become empty all of a sudden?

She sat by the side of her bed for a few moments but she couldn't settle. Her eyes flicked around the familiar room, bright but sparse, ready for whatever was thrown at it. Next week, it might hold another patient, yet Allie wasn't ready to say goodbye to this one.

'What am I going to do without you, Kaz?' she whispered as she stood up to leave.

⌣⌣

Perry was waiting for her back in A&E. 'How is she?' he asked.

Allie shook her head, still wiping at her eyes. 'Did you bag up the money?'

'Yes, boss.' He handed it to her.

'I'm going back to the station. Do you want to shoot off for a bit of shut-eye or are you staying on shift?'

'Both,' he grinned.

⌣⌣

When they arrived back at the station, Nick was at his desk. The room was quiet as most of the phone calls had stopped coming in. Sam had her head down too. Allie grabbed everyone's mugs and made them all coffee.

'What did Ryan say when you questioned him earlier?' Nick asked as she placed his drink down next to him.

'Sorry?' said Allie, her head too full of thoughts of her sister for her to be sure what he was referring to.

'You were going to ask him about the CCTV footage. Even though we now know Jordan was at The Genting Club, he'd still be one of the last people to be with his brother.'

'Oh, I –' Allie lowered her eyes. 'I didn't ask him.'

'Why not?'

'I couldn't.'

'But he might have been able to tell us where Jordan was going. Especially since we now know he should have visited Sophie Nicklin.'

'We knew that anyway,' she snapped.

Nick raised his eyebrows.

'He'd just been to identify his brother. He was really upset.'

'And?'

Allie's hand went up in the air. 'I couldn't just ask him questions that sounded like we were looking into him, too.'

'We needed that information.'

'He was laying flowers with his mother!'

Sam and Perry glanced at each other. Sam pulled a face.

'You should have asked him.'

'But, sir – I –'

'I said if you became too emotional you needed to tell me that too.' Nick's arms flapped about. 'If you're not up to working on this case, then let someone else take over. I need your mind on the job. This is a murder investigation!'

'For fuck's sake, what do you take me for?' Allie stood up. 'I'm not an unemotional brick like you. I have feelings too and I . . .' As all eyes fell on her, she ran from the room. Tears pouring down her face, she rushed into the ladies' toilets and into a cubicle. She sat down on the toilet lid and gulped in big mouthfuls of air.

Although livid at being humiliated in front of her staff, Allie realised that Nick was right, and maybe she shouldn't be working on this case anymore. Her mind hadn't really been on the job for three weeks now but she couldn't tell him every reason why. Last month, while working on the serial rapist case, she had interviewed a woman in her mid-twenties – tidy, yet ageing before her time, bags under her eyes telling the true nature of her life. Dark roots had been showing through her blonde-dyed hair, her nails bitten down to the quick. To Allie it had seemed as if she wanted to look nice but didn't feel she should. Sarah had been raped when she was eighteen and the case had never been solved. She seemed old before her time, painfully reminding Allie of how she herself hadn't really lived while her sister had been suffering.

'Is there anything else you can remember, Sarah?' she had asked her gently.

'I – I don't think so.' The woman looked down at the table. 'It was years ago now and it all happened so fast.'

'Even something tiny might be useful to us.'

Sarah paused. 'Strange though, because sometimes it was as if it happened only yesterday.'

Allie reached a hand across the table. 'I'm sorry to dredge up old memories but we're hoping that with new advances in technology we might be able to find the man responsible for this.'

Sarah looked up through watery eyes.

'We will get him, Sarah. I promise.'

As she rested her head in her hands, thoughts swirled around her mind. She had regretted the words as soon as they had come from her mouth. Was she really so sure they would, after all this time?

She grabbed some toilet roll, wiped her eyes and blew her nose. Keeping busy, that's what she needed to do. Because if she didn't, she would be no good to Karen, just a gibbering wreck. No good to anyone.

The outside door opened and she heard footsteps. A knock on the cubicle door.

'Allie?' Sam's voice was soft.

Allie opened the door and went out to her.

'Nick sent me to find you. I would have come anyway.' She smiled. 'Are you okay? Talk to me.'

Allie remained quiet, the lump in her throat making speech impossible.

'You're not invincible,' said Sam. 'No one thinks ill of you because you're upset.'

'But Nick thinks I wasn't doing my job properly.' Allie wiped at her eyes. 'I – I wasn't.'

'It's late, we've all been on shift for too long and we're tired. And Nick is a thoughtless dick.'

Allie smiled a little through her tears. 'I should have questioned Ryan Johnson. I let my heart rule my head. All I could think about was the fact that that's going to be me soon. I just wanted to let them grieve, you know? I was stupid.'

'It wouldn't have made any difference, though.' Sam placed a hand on her shoulder. 'We'll get them in the end.'

'But will we really?'

'With your expert interviewing skills and my expert camera skills, of course we fucking will.'

Sam's reassurance did it. Allie burst into tears again.

'I haven't been straight with you,' she said. 'I haven't been straight with *any* of you.'

'What are you talking about?'

Allie moved over to the sink, held on to it for support. As Sam moved to put a hand on her arm, she glanced at herself in the mirror. She didn't like what she saw reflecting back at her.

'Last week I was at the hospital with Mark and another rose was delivered to Karen's ward.'

Sam stared at her wide-eyed. 'Why haven't you told anyone?'

'Because!' She looked up at Sam through the mirror. 'I need to do my job, Sam. I don't want to be mollycoddled. It's bad enough with all this risk assessment bollocks since Chloe Winters was raped, as well as having to be babysat.'

'But you still need to be safe!'

'I can't cope if I don't do it, can't you see?' Allie turned to her. 'Doing what I do best blanks everything else out. It's the only thing I'm good at too.'

'You're going to be in so much trouble,' said Sam.

'I know.' Allie touched her arm. 'Promise you won't say anything.'

'I – I –'

'You have to promise! Once things are over with Karen,' Allie took a deep breath, 'then we can go after the bastard that did it to her. But for now, I just need to concentrate on her. And to do that I have to block her out too and do my job.'

Sam stayed quiet.

'Please, Sam.'

'Okay, I'll trust you on this one.' Sam sighed.

'Thanks,' Allie said. 'You're a true friend.'

'I'm a bloody sucker,' said Sam. 'Come back when you're ready. I'll tell Nick you'll be fine.'

Once Sam had gone, Allie took a few moments to calm down. She splashed her face with water, gave herself a good glare in the mirror and, head high again, she went back into the office.

'I reckon it's your shout for the oatcake order tomorrow,' said Nick, his stare a little friendlier than she had anticipated.

Allie's smile was faint but it was there. He was trusting her to get on with it and he wasn't going to give her a bollocking for insubordination. She sighed with relief. She didn't want to be sent home.

Perry shook his head as she sat down again. 'You are one smooth operator,' he teased.

'Why?'

'You swore at the boss man and got away with it.'

Allie smiled faintly. What she was more concerned about was how much Nick would swear at her when he realised she had kept something back from him yet again.

11.00 P.M.

Allie and Nick arrived at The Gables.

'You sure you're okay to do this?' Nick asked.

Allie nodded. 'Sorry about earlier. I was out of order.'

Nick knocked on the door and turned to her. 'You're a good officer, Allie. If your emotions get the better of you every now and then, it's hardly a bad thing. Even though you do try my patience at times.'

Ryan opened the door.

'Mr Johnson.'

He nodded and stood aside for them to pass.

'My apologies for it being so late,' Nick said to him as they followed him into the living room. Kirstie was standing barefoot in front of the fireplace, enveloped in an oversized cardigan and leggings.

'Oh, not you again.' She rolled her eyes after glaring at Allie.

'Can I get you a drink of anything?' Ryan ignored her. 'Coffee – something stronger?'

Allie felt a shiver tickle her skin as she recalled the last time she had been asked that, when she'd been at this house alone with Terry.

'I'm not wasting good drink on the likes of her,' Kirstie retorted.

'Clearly you've had enough of the stuff already,' said Ryan.

'We're fine.' Nick sat down when urged to. 'We just have a few more questions about Jordan. It seems from CCTV footage at Flynn's that you may have been the last person to see your brother alive at the club, Ryan. We wanted to clarify a few things from last night, now that we know the reason Jordan was at Harrison House this morning.'

'You mean he was going to see that trollop,' said Kirstie.

'You knew he was seeing someone who lived there?' said Allie with a frown.

'I thought it was the barmaid, as you know. Ryan told me her name.'

'I didn't want her to find out from anyone else,' said Ryan.

'We've spoken to Miss Nicklin twice today,' said Allie, taking great satisfaction in deliberately using the woman's name. Miss Nicklin was no trollop. 'It seems that Jordan had arranged to meet her there after he'd finished work at Flynn's. You also went to see her this evening, didn't you, Ryan?'

'I bet you loved saying every word of that, didn't you?' Kirstie almost spat the words out. 'You can't wait to get one over on me.'

'Kirstie, for Christ's sake, show some respect.' Ryan turned to Nick, his annoyance clear. 'Yes, I went to see if Jordan had visited her last night. It seems he was supposed to but he didn't turn up.'

'That's bloody convenient, don't you think?' Kirstie folded her arms. 'I mean, what man turns down sex on a plate with a tart?'

Allie bit her lip to stop from shouting out at her to grow up. She'd had just about enough of her selfish attitude.

'We found his car parked in Sparrow Street.' Nick ignored Kirstie. 'In case you don't know, it's a few minutes' walk from

Harrison House. According to neighbours who were questioned, it was often there during the early hours of a morning, but gone before most people were up the next day.'

'So he screws her and comes home to me.' Kirstie looked more disgusted than hurt.

Allie was confused: were she and Jordan still a couple? Had they got it wrong after all?

'Can either of you tell us if he was carrying any money on him?' Nick asked.

A glance between Kirstie and Ryan made Allie and Nick do the same.

'You said you had his wallet,' Ryan answered. 'There would have been a few notes in that, I guess.'

'I'm talking a lot more than a few notes, Mr Johnson. A whole lot more.'

'I don't understand.'

'There was a bag of money near to where Jordan was found. It's possible that he could have been targeted and robbed for it.'

'Killed for money?' Kirstie gasped.

'It's looking that way.' Nick nodded. 'We're trying to establish whether the money belonged to him and also if it was the reason why he was killed.'

'Have you asked her?' Kirstie almost snarled the last word. 'That Sophie woman?'

'We are following that line of enquiry at the moment,' said Allie. 'There was also a woman with long dark hair and a slim build seen going into Harrison House around three thirty a.m., at the same time Jordan was found.'

'Similar to me, you mean?' Kirstie pointed her finger at Allie's face. 'You really have it in for me, don't you? Wasn't it enough for you that you put my father in prison?'

'We're just following lines of enquiry.' Allie looked up, holding Kirstie's gaze to show she wasn't intimidated.

'But why would he have that much money on him? I mean, you can't just shove thirty-five grand underneath your jumper.'

'Thirty-five thousand?' Nick raised his eyebrows. 'What makes you think it was that much?'

Kirstie looked down at the floor with a shrug. 'You've just said it was.'

Nick looked at Allie for confirmation. She shook her head.

'We didn't mention an amount to either of you,' he said.

'I can't have plucked that figure out of thin air.' Kirstie moved to stand by Ryan. 'They did say thirty-five thousand, didn't they?'

The muscle in Ryan's cheek began to ripple as he struggled to keep his features straight. 'It's been a long day,' he replied. 'We're all confused.'

'That's highly possible, given the circumstances, Mr Johnson,' said Nick. 'But to make things easier, we'd also like to check around your and Jordan's rooms again while we're here. Would you mind? We'll make it quick.'

Kirstie shrugged her shoulders. 'Be my guest.'

'And maybe we could take a look in the back of the wardrobes while we're there,' said Allie.

Kirstie burst out laughing. 'I suppose you think you're going to find something in the hidden compartments again, don't you, Detective Sergeant Shenton? Just like last time when you stitched my dad up?'

'Secret compartments?' Ryan frowned.

It seemed genuine to Allie that Ryan didn't know anything about them, but she wasn't taking anything on face value.

'Well, now that you come to mention it,' Allie stood up, 'it's as good a place as any to start.'

'I – I –'

'Mr Ryder had compartments built into the wardrobes for safekeeping, to hide his wife's jewellery,' Allie explained to Ryan. 'But we found some interesting items in there when we searched the property three years ago; we found a knife covered with blood wrapped up.' She turned to Kirstie. 'I suppose *you're* going to tell me that you don't have the key fob?'

'I think you'll need to come back with a warrant,' Ryan glared at them.

'Maybe, but we're investigating the murder of your brother.' Allie's smile was kind but demeaning. 'You did indicate earlier that you want us to cover every eventuality?'

'Oh, don't worry about it, Ryan.' Kirstie padded into the dining area. 'Let them look. There's nothing there.'

'Then we won't keep you long.'

From the sideboard, Kirstie took something out of the top drawer and dropped it into Allie's outstretched palm.

Allie held her stare as her fingers clasped around it.

'Don't think you'll be as lucky as you were the last time you looked in there,' said Kirstie.

⌣

Allie followed Kirstie upstairs, Nick and Ryan close on their heels. Along the landing, Kirstie opened a bedroom door and switched on a light. 'After you,' she said, not taking her eyes from Allie.

'But this is my room,' said Ryan from behind them.

'It was my parents' room, you know that,' said Kirstie. 'I couldn't move into it after all that had happened.'

Inside the room, Allie glanced around as she and Nick pulled on latex gloves. The bed was made, the curtains drawn. Aftershave bottles of all shapes and sizes were lined up in a row on top of a large chest of drawers, next to a pair of cufflinks with a Route 66 emblem on them and a tie, still knotted, thrown on top of everything.

She opened the first wardrobe, full of men's clothes, and pushed them apart. She lifted the key fob, aimed it at the wall and pressed. There was a click and a door in the wall opened.

'What the hell . . .' Ryan stepped forward to look.

'Please stay by the door, Mr Johnson.' Allie raised a hand as Nick came past her.

Inside the compartment was a metal box lined with purple velvet. Nick reached inside and took it out, carefully placing it on the bed as he lifted the lid. He glanced at Allie before pulling out a pack of twenty-pound notes in a red paper band. There were more underneath that one. Then his hand fell upon something inside a roll of purple velvet. Unwrapping it, he revealed a knife, its blade approximately five inches in length.

It was covered with dried blood.

'I have no idea where that came from,' said Ryan, his eyebrows raised.

Kirstie folded her arms. 'Don't look at me. I didn't put it there.'

'Well, one of you knows something about it.' Nick stood up and took out his handcuffs. Allie followed suit.

'Kirstie Ryder, I'm arresting you on suspicion of the murder of Jordan Johnson. You do not have to say anything. But it may harm your defence if you do not mention when questioned something that you later rely on in court. Anything you do say may be given in evidence. Do you understand?'

'Wait! No, I don't understand!' Kirstie stepped away from them. 'I've done nothing wrong.'

Allie reached for her hands and snapped the cuffs around them.

'But I haven't done anything!' Kirstie turned to Ryan. 'What's going on?'

Nick moved to handcuff Ryan. He read him his rights too.

'I'll radio through for another car,' said Allie.

11.30 P.M.

Allie and Nick were sitting in the office. Both Ryan Johnson and Kirstie Ryder had been booked into custody and were sitting in cells waiting to be questioned.

'Get those things fast-tracked, Allie,' said Nick. 'Pull in any favours you can. Sleep with Dave Barnett if you have to.'

'That's not funny, coming from you,' said Allie. 'You're asking me to use my womanly charms again, after I got into so much trouble on the Steph Ryder case?'

'Hell, *I'll* sleep with Dave if I have to.' Nick raised his hands. 'Will that do you?'

Allie smiled. 'I'll ring him but I can't promise.'

'Thanks. Then we need to think how to handle this one. May be a little drip feeding is necessary?'

'Sir?'

'Let's talk money for now until we hear back about the knife. I want to know why she said thirty-five thousand pounds. She knows something – they *both* do. Then once we have more details we can go in for the kill, so to speak. If Kirstie is anything like her old man, she'll be unwilling to cooperate. Once you've tasked her about the money, take a break. Let her stew.'

'Got it.'

'I'll start off with Ryan, see what he has to say about it all.'

'Don't you think Kirstie was a bit quick to give us what we wanted?' questioned Allie.

'Yes. I'm wondering if this is to take us off the scent of something else as well. Get Financial Forensic Unit to take a look into their finances in the morning and see if anything has gone out of any accounts recently.'

'Money laundering?'

'It's possible, although it seems too much of a coincidence to me.'

Allie nodded. 'Considering a knife with blood and no prints was found in the exact same place during the Steph Ryder case?'

'Yes.' Nick yawned and stretched his arms over his head. 'I think it's time you and I paid a visit to the man behind it all.'

Allie didn't want Nick to say Terry's name. If he didn't say it, she could avoid ever having to see him again. It was a nice place to be.

'The one and only Terry Ryder,' said Nick.

Her warm and fuzzy feeling evaporated in an instant.

'We'll interview these two and if we get nothing from them, I'll put a request in and we can go early in the morning after team brief. We can be back by lunchtime. Ryder might speak nicely to us if he knows we have his daughter in custody.'

Sam joined them, looking as if she was ready to drop on her feet. 'There's good news and there's bad news,' she said. 'Forensics have found a DNA match on a cigarette butt found near to the body. The bad news is that it could belong to either of the Granger twins, and it was found on the pathway so may or may not be directly linked to the crime scene.' She folded her arms in frustration.

Allie dropped her head onto the desk. 'Oh, for fuck's sake.'

'I'm just starting to go through the CCTV we have in to see if I can see one or both boys anywhere on their walk home. In the morning, I'll see what I can find from the shops en route, too.'

'Talking of home,' said Nick, 'go and get some rest, Sam. You'll be seeing double anyway if you don't look at it with fresh eyes.'

'I can stay a while longer if you need me.'

'See you in the morning.' Nick shooed her away. 'There's no point in us all staying on.'

'If you're sure? I'll be back in early then.'

'Night, Sam,' said Allie. Once she'd gone, she let out a huge sigh. 'I'm tired – tired of this case. It's like playing one against the other. And now we have those idiots to talk to.'

'The Granger twins will cover for each other,' said Nick. 'They always do.'

11.45 P.M.

Nick went in to Ryan, who was in interview room one downstairs. He sat down across from him and his legal representative at a table.

'Right, then.' Nick got out his notebook after the formalities had been dealt with. 'Can you tell me anything about the items we found earlier this evening?'

'Not a thing. I had no idea there was a secret compartment in that wardrobe until your colleague pressed that key fob. It was as much a shock to me as it was to you.'

'So the money we found won't have your fingerprints anywhere on it?'

Ryan remained steely-eyed.

'Oh, come on. You're saying you don't know anything about it?'

'I'm saying exactly that.'

'What time did you get home this evening?'

'About nine thirty.'

'And this morning?'

'I was out of the house for a couple of hours.'

'And Kirstie was home?'

'Yes. What are you trying to insinuate?'

'Just getting to the truth, Mr Johnson. What was your relationship with Jordan like? Did you get on well?'

'Yes, we did.'

'Well, I suppose that's obvious after he let you move into his house.'

'It isn't his house. It belongs to Terry Ryder.'

'So it was Terry who allowed you to move in?' Nick cocked his head to one side.

'You're putting words in my mouth now, Inspector. I had an argument with my wife a few months back and left the marital home to cool down. I went to see my brother and while I was there Kirstie said I could stay if I needed to. The argument with my wife was beyond reconciliation so I moved into The Gables. It's only a temporary measure.'

'How long have you been there?'

'A few months.'

'That's rather more permanent than temporary, I'd say.'

'I'd say that it's none of your business, actually.'

'So you haven't seen the knife before?'

'I hadn't seen *any* of it before. The hole in the wall, the metal box, the money. And I certainly don't know anything about a knife with blood on it. Is it Jordan's blood on the blade?'

'We're running tests on it at the moment.' Nick ran a hand over his chin. 'Do you have any idea how it would have got there if the blood does turn out to be a match?'

'If it does turn out to be a match, then someone close to me is in very serious trouble.'

Nick met his gaze.

'I didn't put it there,' Ryan elaborated.

'Did Kirstie ever tell you what happened with her mother and father?'

'I knew already.'

'Yet you chose to go and stay at the house of a known murderer?'

'I see no danger in it. He's not there.'

'You're very trusting.'

'Is that a crime now?'

'Not at all.' Nick shook his head. 'So, to clarify, you don't know anything about the secret compartments?'

'No.'

'You don't know anything about the knife and whose blood is on it?'

'No.'

'Or how it got to be at the house?'

'No.' Ryan folded his arms.

'And you're saying the money is nothing to do with you and that we won't find your prints on it anywhere?'

Ryan shifted in his seat. 'If my prints are on it, it's been planted by someone.'

'Oh?'

'I run Flynn's nightclub with my brother – or rather, I did. It's possible that the bundles may have come from there.'

'What makes you think that?'

'I'm just saying that I handle money often so it would be quite easy to get my prints on notes and set me up.'

'So, one last time, Mr Johnson, where were you between one a.m. and four a.m. yesterday morning?' said Nick.

'I was at home. But you already know that, Inspector, as you've asked me before.'

⌣⌣⌣

Allie sat across the table from Kirstie in an interview suite, Perry by her side. As soon as she'd arrived at the station, Kirstie had arranged legal representation, and Ed Woodgate, a solicitor in a three-piece suit with slicked-back hair and round rimless glasses, had appeared in less than thirty minutes.

Even at this late hour, Allie was ready for the challenge of breaking Kirstie's spirit. Kirstie had denied all knowledge of the money and the knife, yet Allie was convinced she had something to do with the murder of Jordan Johnson. There was too much similarity between that and what had happened back in 2011. She wondered how long it would take for a match to come back to the body and the weapon. Dave Barnett had come in to start off the procedure, then left again, saying he'd get a few hours' sleep and come in early the next morning, push it to the top of his list of high priorities.

Allie went through the formalities and began.

'Kirstie,' she smiled politely at the woman sitting across from her, 'can you just go over again for me where you were between one a.m. and four a.m. yesterday morning, please? The morning of February fifth, 2015?'

'I was exactly where I told you I was when you asked me yesterday.'

'Remind me.'

'I was in bed at home.'

'Can anyone verify that?'

'Yes and no. Ryan was home too, but he wasn't in my bed.'

'Weren't you worried about Jordan after you'd fallen out?'

'Why should I be when he was off seeing that tart?'

'How do you know that?'

Kirstie tutted. 'I *don't* know for certain. I'm just using my detective skills – you should try it some time.'

Allie raised her eyebrows. She could feel Kirstie's stare burning into her, as if she was trying to penetrate her soul, but she wouldn't look away.

'The woman you're referring to – is it Sophie Nicklin?'

'Well, I've only just found out her name but, yes, it seems he was with her. And he was found outside where she lives so he must have visited her, or was about to. You have questioned her too, I hope?'

Allie ignored her. 'Do you get on with Ryan, Kirstie?'

'He's okay.' Kirstie shrugged. 'He's a mean bastard, though.'

'You took a shine to him when he came to stay with you, is that right?'

Kirstie clapped her hands slowly. 'Oh, you've worked it out. Well done. Yes, I've been seeing Ryan since the month after he moved in.'

'Did Jordan know?'

'Yes.'

'And he didn't mind?'

'Why should he?' Kirstie shrugged.

'So you were sleeping with both of them?' Allie tried to look surprised but found that she couldn't.

'I was indeed.' Kirstie curled back her fingers on one hand and looked at her nails. 'I obviously have the touch.'

'Didn't it make either of them jealous?'

'Nope.'

'Really?' Allie stuck out her bottom lip. 'Both sleeping with a good-looking woman like you? I would have thought that might cause a little friction.'

Kirstie shook her head. 'Ryan and Jordan couldn't stand each other. They were always arguing.'

'No brotherly love lost, then.' Allie smiled.

'If you say so.' Kirstie folded her arms and sat back in her chair. The room was silent for a while.

'Tell me about the money and the knife,' Allie continued.

Kirstie shook her head. 'I've never seen them before in my life.'

'You honestly expect me to believe that?' Allie couldn't help but snigger. 'We go straight into a room that you allow us to look around and find them in a secret compartment at the back of the wardrobe? The exact same place we found a knife three years ago with another murder victim's blood all over it?'

Kirstie stared at Allie, the atmosphere becoming electric. Silence again. Then Kirstie sat forward.

'What really did happen between you and my father?' she glared at Allie. 'I heard you were the bitch that got away. What does that mean?'

'Answer the question, Kirstie.'

'No, really, I have no idea. You obviously have the same allure as I have with men.'

'Hardly.'

'Don't they all find you irresistible?'

Ed Woodgate coughed to get her attention, shaking his head when Kirstie caught his eye.

'This is about you, not me.' Allie wouldn't be drawn, although she wanted to lean across the table and slap Kirstie hard. 'So you're saying you have no idea how the knife or the money got into the back of your wardrobe?'

'I'm saying exactly that.'

'Someone put them there.'

'Well, it wasn't me.'

'Did Ryan know about the compartments?'

'Of course.'

'So he could have put the items there?'

'Now you're getting it.' Kirstie smiled.

Allie fumed inwardly. Oh, she was getting it, all right. She was naffed off with every word that Kirstie said.

February 6, 2015
12.30 A.M.

Back in her cell after her interview, Kirstie sat in the corner of the small room, knees drawn up and her arms wrapped tightly around them. She rested her chin on her kneecaps to stop her bottom lip from trembling. Despite her bravado in the interview, the truth was she was terrified. It was her first time in a police cell. She didn't like feeling caged in, alone, vulnerable. Hearing people yelling obscenities and banging on walls, doors clanking, keys jangling. She hoped to God she wouldn't have to get used to it any time soon.

The lights were on low, and she'd covered her legs in a blanket she'd been provided with but she knew she wouldn't get any sleep. She didn't like knowing that the police wanted her to trip up, were waiting for her to make a mistake. Despite her distress, she knew she was in good hands with Ed Woodgate. He was a good solicitor, kept on the payroll for this type of thing. But she couldn't help wondering what else the police would find.

In reality, she still didn't quite know who was doing what for her father on the outside. She knew money was being moved around. She knew there were some dodgy dealings but she never saw any of it. Steve Burgess had looked after that side of things and she'd been glad of it.

Because Kirstie was alone and vulnerable, people had used her to get back at her father. But she was on her own for sure now. She would try not to crack under the pressure but if she did, she was going to act like a Ryder to the very end, no matter what the outcome.

2.00 A.M.

Allie was home at last. It was quiet, eerie even, as she retrieved her belongings from the back seat of the car; the only noise coming from a white van that had driven past and parked further up the street, its engine ticking over, its occupants probably saying goodbye. Drained and emotional, she tiptoed upstairs, desperate to see Mark. She opened the bedroom door, saw his familiar shape, his chest rising and dropping as he lay with his arms above his head, and closed it again quietly. She didn't have the heart to wake him. What was the point going to bed anyway? She knew she would be restless and up again in a few hours. It wasn't fair to disturb him.

In the kitchen, she made a quick sandwich and took it through to the living room. She was starving, hadn't eaten anything substantial since lunchtime.

It was nearly twenty-four hours since she'd taken the call about the murder. Never in her wildest dreams did she think she would be visiting The Gables so soon.

Kirstie Ryder – she shuddered as she remembered the look she had given her across the interview room. Those eyes, as cold and as deceiving as her father's, trying to read her every thought. And now all she could think about was Terry. She was so nervous about seeing him again, especially with Nick by her side. She'd have to be careful what she said, ignore him, try not to rise to his bait. Because she had been foolish on the night she'd gone to visit him alone. It had been irresponsible of her, naive even. It still haunted her all the time.

He could have killed her in an instant.

If he had wanted to.

Going to see him again was like facing her demons straight on. But would the devil eat her alive and spit her out or would she climb out of the flames? She could see herself, three years ago, naive yet intrigued by this man whom everyone seemed to fall for. The women loved his sex appeal, the power he exuded; the men loved the danger of working with him, the lifestyle, the image, the whole caboodle.

Yet in some ways Terry Ryder was no more than the drugged-up layabouts who stood on the street corners of any sink estate, selling his wares, making his money illegally, getting others to do his dirty work so that he could stay out of prison and live the life of Riley. He had lived it up – but she, and her team, had put a stop to it. Just in the nick of time.

They hadn't got everything yet but with each investigation, they became a little closer. She hoped they would ruin him before he was due out of prison, so that he would have one sentence rolled onto the next and never see the light of day again. At least while he was locked up they had better control of him, even if he did have people on the outside who were prepared to stick their necks out for him.

One day, sure enough, he would slip up.

The living room door opened and Allie was jolted out of her reverie as Mark appeared in the doorway.

'Hey.' She smiled as he sat down beside her, feeling herself blushing because she was thinking of Terry again. She leaned over to kiss him. 'Sorry, did I wake you?'

Mark yawned and ran a hand through his hair. 'Couldn't settle without you home.'

'You were snoring like a trooper when I came in.'

His smile was slight, lazy, but it was there.

'How's the case?'

Allie told him all she could, and a little of what she shouldn't, knowing she could trust him with the details.

'Tough day,' he sympathised, pulling her towards him. 'I really don't know how you do it.'

'But you mind a lot, don't you?' She nestled in the crook of his arm, flicked her feet up.

'You work sensible hours most of the time. I suppose I can't grumble. And I like my own company. I can watch what I want on the TV.'

Allie was glad he couldn't see her face as her eyes brimmed with tears. 'I was happy to keep my mind occupied. I'm dreading tomorrow in more ways than one.'

He held her closer for a moment. 'I think it's going to be tough all round.'

'Did they say what time the tests would be back?'

'They said they'd call when the consultant wanted to see us, save us hanging around. Well, when I say hanging around – they mean sitting for hours on end waiting for him. I gave them my number and asked them to call me first. Would you like me to hear the results and then let you know?'

'Please, I don't think I could handle that.' She squeezed shut her eyes. Why was he always so good to her when she kept so much from him? She decided to come clean, no matter how much he would be hurt.

'I have to go and see Terry Ryder in the morning,' she said, sitting up and away from him.

Mark's eyes had been closing again but they opened wide immediately. 'In prison, you mean?'

'Yes. Nick wants to question him about the case and he – he wants me to go with him.'

'Why are you telling me now?'

She looked at him with so much love she feared she would burst. 'Three years ago, I didn't tell you about the first rose that was delivered to Karen. You were angry at the time when I had to see Ryder, when his wife was murdered. I didn't want you to think . . . I don't want to keep anything from you.'

The silence that followed became loaded. But she had to accept it, wait for his response.

'Is there anything else you're not telling me?' he said eventually.

She shook her head.

Mark stood up, looked down at her for a moment and held out a hand. 'It's late, come to bed.'

She let him pull her up, kept hold of his hand while he turned out the lights, and followed him upstairs. Who knew, indeed, what the day would bring, but she had Mark. That was all she needed.

Fuck Terry Ryder.

She wouldn't allow him to get under her skin again.

2.30 A.M.

Damn this investigation! He was finding it harder and harder to get near to Allie. Why couldn't that Johnson fool have been offed next weekend? It would have been much more convenient. This was no job for a grieving woman to be doing.

It had broken his heart to watch her for the two weeks she had sat with her sister every day and night after she had been taken ill. She had barely moved from her side, and the hospital cafe had been a perfect place for him to sit unnoticed and watch the doorway. Allie was too busy, too full of dread and guilt, to notice anyone watching her.

He hadn't expected her to be up and out of the house so early this morning. It had thrown him at first. Leaving her road after seeing that her car wasn't parked next to Mark's, he'd been on his way to the hospital when he'd heard the news on the radio. Someone had been murdered – what terrible timing for her. He'd driven down Ford Green Road, excited to clap eyes on her, parked his car in a side street near to Harrison House and gone to see what was happening.

If Allie was at work, then he assumed that all must be well with Karen. He hadn't wanted to go inside since he'd left the rose in the box. He couldn't risk anyone stopping him seeing Allie this late in the game. Karen had been stable for three weeks now, but she could die at any moment.

He wondered if Mark was always happy about the long hours that Allie worked. Having an ambitious wife could go against the grain for some men. Not that he would mind, himself. He'd gladly support Allie if she were his wife. Although he would enjoy the role-play more – she could dress in her uniform and handcuff him to the bed any time that she saw fit. That thought spurred him on tremendously. Not long to wait now.

Looking down at his phone, he paused the video recording of the press conference on the tiny screen, not interested in the slightest in what the lead officer was saying. He ran a finger lightly over Allie's figure. He had footage of her from the last case she'd worked on too – saved on DVD for him to look at on a 50-inch widescreen HD television. He would transfer this clip onto it when he got home, watch it again and again, put it with the rest. God, she was beautiful. He imagined running his hands through her hair, imagined what was beneath the white shirt and jacket that she wore. Had she ever worn a long coat with no underwear beneath it to tanta-lise Mark?

On the seat beside him were photos of Allie through the years. He'd followed her career since she'd been a trainee social worker, before she'd joined the police force. Photographed her on numerous occasions, far too many to count. When she was visiting Karen's that New Year's Eve. He'd sent the first rose then. When she'd been coming and going to Riverdale Residential home to see Karen, at the funeral of her dad and then her mum. At her house, in every car that she'd owned. Photos of her in the new Subaru she'd picked up just before Christmas.

He'd almost come unstuck when, after hearing about his friend from school going around murdering people he knew last month, he'd become obsessed with Karen again. He'd wanted to know how it would have felt if he hadn't hit her so hard, if she hadn't played him along, if she had been willing to let him screw her. He knew she'd wanted it really, no matter how much she had screamed. And that young girl, Chloe Winters, had been in the wrong place at the wrong time. He'd been walking around and saw her. She'd reminded him of Allie with her slim figure and long dark hair, and before he knew it, he'd grabbed her hand and begun to run with her.

He'd left a note for Allie, to let her know that it was him and nothing to do with the serial killer case. He wondered if she had ever cottoned on.

Every time he saw Karen, he still felt sorry for what he'd done, the pain he'd caused Allie. But once the constant reminder of his mistake had gone with her, he would make up for it. It had to be on his terms. It had to be perfect. He had it all planned.

He needed Karen to die first. And then Allie would be next.

His surviving angel.

5.30 A.M.

When Allie awoke on Friday morning, she knew it had been point-
less going back home when she was so wired, but it was equally
important that she had got at least a few hours' rest. Eventually she
had dropped off next to Mark, only to sit bolt upright half an hour
later, wide-eyed and breathless as her nightmare of years gone by
returned.

Downstairs after her shower, over a quick coffee and bowl of
cereal, she pondered what would happen today. Most of all she was
dreading the results of Karen's tests, and she was fighting her guilt
about keeping busy.

Dressing had been more of a chore that morning. She wanted
to come across as confident and assuring but not in any way sexy
or dominant. But she'd ended up choosing a black pencil skirt
with jacket to match, a white shirt with a big collar and black
knee-length boots with a heel. The icy conditions outside didn't
make heels a good idea but she wore them anyway. They were her
confidence booster.

Mark was in the shower as she was about to leave for work. Oh,
how she wanted to join him and stay in there forever. Not go out
into the cold and unforgiving thing that was called life. She went in
to him, a slither of regret running through her as she saw his naked

body silhouetted through the glass rippled with drops of water. She slid the door open a little.

'I'm off now,' she shouted to him. 'See you later.'

He turned towards her, soapsuds falling down his torso, gave her a wink. 'Hang on a tick,' he said.

She waited while he finished. Less than a minute later, the shower went off and he opened the door.

'Are you sure you're okay to go in today?' he asked as she handed him a towel. 'They'll understand if you don't.'

'We're already a man down on our team now that Matt has retired.' DC Matt Radcliffe had worked with Allie as part of her team for several years until he'd been involved in a car collision last year; his injuries had been severe and were mending slowly. So after reaching the age of fifty, he'd decided to call it a day. She nodded her head at Mark, hoping this sudden turnaround was about Karen and not him feeling threatened that she was off to see Terry Ryder. 'I'll come away if necessary, regardless, but for now I need to sort this case out, keep busy.'

She stepped towards him and kissed him gently, overwhelmed by the scent of him. His response was to turn the kiss into a deep, passionate embrace, the romantic yet possessive kind that took her breath away. She felt him harden against her, liked that she could still do that to him.

'I love you, Allie,' he said, staring deep into her eyes. 'I know I don't say it often enough, but I do. You're my world, despite your irritating ways at times.'

'You kinda ruined it with that last statement,' she teased. 'I love you too – always.'

He smiled. 'Just make sure you stay safe and come home to me.'

She left him a minute later, tears welling in her eyes as she got into her car. Lord knows what she would face today but with

Mark behind her she had the feeling that she could tackle anything. Which was a good job, considering what she had lined up for that morning.

6.30 A.M.

Sandra Granger had been awake since half past five, too. She was sipping her second cup of tea. As she clasped her hands around it, she stood staring through the kitchen window. Beyond the walkway, everything was in shadows now but she could see the place where Jordan Johnson had been murdered.

The tent had been removed and the police had gone for now, yet the feeling of impending doom she felt had heightened. She just knew Jacob was involved. If he wasn't, why had he lied to the police about where he was when the crime had taken place? He said he'd been out with Tommy and then he'd said he'd been over at his friend's house. Neither of those was true. She should know. He'd woken her by banging the front door shut at three forty-five.

She'd heard on the news that Jordan had an older brother. She wondered how their mother was bearing up now. Was it beginning to sink in that she would never see her youngest son again or was she still in denial? To have a child taken so brutally, so quickly must be a parent's worst nightmare. So wrong, so unnecessary. Yet she knew if she didn't do something, the same fate could be hers. Worse, one son could be killed at the hands of the other.

Her boys weren't saints, far from it, and, even though they were always in trouble, she loved them dearly and would defend them until there were no more words left in her vocabulary to use.

Losing one of them was beyond comprehension.

She couldn't lose them both.

Which meant sacrificing one for the other.

7.00 A.M.

At the station, Allie checked through her action list and emails as she sat at her desk.

'Sarge,' said Sam, 'we've had a call from Stella Elliott. She was dismissed from hospital late last night and went home. But hubby never showed up. She's worried about him.'

'Well, I'm not – the bloody scrote,' Allie retorted. 'How the hell can she stand by him after what he did to her? He's beaten her black and blue, more than once as well. And she lied to us to cover for him about what time he got home. She's just as bad as him!'

'Who rattled your cage this morning?' said Perry, throwing his keys onto his desk and stretching before he sat down.

Allie shrugged but didn't say anything, knowing that the mood she was in had nothing to do with the Elliotts.

Nick started the team brief and they went through everything that had happened overnight. Allie expressed her concerns about the knife.

'It's too much like the Steph Ryder case to be a coincidence, isn't it?' She looked at Nick for confirmation. 'I think it was set up for us to find.'

'But why?' Sam looked puzzled.

'I don't know,' said Allie. 'It will be interesting to see if there are any fingerprints on this one.'

'We'll get forensics back around lunchtime, said Nick. 'Perry, can you check over Leah Matthews's statement, see if her story is straight, and go and see Stella Elliott, see if Elliott is still missing?'

'Yes, sir.'

'Sam, can you continue checking CCTV around the surrounding streets?'

'I'm on it, sir.' She moved away as the phone began to ring on her desk.

'Anything else?' Nick addressed the room again.

'There were some incidents of noise and shouting last night on floor one but no one would say any more than that,' said Perry. 'No flat numbers, no names were given. Just stuff in general. But we now know that was probably to do with Leah, Stella and Craig's coming and goings.'

Allie sighed. 'Is there anything we *can* say for definite?'

'Yes, there's been a mur-dar.' Perry grinned to lighten the mood.

'Before we leave, Allie, can you ring Simon at *The Sentinel*, see if there's anything in the news recently about the Granger brothers that we didn't know of? Have they upset anyone, etcetera? And get someone from uniform to check out every Car Wash City again. Anything we can get to nail Ryder and add to the investigation, I want to be all over it. Anything else?'

'Sir,' Sam shouted over. 'We've had a call from Sandra Granger. She must have grown a conscience overnight, as she's saying that both boys didn't go out on Wednesday night like they told us. She said Tommy was with his girlfriend and stayed overnight with her, too. Jacob came in about three forty-five a.m. She remembers because he always makes himself something to eat, so she gets up to check that he doesn't leave the grill on and fall asleep. Apparently, he did it once and almost burned the whole kitchen down.'

'Let's bring them both in.' Nick stood up. 'Everyone back here at midday, I think, and we'll go through what we have before we attempt to tidy this all up.' He clasped his hands together and rubbed them eagerly. 'Grab a car, Allie. You and I are going to see Terry Ryder.'

'But what about Ryan and Kirstie in the cells?' Allie asked, hoping he would let her continue to interview them alone, see if she could find out anything else.

'Let them stew,' he replied. 'We're still within our time limits.'

8.00 A.M.

At Harrison House, Perry knocked on the door of flat 404. Three uniformed officers waited behind him.

Sandra Granger opened it.

'Is Jacob still here?' he asked.

Her face dropped and she pointed to a room.

Perry scowled as he went in. He wasn't sure which smell was worse – stale ale, sweaty socks or dirty bedding.

'Wakey, wakey, rise and shine.' He turned on the bedroom light.

Jacob sat up in bed. 'What the –'

'Just a few things to clarify for us down at the station.'

'It's always me, isn't it? It's never Tommy.'

'We've picked up Tommy as well.' Perry grabbed the box of cigarettes that were on the drawers by the side of the bed and tutted. 'You need to be more careful where you throw your butts, Granger. Sometimes they'll put you in the right place at the right time.'

'You've got nothing on me!'

'Well, I guess we'll be sorted by lunchtime and you can come back to your pit. Now get up and put some clothes on.'

'I'm not coming with you!'

Perry barred the door as Jacob made a run for it, then knocked him to the bed. Within seconds, he had a knee in Jacob's back, holding him secure. He read him his rights while he took out his handcuffs.

'You would make things hard for yourself,' he said, fastening them securely around Jacob's wrists. 'Now you'll have to go as you are in your pants and it's a bit nippy out there.'

'Let me put my trousers on!'

'Oh, so now you'll cooperate. Get dressed and shut the fuck up complaining.' He turned to the officer behind him. 'Do the honours and help him into his kegs, would you?'

On his way out, he nodded his gratitude to Sandra. It couldn't have been easy doing what she'd done, and although she would feel guilty for a while, it had been the right thing to do.

———

Allie felt thankful for the cold weather as she popped her hands into leather gloves. Having them covered up might stop her wanting to wring them, as she was prone to do when her nerves got the better of her. She didn't want to alert Nick to how she was feeling.

'He knows something about this money,' Nick said as he drove down the M6 towards HM Prison Long Lartin in Worcester.

'Possibly,' Allie agreed, 'but bear in mind what a sleazeball he is. He and Kirstie could be in this together, and slipping up might have been her intention. I wouldn't put it past her to be double-crossing Ryan even if they are seeing each other.'

'Is that what you think?'

'I wouldn't rule anything out when dealing with a member of the Ryder family. They're slick operators who think they are beyond the law.'

They sat in silence, the temperature rising as the ice made way for heavy rain. Allie couldn't help but wonder how prison had treated Ryder. Would he still be lording it up as he had done outside before being locked up? Would he have his minions working for him on the inside now as well as on the outside? Would his time in prison have been served well?

She wondered if he'd still been taking regular exercise, keeping his body fit as well as his mind – knew the answer, really. Someone like him wouldn't lose the feeling just because there weren't many women around for him to manipulate.

She checked her watch: less than half an hour to go before they would arrive at the prison. She should really stop giving him so much time in her thoughts.

8.15 A.M.

After he had arrested Jacob Granger, Perry went to see Stella Elliott.

'And you're worried about *Craig*?' he asked incredulously when she opened the door. Stella's face was a riot of blacks and purples, her top lip, nose and left eye swollen. She had a bandage around her wrist and two fingers taped together. She held on to her chest as she shuffled through to the living room.

'I haven't seen him since last night and now he's not answering his phone,' she said as she lowered herself down slowly onto the settee.

'After what he's done to you, I'm surprised you want to speak to him at all.' Perry couldn't stop his anger from spilling out. He sighed. 'Would you like a cup of tea making?'

'No . . . Thanks.'

Perry nodded. 'When did you see him last?'

'When do you think?' She glared at him. 'You were with me last night after what happened.'

'Routine questions, Stella. Did you see him after he beat you up?'

'No, I tried to ring him when I was released from hospital but he didn't pick up.'

'Was the phone switched on?'

'Yes.'

'Does he stay out at Flynn's? You know, in that stay-over room.'

She shook her head. Perry saw her wince in pain.

'And there's nowhere else he would be?'

'Not unless he's cheating on me again.' A tear dropped down Stella's face. 'Don't judge me. I can't help loving the bastard.'

'There's nothing we can do for now but report him as missing,' said Perry. 'I'm sure you'll understand that Jordan Johnson's murder takes precedence, but we'll do our best to find him for you.'

9.00 A.M.

If the prison surroundings weren't enough to intimidate her, sitting in a room waiting for Terry Ryder to be brought in to them was making Allie's heart leap about inside her chest. She could hardly hear the sound of clanking doors, keys in locks and the faint shouts of men for the sound of it. Now she had removed her gloves, she had no choice but to rub her hands together. She sat on them eventually and turned towards Nick as they heard noises outside in the corridor.

'Here he comes, the suave bastard,' Nick muttered as the door opened.

It was like stepping back in time. Terry's skin was paler than she remembered, although other than that it seemed prison life had been kind to him. She was right about his fitness: he still kept himself trim. His hair had more grey at the roots but it was still dark, short and tidy. His lines had deepened a little, but his eyes had the same come-to-bed vibes that she remembered so well from that night three years ago.

He sat down across the table from them.

'Allie, how marvellous to see you after so long.' His smile seemed sincere. 'But I'm disappointed. Not a card, or a phone call, a visit to say hello, perhaps? Have you missed me?'

Allie ignored him, mortified as she felt the telltale blush rising across her cheeks.

'Cut the crap, Ryder,' said Nick. 'We have a few questions for you, concerning your daughter.'

'Is she okay?' Terry sat forward, a concerned look on his face now.

'She's fine. She's in one of our cells at the moment.'

'What do you mean?'

'Jordan Johnson has been murdered. Surely you know?'

'Jordan?' Terry sat forward. 'I had no idea.'

'You don't watch the news on TV?'

'Not if I can help it.' His eyes fell on Allie again. 'How have you been?'

Allie stared at him, but eventually she was intimidated enough to drop her eyes.

'So why is Kirstie at your place?' Terry shook his head. 'What's going on?'

'Jordan was beaten and stabbed. He had a large quantity of money with him. When we questioned Kirstie and Ryan, we never mentioned an amount. Kirstie then said something about thirty-five thousand pounds.'

'You found that much money at my house?' Terry raised his eyebrows.

'We found ten thousand pounds.'

'Where exactly did you find it?'

'It was hidden in one of the compartments in the wardrobes,' said Allie. 'The last time we spoke, not many people knew about it if I recall rightly.'

'It's been three years since we last spoke, Allie.' Terry looked meaningfully at her. 'I've dreamt about you every night, though. Please tell me you've missed me.'

Allie rolled her eyes. God, he really was playing a blinder. But she was prepared, despite her flushing skin.

'Who knew about the compartments?' asked Nick.

'Kirstie's young, trusting. She could have told anyone about them.' Terry pouted. 'How do you know it has anything to do with her? Does the money have her prints on it?'

'We have it with forensics at the moment. It will become clear soon.'

'So you've arrested her for what, exactly?'

'We're trying to make things better for Kirstie by understanding how the money got into the compartment, where it came from in the first instance and why she mentioned a figure of thirty-five thousand pounds.'

'I thought as detectives you might be able to tell me that.'

Nick fidgeted in his seat. 'We also found a knife with the money. The blade had dried blood on it. Sound familiar to you?'

'You can't trust a soul in Stoke these days.' Terry shook his head as if mocking them.

'We just wondered why it would be found in your house, in a place that only Kirstie knew existed.'

Terry looked at them again. 'Can you be certain that only my daughter knows about it?'

'No.'

'Then she has no case to answer to. I'm sure Mr Woodgate will tell you that too.'

The air thickened as Terry looked from one to the other over and over again. A silence fell in the small room.

'Was Jordan put in to look after Kirstie?' Allie broke into it.

Terry sighed. 'Yes. She's a young woman, who lost both of her parents in the space of a month. I couldn't leave everything under her control.'

'But he's young, good-looking, power-hungry even. I'm sure a man of your intelligence would have seen that as a threat rather than an advantage?'

Terry laughed. 'What planet do you live on, Detective Sergeant? He's just an employee of mine.'

It still irked Allie that nothing of Ryder's could be taken away from him until they could prove he was doing something illegal.

'What did Jordan help you out with?' asked Nick.

'Well, as you know, he helped to run Flynn's nightclub and he kept an eye on Kirstie and the house.'

'So he didn't work for you regarding Car Wash City?'

'Ah. You mean the best hand job in town.'

Allie drew in her breath.

'Sorry?' said Nick, frowning at him.

'It's a new tagline I thought up while I was in here. Good, isn't it?'

Allie wanted to lean across the table. She would punch his lights out if she had the chance, or courage to fight. An obnoxious twat – that's all he ever was.

'Do you have people running around doing everything for you on the outside?' Nick continued.

'It seems I do.'

'And do they know everything that goes on?'

'I'm not with you.'

'Do they know where that large amount of cash came from?'

'I'm not sure I follow what you're getting at.'

Allie raised her eyebrows.

'You think I'm money laundering, as another side of the business?' Terry laughed. 'Just exactly how much do you think I can do from my cell?'

Perry joined Jacob in the interview room and sat across from him and a duty solicitor. Liz Harding was a heavy-built woman, mid-thirties, dressed in a black trouser suit, the frame of her glasses almost the same shade of red as her short hair. Perry had known her for a few years now.

'Jacob, where were you between one a.m. and four a.m. yesterday morning?'

'I was out with Tommy.'

'For the benefit of the recording, please confirm who Tommy is.'

'My brother.'

'You told me that you were in Burslem and had a few pints at The Leopard. Is that right?'

Jacob folded his arms and sat back in his chair. 'No comment.'

'What time did you get home?'

'No comment.'

'What time did you leave the pub?'

'No comment.'

'Did you go anywhere else?'

'No comment.'

'Are you covering for Tommy, Jacob? Did you really go out together last night?'

'No comm –'

'No comment. Yes, I get it.' Perry shook his head, folding his arms and then unfolding them again just as quickly. 'Do you smoke, Jacob?'

'No comment.'

'And Tommy – does he smoke?'

'No comment.'

'There was a cigarette butt found near to the body of Jordan Johnson and it has your DNA on it.'

Jacob met his eye with a steely glare. 'No comment.'

'Do you think Tommy could stick a knife in Jordan Johnson?'

'I doubt it. He's a wuss.'

'I think that you could.'

'No comment.'

'So it wasn't you who stabbed Jordan Johnson?'

'No comment.'

'And the only alibi you have is your brother, Tommy Granger?'

'No comment.'

'Interview paused at twelve forty-five. I'll grab you a brew, Jacob. Tea or coffee?'

'Tea. Two sugars.'

Perry sighed. 'Those three words were easy enough to say.'

10.30 A.M.

'Can you believe the gall of the man?' Allie almost spat out fire when they were in the car on their way back to Stoke-on-Trent again. 'He's laughing at us. I hope that he hasn't had any more secret hideaways made for Kirstie that we don't know about. Oh, he would love that, the self-centred bastard – making this all about him. I feel like I want to –'

'What went on between you and him?'

'What?'

'You know exactly what I mean.'

'Nothing, sir.' Allie looked out of the window quickly.

'Really – off the record.' Nick glanced her way before indicating to change lanes and manoeuvring out. 'I've worked with you a long time now. You're a passionate officer and fantastic at using your emotion to gain respect so that people confide in you. And you're a bit erratic at times but I've never seen you this wound up about anyone – anything! He's really got under your skin.'

'It's not like that. I –'

'Did you sleep with him?'

Allie turned to him sharply. 'No, I bloody well didn't . . . sir!"

'You wouldn't be the first officer to step over the line.'

She shook her head. 'You told me to work closely with him to get the truth. He wanted to get a lot closer than was necessary. I was only following my gut instinct. I did my job. Sir.'

Allie's phone rang and she gave silent thanks as she answered it.

'That was Sam,' she said after she'd disconnected the call. 'She's been going through camera footage taken from some of the shops on the route home that the Granger twins would have taken on Friday night. There's only one of them seen walking alone – although we can't be certain whether it's Jacob or Tommy.'

'Great. We'll be back in time to put it to them.'

'Oh, I have much better news than that.' Allie couldn't help but feel a bit breathless as the adrenaline kicked in. 'While she was looking for those two, she spotted Kirstie Ryder's car going down Ford Green Road and then parking up in Regina Street.'

'That's only streets away from Harrison House.'

'And exactly the same place where Craig Elliott's car was seen too.'

'What time?'

'Three o'clock yesterday morning.'

———

Perry had been called back to his desk by Sam.

'Here you go.' She handed him several photos of a lone male at various points on Moorland Road and Ford Green Road.

'Brilliant!'

'Oh, there's more. Guess what else I found while I was looking for these?' Sam showed him the images she had of a car, its number plate clearly visible. 'That belongs to Kirstie Ryder.'

Perry's eyes widened. 'Great job, Sam! So that puts her near to the murder scene too. Allie will be pleased when she gets back. Did she say how long she'll be?'

'Another half hour.'

After a short break, Perry interviewed Tommy Granger next. Liz Harding had joined them again.

'What's happened to your face, Tommy?'

'Oh – I fell.' Tommy put a hand to his nose and winced.

'Okay . . . Tommy, where were you yesterday between one a.m. and four a.m.?'

'I told you – I was with my brother.'

Perry made a show of looking back through his notebook. 'You told me that you were in Burslem and had a few pints at The Leopard. Is that right?'

'Yeah.'

'What time did you get home?'

'About half one.'

'What time did you leave the pub?'

'Around midnight, I guess.'

'So what did you do in the time it took for you to get home, which is,' he shrugged his shoulders, 'forty minutes at staggering pace?'

'Can't remember. We'd had a few pints, like you've said.'

'Can anyone vouch for you?'

'My brother, Jacob.'

Tommy folded his arms and looked on a little unnerved. Perry had a sense of déjà vu as his actions mirrored Jacob's earlier.

'Were you with him all night?' he asked next.

'Yes.'

Perry frowned. 'That's strange, because we only have one of you on CCTV.' He pushed a video still across the desk. 'Is this you, or Jacob, seen walking down Moorland Road?'

Tommy shrugged. 'I was drunk.'

'If it is you, where is Jacob?'

'I – I don't know. I can't remember.'

'Are you covering for your brother, Tommy? Did you really go out with him on Wednesday night?'

'No! Yes, I went out with him!'

'So is that you on the photo or your brother?'

Tommy spoke to Liz for a few moments and then turned back to him.

Perry waited patiently for him to work out what to say next. Either answer had ramifications for him and he could almost hear Tommy's brain whirring as he tried to figure out the best thing to do.

'I – I – what's this about?' said Tommy. 'I haven't done anything wrong.'

'Is that or is that not you in the photo?'

'I can't remember.'

'But you can remember getting in around one thirty a.m.?'

Tommy looked at his fingernails as he picked at the skin around them.

'Do you smoke, Tommy?'

'Not really.'

'Not really?'

'I gave up – but I have the odd one every now and again.'

'And Jacob – does he smoke?'

'Yeah.'

'Ah, then you see, this is where I have a problem.' Perry paused for a moment and stared at Tommy, scanning his body language for signs of agitation – eyes flitting everywhere around the room but not catching his, perspiration on his forehead despite the chilly temperature, left knee jigging.

'There was a cigarette butt found near to the body of Jordan Johnson and it has DNA on it.'

'It isn't mine!' Tommy scraped his chair back and stood up. 'I didn't have anything to do with that.'

'Sit down, Tommy.'

'It isn't mine!'

Perry remained quiet while he waited for him to sit down again. Once he had, he continued.

'Something doesn't add up here, Tommy,' he said. 'Look at it from my point of view. You won't tell me if the image on the photograph is you or if it's your brother. I have a cigarette butt with DNA on it and again it could be from either one of you. As you know, we can't yet distinguish saliva for identical twins.'

'But that could have been there for weeks!'

'I guess you're right.' Perry nodded.

'I could never stick a knife in anyone and kill them!'

'Do you think Jacob could?'

Tommy shook his head vehemently.

Perry let him stew for a moment before continuing. 'Tommy, you need to come clean with me if you don't want to be arrested for the murder of Jordan Johnson. Was it you or was it your brother on the CCTV footage?'

Tommy kept on shaking his head.

'We have several images of this person,' he pointed to the photo, 'in different places walking up Moorland Road and down Ford Green Road. Several small shops along the way, you see.'

Tommy held his head in his hands.

'It wasn't you, was it?' said Perry.

Tommy looked up for a moment between his fingers. 'No comment.'

11.45 A.M.

As soon as Allie and Nick got back to the station, Allie headed for her desk. She looked around in expectancy.

'What?' said Sam, as she clocked what she was doing.

'Please tell me you got my usual order from Graham. I'm starving and two oatcakes would just fill the gap nicely.'

'He hasn't been yet.' Sam checked her watch and frowned. 'He's late today.' She beckoned Allie over to her desk. 'Come see what I've spotted.'

'You look as excited as Emily at a birthday party,' Allie remarked. Emily was Sam's five-year-old daughter. 'Good job on the CCTV footage, by the way.'

'That's nothing to what I spotted afterwards.'

Intrigued, Allie rolled her chair along to Sam's monitor and sat down beside her.

'Sir!' Sam shouted when she saw Nick come into the room. 'You have to see this.'

Nick came over and stood beside them.

'Ready for the finale?' Sam looked up at them.

'Just press the button!' Allie cried.

'Right, then. You know I spotted Kirstie's car at 03.02 going down Ford Green Road yesterday morning?' Sam pointed to the screen. 'Well, I started checking the streets around to see where she went and I spotted . . . him.'

Allie saw a lone male walking out of the pathway by the side of Harrison Road. Sam zoomed in.

'Is that..?'

'Yep. A Granger twin.'

'Good work, Sam,' said Nick.

'That's not all.' Sam's smile widened.

They continued to watch as he crossed over Ford Green Road and stopped at a car. Sam zoomed in closer.

Nick leaned forward. 'Did he just give something to the driver?'

The driver's face was partly covered by a scarf, so Sam zoomed in again. They could see dark hair.

'Is that Kirstie Ryder?' Allie sat there open-mouthed as the two people on screen spoke for a moment or so.

'I can't be certain, but I'd like to take a bet on it before it's enhanced,' said Sam.

The male walked off. Seconds later, the car moved away too.

'It looks like her,' said Nick.

'It's her,' said Allie, nodding her head profusely.

'It's not enough yet.' Sam handed Nick several stills of the footage that she had printed off. 'But once it's been printed out professionally, it will show her properly.'

Allie turned to her and kissed her full on the lips. 'You wonderful, wonderful woman.'

Nick moved forward to do the same but Sam squirmed away. He grinned. 'Allie, I'll come in with you for the next interview. But first, can you have a go at Jacob and then we can discuss how best to deal with Kirstie afterwards.'

Perry was back in an interview room with Tommy Granger.

'Do you get on with your brother, Tommy?' said Perry.

'Yeah, why wouldn't I? He's my brother.'

'Okay, let me rephrase that, while there's only us in this room. Are you scared of your brother?'

'No.'

'Does Kayleigh get on well with him?'

He watched Tommy's facial expressions change.

'I checked with her earlier – Kayleigh Smith, isn't it? She seems to think a lot of you.'

There was a hint of a smile. 'Yeah.'

'You been seeing her long?'

'A few months.'

'Things going well?' Perry smiled too. 'Seems that way from how she spoke about you.'

Tommy raised a shoulder. 'She's nice. I like her a lot.'

'I got the impression she's heard those three words that women like to hear quite a few times from you so far. I certainly got the impression that she says them back to you too.'

That smile was there again.

'So why did you want her to lie for you? It's not a nice thing to ask anyone, especially someone you obviously care so much about.' When Tommy remained silent, Perry went on. 'She says that you spent the night at her house on Wednesday, that you weren't with Jacob at all. So . . . which one of you two is lying?'

Still Tommy said nothing, just chewed at his nails.

'We also found a substantial amount of money in your room. Does it belong to you or Jacob?'

'I don't have any money! Fuck, where did you find it?'

'Under his bed.' Perry couldn't help but smile. 'He didn't have the nouse to hide it anywhere decent.'

Tommy shook his head in despair.

'Why did you lie about being with Jacob? Was it because of what he'd done? Or because of what he would do to you if you didn't stick by him?'

'I don't know!'

'You weren't with Jacob on Wednesday night, were you?'

Tommy shook his head. 'I was with Kayleigh.'

'All night?'

'Yeah.' He looked at Perry. 'I didn't know anything about Jordan at first. And when I did, I was in too deep and had already lied to you lot. And then Jacob made it worse by saying something different.' He put his head in his hands. 'But you don't know my brother. He threatened me, and my mum. Said that if I grassed him up, he would get Kayleigh and throw acid in her face. He would, too. He's a nutter.'

'So are you saying that Jacob stabbed Jordan Johnson?'

'I don't know.' Tommy's face lost its colour in seconds. 'He came at me with a knife the last time I saw him. He gave me the bruised face. He owed money to Kenny Webb, got himself in bother because of it. He was after money to pay him back.'

'A bit heartless, don't you think?' Perry shook his head. 'There can't be many people, no matter how much money they get, who would have the guts to stick a knife in someone to kill them.'

'Our Jacob would. He's always going on about doing someone in, wanting to know how it feels to take a life.' Tommy looked at Perry with eyes like a child who thought he'd seen the bogey man under his bed. 'He scares me. That's why I've always been in trouble.'

'Has he used you as a scapegoat before?'

'Yes, lots of times. I couldn't tell anyone!' Tommy was almost crying.

'Have you done time for him?'

Tommy nodded. 'Once for theft.'

Perry struggled to keep his emotions in check. How could one brother do that to another? Tommy seemed so scared of Jacob that he didn't dare admit the truth for fear of repercussions.

But there was a glimmer of hope for Tommy.

'Jacob has a son, right?' he asked, looking back through his notebook.

'Yeah, with Malory Victor. He's not with her anymore, though.'

'Do you know there are tests we can do now that will give us definite DNA from the two of you if one of you has a child?'

Perry's hard exterior nearly cracked as Tommy looked at him, so eager to learn more.

'You might be his identical twin but you won't have the same DNA as the child – only the father will. If necessary, and if we could persuade the powers that be to run those tests, because they are expensive, it would determine whose DNA is on the cigarette butt.'

Tommy's shoulders sagged.

'It might not be enough evidence but we have more coming in that we're going to talk to Jacob about. In the meantime, if I were you, I'd perhaps think about trying to get some help. If Jacob is involved in Jordan's murder, it could be time for you to make a fresh start.'

'What's going to happen to Jay?' Tommy asked as Perry stood up to leave.

Perry turned back to him. 'That depends on what he tells us when we interview him.'

12.30 P.M.

During a quick briefing, Nick told everyone that he and Allie had got nothing substantial from their visit to Terry Ryder.

'He was playing with us,' he addressed the team. 'One minute he was concerned about Kirstie being arrested; the next he was joking about his life in prison and the fact that he could still run his businesses from his cell. He was trying to get our backs up.'

'Smarmy bastard,' muttered Allie. 'He knows more than he's letting on.'

'Maybe, but it wasn't anything he was willing to share.' Nick pointed at his desk. 'Forensics are back. The blood is a match to Jordan Johnson but there are no prints on the knife.'

There was an audible groan around the room.

'I know, I know.' Nick held up his hand for quiet. 'But let's face it, we didn't expect there to be any prints. At least we know we have one of the murder weapons used now. There's still no sign of the bat?'

'No,' said Allie. 'It's a good job that Sam has unearthed CCTV footage. Sam?'

Sam showed everyone the footage of the Granger twin walking to Kirstie Ryder's car and giving her something before walking away.

'How did you get on with the Granger twins, Perry?' asked Nick.

'I spoke to Tommy Granger's girlfriend, who confirmed that he was with her all night, so that must be Jacob on the CCTV footage. When I told Tommy, he confessed. Said he wasn't with Jacob but that his brother expected him to cover for him.'

'And Jacob? What did he have to say when you gave him this new information?'

'I've left him with his legal rep for a moment while she goes through his position now. It's not looking good for him either way.'

'And now we're going to interview Kirstie Ryder and show her what we've uncovered,' said Allie, standing up quickly.

'Go in with Perry first,' said Nick. 'See what Jacob has to say for himself.'

1.00 P.M.

'So Ryder was as cocky as ever when you saw him, boss?' Perry asked as they walked down the stairs to the interview rooms.

Allie grinned and lightened her step. 'Is it that obvious I'm stomping?'

'Can't say I blame you.'

'The man is a loathsome cretin.' Allie nodded vehemently. 'I can't bloody wait to speak to Kirstie. Just let her try and talk her way out of this one. I'm going to –'

Perry held up his hand. 'I think you should lead on this interview with Jacob.'

Allie turned to him with a puzzled look. 'But you brought him in and you're almost done, aren't you?'

'You could use your womanly charm,' he grinned.

'Why, you –' Allie went to slap him playfully but he jumped out of the way. He was right, though. Maybe she could use her pent-up feelings and get Jacob to confess.

They both went into the interview room. Allie slid the new evidence across the desk to Jacob and watched for a reaction.

'You can't be sure that's me on there,' he said to her. 'It could be Tommy.'

'Tommy has an alibi.'

'What, that tart he's sleeping with?'

'We also have a witness who says you went into your home at three forty-five yesterday morning.'

'Who?' Jacob stared at him.

'That's irrelevant right now.' Allie looked at him pointedly. 'Did you get home at quarter to four on the morning of February fifth?'

'All lies.'

'Is it a lie that you have nearly five thousand pounds stashed in your room?' said Perry.

Jacob's eyes widened. 'That's Tommy's money,' he muttered, turning to look at Liz Harding.

'For God's sake, Jacob.' Allie slammed her palm down on the desk. 'How much more evidence do we have to provide before you'll come clean?' She paused before their final reveal. 'We've found the knife with Jordan's blood on it. Perhaps you should start talking.'

Jacob swallowed. 'I had no choice. I owed money and I was in big trouble.'

'Trouble enough to put a knife in someone?' Allie scoffed. 'You really expect me to believe that? It's murder – it's not as if someone stood over you, egging you on to "just do it" until you're brainwashed enough to attack. *You* had to stick a knife in someone, all alone, with the fear of getting caught. A man who had been beaten up even, unable to retaliate. You knew exactly what you were doing. You can't blame anyone but yourself.'

'If I didn't pay the money back, I would have been dead myself!'

Allie threw down her pen. 'It's too convenient. Just like it's been too convenient for you to blame everything on your brother and let him take the rap for you because of his DNA.'

'I never did that! And you can't prove it. It's my word against Tommy's.'

'You're saying your brother is a liar?'

'Yeah, he is.'

'Jacob, we have the knife that was used to murder Jordan Johnson.' She shoved another photo across the desk. 'We have CCTV footage of you approaching a car we know belongs to Kirstie Ryder a few minutes after we believe Jordan was killed. It clearly shows you giving something to the driver. A few hours later we find the knife at her house. How do you think it got there?'

Jacob placed his head in his hands and wouldn't look at anyone. 'He paid me good money.'

'Who did?'

'Steve Burgess. He said he'd pay me five grand to hit Jordan in the heart. I had to wait until Jordan was beat up and then do it.'

'Wait a minute,' said Allie. 'You saw someone beating him up?'

Jacob nodded. 'It was Craig Elliott. He was told to knock Jordan about a bit. I was told to wait for him to leave and then finish him off.'

Allie frowned, not entirely sure she understood everything. 'And then what happened?'

'I took the knife to that woman – Kirstie Ryder. Just like I was told to do.'

1.30 P.M.

Allie had a spring to her step when she went back into the office and enlightened the team as to the outcome of their interview with Jacob.

'Well done, everyone,' said Nick. 'Great work, Allie.'

'Thanks, sir,' she replied. 'Although to be fair, Perry would have got the same results. He worked hard getting to the stage we were at with both twins.'

'I'm not so sure,' Perry disagreed. 'I'd have lost my temper with the little scrote and dragged him across the table.'

'No, you wouldn't! You're a gentle giant underneath that bulk.'

Perry grinned. 'I suppose I'll give you that one.'

'Never mind who got him,' said Sam, raising a mug of steaming coffee into the air. 'We *got* him, that's all that matters! And it looks like we've got Kirstie Ryder, too.'

'Yes!' Allie raised her hands in the air and whooped. Then she laughed. It felt so good to hear it. 'Curry to celebrate is on me, Nick, seeing as I missed buying oatcakes this morning.'

'Absolutely.' Nick smiled for a moment and then became serious again. 'Has uniform been sent to pick up Steve Burgess for questioning?'

'Yes,' said Perry. 'They're also checking to see if Craig Elliott has returned as well so we can talk to him, too.'

'Right, I think it's time for you and me to talk to Kirstie,' said Nick.

'Bring it on,' said Allie.

1.45 P.M.

When she and Nick brought her out of her cell and into an interview room again, Kirstie was none too pleased.

'Why the hell have I been kept here since last night?' she snapped as she sat back and folded her arms.

'We've had a lot of evidence that has come in,' Nick explained. 'We've been trying to process it as quickly as possible.'

Kirstie's aggressive demeanour dropped a little. 'What kind of evidence?'

'Do you know whose blood we found on the knife, Kirstie?'

Kirstie remained stone-faced.

'It's Jordan Johnson's blood. It was the knife used to kill him, but then you already knew that, didn't you?'

'No.'

'The knife was found in your house along with ten thousand pounds.'

'I know.' Kirstie glared at him insolently. 'I was there, remember.'

'But you don't remember how it got there, do you?'

'No. I told you – you should be asking Ryan about it.'

'We have. He denies ever seeing the knife, or the money.'

'He would, wouldn't he? He's trying to blame me.'

'Why is that?'

'Because he knows he's in trouble. Look, I don't know anything about that knife, or the money.'

'So you had nothing to do with the murder of Jordan Johnson?'

'Of course I didn't. I couldn't kill someone in cold blood.'

'But you did collect the knife from Jacob Granger, didn't you?'

Kirstie's eyes met Allie's.

Allie opened up her laptop, pressed a few buttons and swivelled the screen round to show Kirstie. She watched her face drop as she was shown the footage that Sam had found.

'Is that you?' Nick pointed to the woman clearly visible in the front seat of the car.

'No comment.'

'Is that Jacob Granger?' Allie pointed to the man who walked over to the car.

'No comment.'

Nick leaned forward. 'It will look better for you if you start telling us the truth.'

Kirstie looked to Ed Woodgate.

'I think we need to take a break here,' he said.

Nick nodded. He and Allie stood up.

'So what happens now?' Kirstie asked before they left the room.

'You can either talk to us, tell us what you know,' said Nick, 'or you can keep quiet, and anything else we have, or find out against you, well, it could mean the difference between a medium sentence or a more lenient one. That also depends on whether we find any more evidence against you. We've found so much that's mounting up now, who knows.'

'Wait!' Kirstie cried, her voice breaking with emotion. 'You're saying I could go to prison?'

Allie sighed inwardly. Finally, it was about to hit Kirstie how serious everything was going to get. Did she really think she would get away with whatever had been planned?

Nick nodded. 'You talk to your solicitor, decide what else to say and then we'll come back to you. It would be much better for you if you're seen to cooperate at this stage rather than not.'

Allie and Nick left the room to the sound of Kirstie's raised voice as she took out her frustration on Ed Woodgate. Ten minutes later, they were called back. Kirstie's eyes were red and teary.

'My dad found out that Ryan and Jordan had set me up,' she said before they had settled down. 'When Jordan and I bought Flynn's nightclub, there was a clause in the contract that after two years the club would belong to Jordan and Ryan. I hadn't read the contract and when my dad found out, he went ballistic.

'Ryan brought thirty-five thousand pounds home. It was meant to be passed to Steve Burgess via Jordan, but it was only to lure Jordan to a place where Ryan would get him beat up. Ryan must have thought that if Jordan was out of the picture for a couple of weeks, then he would be able to sign the club over to himself. He was willing to cut out both me and Jordan and that wasn't part of the plan.'

'This was all planned?' asked Nick.

Kirstie nodded. 'Steve Burgess set up Craig Elliott to rough Jordan up but not to kill him. That was Jacob's job. But Ryan didn't know that.'

'So you knew all along that Jordan was going to be killed?'

She nodded again, a lone tear running down her face.

'Jacob was paid five thousand pounds to kill Jordan. If it was one-on-one he would never have had the strength but if Jordan was beaten by Craig first, it would obviously be easy for him. Though I don't know how anyone sticks a knife in someone. He must be mental.'

Allie tried hard not to show her true feelings. The girl actually thought that Jacob was vicious? It defied belief.

'So how did that happen?' asked Nick.

'He was waiting in the bushes for Craig to do his job and then he did his. Then he brought the knife to me.'

'Why?'

Kirstie shrugged her shoulders.

It was beginning to make sense to Allie now. That bastard Terry Ryder *was* playing them. He'd used his daughter to get back at them, to taunt her even, about the knife in the wardrobe three years ago. There had been blood but no prints found on that either, so they hadn't been able to charge him without evidence. Ryder must have thought he would get away with the same thing by using Kirstie to set things up the way they had been before. But this time, it had backfired. This time they had the evidence. His daughter was going down.

'Did your father set all this up, Kirstie?' asked Allie.

'No.' Her tone was sharp.

'Are you sure? Because if he did, you're probably looking at a lesser sentence if we can say that you were coerced into doing –'

'You really would like that, wouldn't you?' Kirstie stared at her for a moment before continuing. 'It had nothing to do with my father.'

'And the ten thousand pounds that we found?' said Nick.

'Thirty-five thousand was in the bag that Ryan packed,' Kirstie explained. 'He told me that only twenty-five thousand of it got to Steve Burgess. Jordan must have hidden some of it and someone else found it. I assume that's the woman who went into the building at three thirty?'

Nick wouldn't confirm anything. Instead he looked at her, kept her gaze.

They had her.

2.30 P.M.

Nick went in to Ryan.

'We have the blood results back on the knife,' he said as he sat down opposite him. 'I'm sorry to have to tell you that it is one of the weapons that was used to inflict harm on Jordan. The blood is a match to your brother's.'

Ryan's shoulders dropped. 'And fingerprints? Any matches?'

Nick shook his head. 'I'm afraid not. It's clean.' He slid a photo across the desk to him. 'Do you know who this is?'

Ryan looked at the image for a moment. 'His face looks familiar but I don't think so. Should I?'

Nick showed him the next photo, where Jacob Granger was handing something to the driver of a car. 'What about this one?'

Ryan frowned and pulled it closer. 'Is that Kirstie?'

'Yes, she's just admitted to putting the knife in the wardrobe along with the money.'

'But how?' He sat forward. 'When?'

'She went out in the early hours of the morning. This was taken at three-thirty.'

Ryan looked perplexed. 'Are you saying she sneaked out of the house, collected the knife and then came back home? And I didn't hear a thing?'

'Did you not hear a thing?' questioned Nick.

'No! I had no idea. Why would she do that?'

'She wanted to set you up for the murder of your brother. Something to do with you double-crossing her, she said, about Flynn's nightclub.'

Ryan shuffled in his chair but he didn't speak.

'Steve Burgess has been implicated in it too. We're bringing him in for questioning.'

Ryan glanced up, remained calm.

'You don't want to comment on any of this?' asked Nick when he'd stayed silent for a while.

'What do you think?' Ryan's shoulders went up. 'Kirstie will have the best legal advice going. I can't go up against Terry Ryder. It would be more than my life is worth.'

3.00 P.M.

'Did I ever tell you that I have the best team in the world?' Allie said as she joined Sam and Perry back at her desk. 'We may be a man down but we've just nailed Jacob Granger and Kirstie Ryder for the murder of Jordan Johnson.' She leaned across and high-fived first Perry and then Sam.

'Fantastic,' said Sam with a grin.

'More than fantastic,' said Perry. 'Bloody amazing.'

'More than amazing,' said Allie. 'It's bloody epic!' Her mobile phone rang. 'Oh,' she said, her shoulders dropping. 'I have to take this. I – Mark?' She listened to him, her world falling apart with every word he spoke. 'Oh, no. I'm on my way.'

She disconnected her phone with shaking hands and turned to her team. All eyes were on her.

'Karen's had another bleed to the brain.' She gulped in air. 'I – I have to go.'

There was a moment of uncomfortable silence before they all spoke at once and offered their help.

'Would you like me to drive you there?' asked Perry.

Allie blinked back tears but they fell anyway. 'No, thanks. I – I need . . . no, thanks.' She was already running out of the office.

3.30 P.M.

Allie parked in the multi-storey car park, killed the engine and reached into her bag for her purse. Almost automatically now, she switched her mobile phone to silent just in case it went off while she was on the ward. Mobile phones were allowed on some wards now but she couldn't stand the incessant ringtones and voices babbling away on them when she was conscious that some patients needed peace and quiet.

Knowing that the hospital would wait until she arrived to give consent, she took a few minutes to gather her wits. The longer she stayed there, the longer she was putting off the inevitable, yet it was the only way she seemed able to gain control of the situation. The time had finally come. Karen was going to die. It was up to her and Mark now, but ultimately she was her sister's next-of-kin.

So much responsibility was falling on her shoulders. After all this time of blaming herself for the attack on Karen, she *was* going to be the one who ended her life. Seventeen years – it now seemed to have gone in a flash, yet she couldn't even remember the sound of her sister's laughter. She took a few deep breaths to stop the tears from coming. *Not yet*, she told herself as she caught her reflection in the rear view mirror. *There's something I have to do for Karen first. Then I can grieve.*

She watched two teenage girls walk past in fits of giggles. That had been her and Karen once, not a care in the world. How on earth had it come to this?

With a few more deep breaths, she got out of the car and went across to the ticket machine. As she pressed the green button to retrieve a ticket, she heard a noise behind her. She turned to see someone she knew. He held a small fire extinguisher in his hand.

'Hi there, Graham,' she said, swiping tears from her eyes. 'Didn't expect to see you here. Everything okay, I hope? The others mentioned that you didn't deliver the oatcakes this morning.'

'Hello, Karen.' He smashed the fire extinguisher into the side of her face.

The force of it made her stumble and a burst of light flashed before her eyes. He grabbed her arm, almost running with her to the back of a van parked a few bays along. The rear door was already open and he pushed her in. Climbing in too, he slammed the door behind him.

Allie screamed, hands and feet hitting out. He punched her twice in the side of the head and once in the face. Before she could gather her senses enough to fight back, he'd bound her hands together. She tried to scream again as he lifted them above her head and looped the rope through a tie-down ring attached to the side panel of the van.

'No!'

He forced what she thought was a scarf into her mouth and fastened it around her head. She gagged as the wool hit the back of her throat. Kicking out as she pulled at the binding, he grabbed for her feet and tied her legs together with rope at the ankle.

Kneeling beside her, he smiled. A hand came towards her and she screamed. It came out muffled as he stroked the top of her head, his fingers flicking through the length of her hair.

'Be still, my angel,' he smiled, pressing a finger to his lips.

Allie felt a tear drop down the side of her face as she watched him climb out of the van. The slam of the door made her flinch.

As the engine started and the van began to move away, she thought back to what he'd just said in the car park.

He'd called her Karen.

———— ————

Above the sounds of the blood rushing to her head as fear took over her senses, Allie tried to work out what the hell was going on. Why had Graham Stott done this to her? He was someone she knew – the man who had delivered oatcakes to the station every Friday morning for as long as she could recall. She'd always liked him, even though he seemed a little quiet; always thought she had been kind to him, so he couldn't be angry with her for her attitude towards him. But then thoughts came crashing at her, making her stomach flip over. He had called her Karen – this must be the man who had attacked her sister, which meant that Graham was the man who had been watching her.

A scream became stuck in her throat as she thought of how long she had known him. The years he could have been watching her at work as he delivered the oatcakes that they all loved. Should she have recognised that he was specifically fixated on her?

She thought back to the case before this where he'd stopped to talk to her about the serial killer terrorising the city. Had he given her any clue then, any inkling? Had there been any double meanings to his words that she had missed? She couldn't remember.

Another gasp as her mind went wild with images she didn't want to think about. Oh, why the hell hadn't she told Nick about the rose that was delivered last week? Stupid, stupid, bitch.

Wait! Was that why Graham had been missing that morning? Had he been watching her all day? She felt bile rising in her throat. She was going to choke if she didn't calm down.

Finally, her police training kicked in and she made an effort to remember every detail that she could. She felt like she was on a roller coaster as they dropped down two floors to ground level on the car park, her body taking the brunt of every turn as she rolled from right to left on the floor of the van. It was strange to feel glad that she was tied to its side, but at least it kept her more secure, saved her injuring herself more as she tried to keep her wits about her.

The van slowed down, came to a halt. She could hear traffic sounds as they stopped for a moment before moving off again. She veered to the right as he made a turn, groaning as her leg hit the wall of the van. He had driven on to Hilton Road, she was sure. Her survival instincts taking over, she concentrated on the roads they would be turning in to, see if she could work out where they would be when they stopped.

He braked sharply and her whole body shot forward. She heard him curse and the beep of a horn just before her head slammed into the back of the seat. For a few seconds, she lost her bearings again. Before she knew it, they had gone around a roundabout and she no longer knew what road they were on. She whimpered as panic began to set in. How would she tell anyone where he had taken her?

He put his foot down before slowing again, this time not stopping but crawling in traffic. A few seconds later and once more they were going at some speed. They were on a long straight road.

Had they left the slower side streets behind them? Were they on the nearby A34?

Her left eye was swelling from the force of the hit she'd received, but she looked around the van, trying to get a grip on her senses, looking for clues, things she could remember if she ever got the chance to talk about them. A whiff of petrol caught her nose as they went around another corner and her feet slid across the floor. More than that, she could smell her own sweat, her own fear.

A garbled sob escaped her as she thought of Mark waiting for her at the hospital. Mark, her soulmate. The only man she would ever love and who would ever put up with her work ethics, her foibles, her silliness. He would be pacing the corridor waiting for her, worried where she was.

She thought of Karen. *Was* she going to fail her again? Unable to be there for her during her final moments because she was here, trapped in this filthy, stinking van with a man she vaguely knew.

Her bag slid along the floor at the same time she did as he veered to the left again. This time the van began to slow, seemed to swerve in and out – maybe through parked cars? Were they on a narrow street or a popular street for parking, a row of terraced houses perhaps? She had no idea.

Her phone! At least it was on silent. Maybe the team could trace her in time. It would give her something to focus on, help her through this ordeal. They would find her. They had to find her.

Finally the van stopped, the engine stilled and she heard the driver door open and close. For a moment she struggled to breathe, knowing that any second now the door would open again and she would be faced with her worst nightmare. Alone, unsure where she was, unable to get away from someone who was hell bent on hurting her. Tied up and gagged.

The van started to move, only metres forward before it stopped again. Allie blinked away tears, determined not to show him how terrified she was as she heard footsteps outside. The back door opened with a creak.

3.45 P.M.

At the station, Sam answered her mobile phone.

'Sam, it's Mark.'

'Hi . . . I'm sorry to hear about Karen.'

'I'm ringing about Allie.' His tone sounded frantic. 'She said she was on her way about forty-five minutes ago. I didn't think she'd be this long. Has she been waylaid?'

Sam sat forward in her chair. 'No, she left as soon as she'd taken your call. You've tried her mobile? Sorry, daft question.'

'Yes, it keeps ringing out. Oh, Christ.'

'You don't think . . . Oh, Mark, we let her go alone without thinking.'

'But it'll be dark soon. Nothing can happen to her! Fuck!' A pause. 'Is Nick there?'

'I'm walking down to him now. Stay on the line.'

Sam ran to Nick's desk. 'Mark Shenton's on the phone, sir. Allie hasn't made it to the hospital.'

Nick paled as she passed the phone to him. Her right foot jigged up and down as she waited for him to take the call.

'Check in with the control room,' he told her, almost toppling his chair over in his rush to stand up. 'See if the roads are clear. No accidents reported, no ambulances on calls.' He clicked his finger at Perry who had joined them. 'Allie's gone missing. Can you run her registration number through the system to see if we can see where she was last seen? And get the security guards checking for it on the hospital car parks too. I want her found right now!'

'Sir,' said Sam, with a gulp as she knew how much trouble she and Allie would be in when she spoke. But she had to tell him now.

'Allie received another rose last week.'

'It started when I saw you again at the police station,' said Graham. 'When I began to deliver oatcakes every Friday. But I've known you much longer than that.'

Allie turned her head, trying to focus on him. Her left eye had almost closed now and the other was blurry from her being knocked about in the van. She blinked a few times, struggled in vain again to release her hands. Already her arms, strapped behind her head, were beginning to ache. She was trussed up like a pig ready for slaughter. She couldn't hear a thing. Not a passing car, no horns beeping, no voices. It was so quiet she wondered if they were in a warehouse or something similar, although she couldn't recall hearing a door being opened.

She took a peek at him. He could do anything to her here. She was completely helpless, completely alone. Her breathing began to rasp and she concentrated on keeping it as regular as possible. Count up to ten. Count down from ten.

She glanced around. There was nothing she could use even if her hands were free. She was the only thing in the back. And him – Graham Stott.

He was sitting at the side of her on his knees, looking at a photograph. He turned it towards her. She blinked again. It was the same as the one that used to hang on Karen's wall at Riverdale Residential Home. She'd taken it down recently when they'd been to fetch Karen's belongings, say goodbyes to staff because they knew she would never go back there.

The six teenagers including Karen. Of them, only three were alive. Three of them had been killed on her last case; one had survived a stabbing. The remaining girl was Karen. The remaining boy was Graham. She had gone to the same school as him, was in the same year, too. Allie recalled taking the photo from the wall, the list of names written on the back of it. He must have been Gray – it was obvious to her now that it was short for Graham – and the one she had recognised vaguely.

'Karen and I knew each other at school,' he glanced her way for a moment and then back at the photo, 'and when we hooked up we were having a great time – or so I thought.'

Allie turned her head away from him. She didn't want him to say anything but she knew it was what she had been waiting to hear for seventeen years. The truth about what had really happened to Karen that night.

'I bet you want to know about Chloe Winters, too, don't you?'

Allie whimpered. She didn't want to hear about any of them. Maybe it was better after all this time if she didn't know. After all, Karen was dying. There would be no need for closure from him, too.

But even though she didn't feel strong enough to cope with the fallout, she did need to know.

'If I remove the scarf, there won't be any point in screaming, you do know that?'

Allie nodded slightly. She wouldn't scream; he knew she wouldn't scream, because she wanted to know. Needed to know what had happened to her sister.

Once he'd loosened it, he ran a finger down the side of her cheek. She turned her face and squirmed but he grabbed her chin, made her look at him.

'You knew it was me, didn't you? You knew it didn't fit in with the investigation – the serial killer in Stoke. Who would have thought that little geek Patrick would overshadow me? I knew him too – when I was younger. I used to bully him when we were all at junior school together but then I grew up and realised he was just the same as me. A loner, a loser. I wondered if he would come after me when I'd worked out we all went to the same school.'

There was so much anger in his eyes that she flinched.

'I had it all under control until then,' he seethed. 'But he released memories that had been buried a long time ago.' He moved to the other side of the van and sat down again. 'They weren't looking for me, though, were they? They were looking outside of the box and not necessarily at what was right under their noses. But you knew.'

'Y.N,' Allie whispered.

He smiled. 'I planted that note for you to find. I tried to fight my feelings but the more I heard about you, the more I saw you on the television and in newspapers, the more I couldn't keep everything back. I'd gone out that night and coming across her, and thinking it was you, it was just bad timing. A moment of lapsed concentration. Everyone was talking about Patrick and it reminded me of school, of Karen.'

Another smile that turned Allie's stomach.

'Did you work out what the letters stood for before I sent you the second rose?'

'Yes.' *You're next.* She would remember them forever but she wouldn't give him the satisfaction of saying them out loud.

'Clever girl. I'd overheard someone at the station talking about alphabet letters when I was doing my Friday delivery.' He raised a hand. 'It was no one's fault. Just chit-chat as I was in the car park. I thought it would be a great way of getting a message to you.'

Tears poured down Allie's face as she thought of the words Chloe Winters had screamed at her. *Did he do this to me to get back at you?* Chloe had been right: he'd ruined another life because he could. How was she ever going to live with that?

Her breathing began to go out of control. As she gasped for air, he noticed her struggling so she played on it.

He came closer.

4.00 P.M.

'You and me, Allie,' he said, 'we're both the same really. We like to be in control. We want to be liked, considered worthy to know. We want people to accept what we do. We want justice. We want power.'

Allie shook her head. She was nothing like him, didn't he realise? She pulled again on the rope binding her hands and feet. Her fingertips began to tingle. She tried not to think that her nightmare of the past few years might suddenly become reality. Her chest rose and dropped rapidly. *Stop panicking. Think of Mark,* she told herself. *He's all you need to focus on.*

'I was having a great time in Flickers with Karen,' he continued. 'The bar was packed, and buzzing. We squeezed into seats at the back. I bought her lots of drink, and we were getting on fine until she checked her watch and stood up, saying she was half an hour late for you.'

Allie's shoulders dropped. So she hadn't missed her sister. Karen hadn't been outside waiting for her: she'd still been in Flickers. They must have missed each other by minutes as Allie had waited around for a while, then gone to look for her.

Graham's eyes narrowed. 'I was on to a good thing until she mentioned you.' He grabbed her chin and squeezed hard, forcing her to look at him again. 'I took her outside but you weren't there, so I used my tactics of persuasion and lured her away. It was easy really. She was quite out of it by then.' He pointed a finger close to her face. 'She was a feisty one, I can tell you. Didn't complain much at all until I pushed her down the side of St John's Church. She started to scream but I soon shut her up with my fists. She was still putting up a fight and well, I just saw red and I punched and I punched.'

'Stop!' Allie sobbed but Graham continued regardless.

'My hands were around her neck and I was strangling her.' Graham dropped his hand from her face and mimed what he had done in the air, but then he began to cry. 'I didn't realise what I was doing, I swear.'

His shoulders began to shake as sobs wracked his body.

Allie didn't have any sympathy for him.

'When I left, I was convinced she was dead,' he wiped at his face, 'but she was still alive.'

'No, she wasn't.' Allie found her voice at last. 'You should have killed her. You shouldn't have left her how she was. It was cruel. I've had to watch her for seventeen years, you bastard. You should have finished the fucking JOB!'

He leaned forward and slapped her across the face. 'Don't play mind games with me. You wanted to know what happened to her and I'm telling you.'

'No, I don't want to know!'

'Oh, I think you do.' He grabbed for her feet, loosening the rope around them.

As soon she could, she took the opportunity to kick out but he stilled her with a punch to the chin, dazing her once more.

'You might as well give in now,' he told her, calm again. 'I'm not going to stop until I've had you. I've waited long enough for this moment.'

The hand holding on to her foot pushed it up so that her knee was upright. The fingers of his free hand traced a line over the knee and up her thigh, moving over her skirt, inching slowly up her towards her body. Her breathing erratic again, she shivered as his hand found her blouse and pulled it out. Forcing her knee down to the floor of the van with his own firmly on top of it, he took hold of each side of the material and pulled. Buttons pinged across the van, leaving her skin exposed. Goosebumps sprang out all over her.

'A white virginal bra,' he smiled as he gazed at her chest. 'How apt for my angel.'

Allie burst into tears at the mention of the word.

He ran his fingertips up and down, from the waistband of her skirt to the bottom of her bra and back.

'Please,' she whispered, failing to keep her feelings in a box. 'You have to –'

'I can't hear you.' He came closer.

'Please kill me afterwards. Please don't leave me like you left Karen.'

Graham sat up. 'Who the fuck are you to give me orders?' He prodded himself hard in the chest. 'I'm the one who says what goes on around here.'

He undid the button on his trousers. Allie sobbed when she heard the zip go down and felt his hands fumbling around as he lay on top of her. He forced her legs a little wider and she closed her eyes.

'Open them,' he demanded.

She shook her head. She wouldn't give him that last bit of satisfaction.

'Open your eyes!'

'Never!' She squeezed them tighter to prove a point. 'You can violate me by forcing yourself into me but you will not take *me* along with you.'

Graham froze. 'Violate you. Is that what you think I'm going to do to you?'

'Yes.' The tremble in her voice matched the one in his.

He sat up, pulled her blouse around her nakedness and smoothed down her skirt.

Allie was close to passing out with her next thoughts. At the very least her bladder was about to give way. He was going to get a knife, wasn't he? If he couldn't violate her, wouldn't he kill her instead?

'I don't want to touch you if you think that,' he said, his voice emotionless.

'What else could I think?' she said.

'I can't do that.' He began to sob. 'You're too special. Don't you understand? I love you! And seeing you with Mark all the time, I . . .'

Allie cried now. He knew Mark's name. Did he know everything about her?

Graham stood up, paced the van, grabbing handfuls of his hair and pulling at it. He looked down on her, spittle at the corner of his mouth.

'After all this time,' he said, 'I thought you loved *me* but you love *him* more.' He punched her in the face again. 'You've ruined everything!'

She groaned as pain creased her once more.

'You're nothing but a whore. Just like your sister. A dick tease.' He grabbed the collar of her blouse, pulled her up to his face. 'You're going to pay for that.' With his knee putting pressure on one of her legs, he untied her hands and dragged her to the edge of the van by her hair. She screamed as he opened the door and threw her to the ground. The concrete scraped into the palms of her hands but she managed to land on all fours.

She looked around. It looked like they were in a garage, a double. Over on the far wall, there was metal shelving – paint tins, paraphernalia collected over the years by the looks of it, oily rags, an old newspaper. In desperation, her eyes searched for something she could use as a weapon if he came at her again.

'This is all wrong.' Graham slapped himself around the face. He opened the garage door.

Allie shuffled away from him, as near to the wall as she could. She wanted to run for the open door but she couldn't be sure what he'd do next. The state of mind he was in, he might just reverse the van over her. The van that she now realised had been in her street with its engine running last night as she'd got home. How long had he been watching her yesterday?

As he moved past her, he grabbed her by the hair again.

'How dare you reject me?' He screamed. 'I'll make sure you pay for what you've done.'

'No, please!' she cried.

He pushed her away and got into the van. Within seconds, he reversed it out of the garage and screeched off.

Allie was already running out of the building.

She was certain he was going for Mark.

4.20 P.M.

Allie ran outside and stopped. She was in front of a line of garages. Behind she could see a row of back gardens up a bank. They didn't seem familiar to her. Where was she? She ran along the tarmac driveway towards the entrance gate. There would be people on the road, if not in the houses. Her bag was still in the back of the van. She needed to find a phone to use.

Her blouse flapped behind her, her bra was on show but she didn't stop. She ran until her knees buckled and she fell to the ground, sat there gasping for air. Painful sobs escaped her. Mark would be wondering where she was. He would have rung the station. She got to her feet again.

With every step she took, she sobbed, trying not to think of Graham Stott. Images of him plunging a knife into Mark's chest; of Mark falling to the floor; of her being too late, not being there for him as she hadn't been there for Karen.

It was only minutes but it felt like hours. She ran through the gate and onto the pavement, remembering to pull the blouse around her middle. She hadn't got her warrant card on her. She needed someone to trust her.

Ahead, she could see a row of houses and then a sign for a shop. In a split second, she chose to run to the shop.

The tinkling of a bell marked her arrival and she ran to the counter at the far end. A shop assistant was ringing through the goods of an elderly man at the till. She pushed past the man and, before he could protest, caught her breath enough to speak.

'My name,' she said through tears, 'is Detective Sergeant Shenton. Please, I need to use a phone.'

The man's mouth dropped open. Allie leaned on the counter to steady herself, forgetting that her blouse would drop open too.

'Please.' She took another breath. 'I need to use your phone.'

'Yes, of course.' The shop assistant handed over a cordless handset. 'Are you okay, duck?'

As she took the phone, Allie's knees buckled again and she dropped to the floor. She rested her back on the counter behind her while the phone connected.

'Nick! It's Allie. Oh, God, you have to help me. I know who attacked Karen and he's just come after me –'

'Where are you?' Nick interrupted.

'I'm . . .' She gasped for breath again and looked up at the woman. 'Where am I?'

'You're on Newport Lane, duck. In the Spar shop.'

'I'm on –'

'I heard her, Allie. Stay where you are. I'll send someone for you and I'll get over to the hospital.'

'He's going after Mark,' she sobbed.

'Do you know who he is?'

'The oatcake man.'

'The oatcake man?'

'Graham Stott. The bloke who delivers our oatcakes.'

'Jesus Christ! He could have been watching you for years!'

'I don't care about that anymore. Just don't let me lose Mark. He's all I have.'

'You stay put, do you hear? I'll get someone to you right away.'

Allie nodded into the receiver, sobbing so hard she couldn't speak.

The woman behind the counter took the phone from her and guided her into a room at the back of the shop. She handed her a bottle of water and a white T-shirt with a bright logo splashed across it.

'I'm not sure if you can use this but . . .'

Allie removed her tattered blouse and put the T-shirt on. Shivering with shock, she put her jacket over it. She tried to remove the top from the water bottle but her hands were shaking too much.

The woman took it from her, snapped off the seal and gave it back to her. 'I'm Margaret,' she told her. 'What was your name again?'

'Allie.'

She began to shiver uncontrollably as all sorts of thoughts rushed through her mind. What happened if Nick didn't get to the hospital in time? Did he know which ward Karen was on? Was Mark with Karen or was he looking for her? Did Sam know where Karen was?

All she could do was sit and wait. And make another call. She dialled a number.

'Mark!' Tears of relief poured down her face when she heard his voice.

4.35 P.M.

'Everyone, listen up,' Nick grabbed his coat from the back of his chair and pulled it on as he walked towards the door. 'I've just spoken to Allie. She's okay but she was snatched by that bastard who attacked her sister.'

'What the fuck!' Perry stood up, reaching for his stab jacket.

'Where is she?' Sam followed suit.

Nick marched down the office, several officers on his tail. 'She thinks he's going after Mark,' he spoke over his shoulder. 'He's with Karen at the hospital. We need to get up there and keep him safe.' He turned around and walked backwards for a few steps. 'Sam, do you know which ward Karen is on?'

'One oh six – unless she's been moved to ITU.' Sam was already getting out her phone as they thundered down the stairs and out into the car park. 'I'll ring the ward staff, get the security set up there.'

'I'll do it on my way.' Nick opened a car door. 'Go and pick Allie up – she's in the Spar shop on the corner of Newport Lane. Perry, come with me. Anyone else, get up to the hospital.'

4.45 P.M.

Graham drove to the front of the new hospital block, went around
the mini roundabout and parked the van outside the main doors,
behind an ambulance. Despite the cold weather, there were a few
people huddled together. A couple walked out holding a young
baby, a teenager who looked as if he would rather be anywhere else
lagging behind.

'You don't want to leave your car, there, mate,' a man in a
wheelchair puffing on a cigarette told him. 'It'll get clamped.'

Graham ignored him as the automatic doors swooshed open
and he went into the building. He glanced quickly into the cafe
where he had spent endless hours over the past few weeks, keeping a watchful eye on his surviving angel. He followed the corridor
that he'd walked along so many times that he had lost count. It had
been hard not to go in to see Karen too many times but he hadn't
wanted to rouse suspicion. So sometimes he'd grabbed a newspaper and a cup of coffee, sat where he could watch the main doors
for her to arrive. See Allie for a few moments while she went to see
her sister. Sometimes she would be with Mark, other times alone.

He walked on until he came to the sign, ward 106, and
turned left.

Sam broke the speed limit on her way to pick up Allie. As she tried to concentrate on her driving, she couldn't believe what had happened. All that while, all those years and it was someone Allie knew? Someone they *all* knew. Graham Stott had visited the station at least once a week for as long as she could remember. She'd had him down as a quiet soul. How could they all have missed it?

In Newport Lane, she screeched to a halt outside the Spar shop and ran inside.

'She's in the back,' the woman pointed to a door.

Sam went through quickly, her heart pounding, tears of relief pricking at her eyes when she saw her friend sitting amidst a pile of boxes, bottles of water and tomato ketchup and a stack of toilet rolls. Her left eye was half-closed and looked dreadfully painful. Everything on her face was swollen, her top lip was split and still bleeding, her hands and boots covered in mud.

'Allie!' She rushed to put an arm around her.

'Sam!' Allie burst into tears, but she scrambled to her feet. 'We have to stop him. We have to go now.'

'I don't think you should go. You're in no fit state to be of any use to anyone.' Before Allie could protest, Sam held up a hand. 'But I know better than to try and stop you. Come on.'

Sam thanked the assistant and manoeuvred Allie out of the shop. Carefully, she helped her into the passenger seat and then got in herself. Before starting the engine, she looked across at her.

'Let's go and nail this bastard once and for all.'

4.55 P.M.

The relief Mark felt once he'd spoken to Allie quickly turned to anger. Let the bastard come here for him – he'd pay for attacking Allie. He made his way quickly back to the nurses' station to warn them and put the hospital on alert, before going to Karen's room to see how she was. He pushed the door open. There was a man standing next to Karen's bed. Mark gulped when he saw he was holding a knife.

'Well if it isn't the main man himself – at last,' he said.

Mark glanced back along the corridor. The two nurses at the station weren't looking his way. He had two choices. He could alert them to the danger, therefore putting Karen at risk too. Or he could go into the room and wait for the police to arrive.

What would Allie do? He wondered.

'Hi, Graham,' he said.

Graham seemed taken aback that he knew his name.

'You! You spoiled it all. All she ever wanted is you. I've watched her. I've seen you together, the perfect couple, while I had to watch her,' he pointed to Karen in the bed, 'deteriorate year after year.'

Mark tried to stay calm, in control of the situation. He stepped forward. 'I have a few questions for you, if you don't mind.'

'Fire ahead. I have all the time in the world,' Graham sniggered.

'Why did you leave Karen like that? After you caused her all that damage, didn't you have the guts to punch her one more time, finish her off?'

When he didn't speak, Mark took a step forward.

'I thought I had killed her.' Graham's face fell forlorn. 'I thought she was dead.'

'And did it hurt when she wasn't?'

'Come any closer and I'll damage her!' Graham shouted.

Mark held up his hand to pacify him, wondering if there was a way for him to alert the staff from inside the room. He glanced at the emergency button but he was too far away. He stepped closer.

'Please, this has nothing to do with her. It's me you're after.'

'I want her, too. I've always wanted her. Can't you see?'

'Graham, have some mercy. She's at the end of her life – let her die in peace. You owe her that at least.' He looked at Karen.

'Not her, you stupid fuck!' Graham roared. 'It's Allie I want. Karen means nothing to me. I could finish her off right now if I wanted to – I could! I do have the guts to do it. You were wrong.' He raised the knife in the air.

'Wait!'

Their eyes met, and suddenly Mark feared for his life. How the hell had Allie got away from this monster?

He needed to get him out of this room. If Allie wasn't there when Karen died, it would destroy her.

He said the one thing he knew would make Graham react.

'You can't have Allie,' he said. 'She's mine.'

'No!'

As Graham came running at him with the knife, Mark prayed he could be as strong as his wife.

5.00 P.M.

'What if we're too late?' said Allie, as Sam went full pelt along the A34 towards the hospital, sirens wailing. 'What if he's . . . if he's . . .'

'We won't be,' she said, slamming on her brakes as someone took longer than necessary to move out of her way. 'No wonder he didn't turn up with the oatcakes on his rounds this morning. He –'

Sam stopped but Allie had guessed what she was about to say. Graham Stott had probably been following her around all day, waiting for the most opportune moment to grab her. All those times she'd thought someone was watching her – could it have been him?

They were at the main entrance to the hospital. 'There's his van!' she cried.

Sam switched off the sirens and killed the engine. She left the car there, much to the amusement of the man still sitting by the doors in his wheelchair.

They ran down the corridor, people moving out of their way as they heard their feet clapping on the floor. Allie caught a glimpse of herself in a window as she went past, hair flying behind her, one eye swelling, almost closed, oil on her skirt from the floor of the van and an oversized T-shirt flapping around.

They turned left into ward 106, continuing to run down the corridor. Ahead at the nurse's station, Allie could see so many people that she couldn't make out what was happening. But she couldn't see the one face she needed to see.

'Mark!' she cried. 'Mark, where are you?'

Several ward staff in various coloured uniforms turned to look at her. She could see hospital security men and two uniformed officers from the station.

She could see Nick; she could see Perry.

Her heart skipped a beat as she spotted blood on the floor.

'No,' she whispered.

Graham Stott was standing with an officer, hands cuffed behind his back. Her eyes scanned him quickly. It wasn't his blood, he was clean.

Oh, God, please let him be okay. She pushed past. Where was he? She couldn't see him. Oh, please, no . . .

And then, there he was. He was sitting on the floor, his back to the wall, the palest she had ever seen him since they'd met.

'Mark!'

Tears poured down her face as he looked up at her and gave her that smile. The smile she'd fallen for all those years ago. She knelt down next to him.

'Are you okay?' he hugged her tightly. 'Sam told me what happened but I know she wouldn't tell me everything. God, look at your face. Did he – did he . . . ?'

'No,' Allie told him, her hand coming up to his face. She needed to touch him. She'd thought so many times in the back of that van that she would never see him again. 'What happened?' she asked, spotting his hand.

'Your fella cracked him one good and proper,' said Perry as he came over to them. 'Stott came at him with a knife and he wrestled him to the ground, punched him a couple of times before I got here to help him out.'

Allie sat wide-eyed.

'Good thing I'm a lover, not a fighter,' Mark grinned. 'It bloody hurt like hell.'

'The blood.' She pointed to the floor, where the pools she'd imagined seconds earlier turned out to be droplets.

'He slashed at my arm too. It's nothing.'

She hugged him again, felt his body relax and his shoulders start to shake as tears of relief came from them both.

They were safe.

Graham Stott had been caught.

There would be no more nightmares. No more thinking about him, obsessing about him. No more wondering who he was, where he was, if he was going to strike again.

Allie pulled away from Mark slightly to look up at him. He ran a finger over her swollen eyelid before kissing her gently on the forehead. She felt tears escape her eyes again.

'Nice T-shirt you have on there,' he smiled.

She looked down at the white monstrosity with a potato-head man on its front, the bright logo colours of a brand of crisps. It was at least two sizes too big.

'I bet people think your wife is so classy,' she grinned.

'I bet people think your husband is a pushover.' He hesitated slightly. 'Sometimes I hate what you do so much. The long days, the times you bring it home with you. The worry you put me through. But most of the time I realise that you are who you are because of it and that's . . . well, that's what I love about you too.'

'Mark Shenton,' she slapped him playfully on his arm, 'you big soppy Stokie.'

Allie stood up as Sam came over to them. They hugged in silence for a moment.

'Your face looks so sore,' Sam told her afterwards.

'It will heal.' Allie tried to smile but winced in pain. 'It looks worse than it is, no doubt.'

'It looks a mess,' Nick said as he joined them too. 'I'm glad you're okay though. Still, you and I need to talk after all this is over.' He lowered his voice. 'Especially before the DCI gets here. Trevor isn't going to be too pleased. Sam told me there was another rose delivered?'

Allie dipped her head. 'I couldn't tell you. I didn't want to be a burden on anyone.'

'A burden, Allie?' Nick baulked. 'You're one of my best officers. I don't want to lose you. You should have told me.'

'I just wanted to do my job, sir. I couldn't do it with any more restrictions.'

'They were put there for your own safety.'

'I'm sorry.'

Nick relented. 'At least it's all over for you now.'

'Almost.' Allie was dreading the thought of what was to come but it still needed sorting soon.

'We'll take you over to A&E to get you looked over.'

'I'm fine, sir.' She shook her head.

'Karen?' he asked.

Allie gulped. 'I – I need to decide whether to turn off the machines that are keeping her alive.'

February 7, 2015
8.30 A.M.

Allie stared at the rows of greeting cards on the bedside cabinet in Karen's hospital room. Cards from Sam, Perry, Nick and a few officers she knew well. Cards from Mark's family and work colleagues. Cards from her friends Ruth and Kate, friends that she needed to reconnect with again, if they would have her. One from the staff at Riverdale Residential Home. Allie had been touched by how many of them had come to visit Karen once she had taken ill. She would miss them all as much as she would miss the routine of going to Riverdale two or three times a week. They had become a huge part of her life over the years. But she would miss nothing as much as her sister.

Karen had been transferred to ITU. Allie had come in alone to say a final goodbye before they switched off her life support machine. The rain was coming down heavily, bouncing off the window ledge. For once she'd rather be outside getting a good soaking if it meant that she didn't have to be here.

So much had happened during the past forty-eight hours that Allie had hardly had time to catch a breath. In the space of two days, they had solved a murder, an assault from over seventeen years ago, and she'd been kidnapped and set free without being raped. Kirstie Ryder was on her way to a long prison sentence. They still hadn't got Terry Ryder for anything, but they would.

She placed a hand on Karen's cheek. Her eyes had been closed for some time now, so Allie was spared the pain of looking into them. It didn't make it any easier though.

'I'm so sorry, Kaz.' A tear dribbled down her cheek and she flicked it away. 'I should have spent the final hours with you, not gone running around Stoke-on-Trent on a case. I know I've been a lousy sister when it came to sparing time for you, but it was hard, you know? I don't want to remember you like this. I want to remember you as you were – vibrant, carefree, always laughing.

'I don't want to say goodbye but . . . but I have to.'

For the last time, she wiped Karen's fringe away from her forehead and leaned over to kiss her. Another tear dropped on to Karen's cheek and she wiped that away too.

'Take care, sis,' she whispered.

'Allie.'

She looked up through her tears to see Mark, good old Mark who had stood by her through everything she had thrown at him. She hadn't for a moment forgotten how awful this would be for him but she had taken it for granted that he would be with her through everything. That needed to change.

'It's time, isn't it?' she said, suddenly realising the enormity of what was about to happen. It wasn't something that could continue and she didn't want to say goodbye, but she was going to be there when Karen died.

'Yes,' said Mark, 'it's time.'

'At least I'll be with her when she – when she . . .'

Mark took hold of her hand. 'You've always been there for her, Allie, and she has always known that.'

Epilogue
March 3, 2015
10.30 A.M.

Ryan parked his car on the drive of The Gables, killed the engine and sat there for a moment. After the drama of the last month, plus Jordan's funeral yesterday, he relished the silence. Once Kirstie and that Granger twin had been charged with murder, he'd made bail while the police looked into things. He'd stayed at his mum's until the funeral but he wasn't sticking around for now. He needed to grab a few belongings from the house and get out of Stoke-on-Trent until the heat had died down.

Somehow, Ryder must have worked out that he'd fooled Kirstie in to signing over the club to him and Jordan. Christ, he'd been such a fool believing Steve Burgess when he'd told him that the thirty-five grand was a down payment to get rid of Kirstie as Terry wasn't happy with her. If it was true what had happened to his wife – why wouldn't he do the same to his daughter?

No, he wasn't going to wait for Ryder to get his revenge.

He wondered how Kirstie would cope, locked up in prison too – then found that he didn't actually give a stuff. Somehow he'd known that she would be involved but even he didn't think she would be capable of trying to pull off what had happened. He had to admit that it had been a genius plot to plant the knife and the money, try to blame him for it, but luckily it had backfired and left her more in the frame. Why the knife was there was beyond him. There were bound to have been no prints on it – no one would be stupid enough to leave any behind. But he had heard something similar about a knife being found at Ryder's house with no prints around the time his wife was murdered. He wondered if it was some sort of in-joke to get at the police.

In the house, he went upstairs to his room, grabbed the large suitcase he had come with and quickly began to throw his things into it.

A noise in the doorway made him look up.

'What the fuck do you want?' he said.

A gun was raised, aimed straight at him.

All that went through his mind in the split second before the shot rang out was the realisation that it had all been for nothing.

Acknowledgements

A huge heartfelt thank you to Steve Burgess who bid a handsome sum of money in aid of a local charity, The Donna Louise Trust, to be named as a character in this book. As I was writing *Only the Brave*, I contacted him to ask how 'mean' he wanted to be and his response was 'the meaner the better.' I hope I did you proud, Steve. Thanks for your kind donation.

I can't believe that *Only the Brave* is my seventh novel. It's special because of that alone, but also because DS Allie Shenton, who has been the main character of three of my books now, has burrowed under my skin so much that I'm going to continue to write about her. So special thanks must go to Maddy Milburn and Emilie Marneur for their encouragement, passion and friendship, which helped to get me to this stage.

Thanks to Alison Niebieszczanski and Talli Roland for all your support, always. A writer's life is a lonely one and I don't know where I would be without good friends. Thanks to Sharon Sant, Maria Duffy and Rebecca Bradley. Thanks to everyone at Amazon Publishing – Eoin, Sana and Neil, Victoria and Jennifer. Thanks to everyone at Kindle Direct Publishing too – Darren, Amy, Kelly and Victoria. Thank you to all my police colleagues who help with research – mistakes are almost certainly mine if there are any. Thanks to all my family and friends who have helped and supported me along the way, and the Harrogate gang that just keeps growing every year. And, last but in no ways least, thanks to the readers who make me smile each and every day.

Finally, to my fella, Chris. My top bloke and my soulmate. A special thank you goes out to you for sharing it all with me. You really are 'too good to be true.'

About the Author

Photo © 2013 Martin Brough

Mel Sherratt has been a self-described 'meddler of words' ever since she can remember. After winning her first writing competition at the age of eleven, she has rarely been without a pen in her hand or her nose in a book.

Since successfully publishing *Taunting the Dead* and seeing it soar to the rank of #1 bestselling police procedural in the Amazon Kindle store in 2012, Mel has gone on to publish four more books in the critically acclaimed The Estate Series and a psychological thriller, *Watching over You*.

Mel was shortlisted for the Crime Writer's Association Dagger in the Library Award 2014 and has written feature articles for *The Guardian*, the Writers and Artists website and *Writers' Forum* Magazine, to name just a few. She regularly speaks at conferences, events and festivals.

She lives in Stoke-on-Trent, Staffordshire, with her husband and her terrier, Dexter (named after the TV serial killer, with some help from her Twitter fans), and makes liberal use of her hometown as a backdrop for her writing.

Her website is www.melsherratt.co.uk and you can find her on Twitter at @writermels.